Naughty

Kokomo-Howard County
PUBLIC
LIBRARY

Naughty

ROCHELLE ALERS

Recycling programs for this product may not exist in your area.

NAUGHTY

ISBN-13: 978-0-373-83128-9
ISBN-10: 0-373-83128-5

www.kimanipress.com

Printed in U.S.A.

When pride comes, disgrace comes;
but with the humble is wisdom.
—*Proverbs* 11:2

PART ONE

Love Lost

chapter one

"I need your license and registration, miss."

Bree held up a hand to shield her eyes from the beam of light coming from the police officer's blinding flashlight. "Wha-at… off-officer," she slurred. She felt sick, sicker than she'd felt in a very long time. "I… I have to… get home."

"You're not going anywhere, miss."

"I need to call my daddy."

"You can call your *daddy* after you give me your license and registration."

Bree reached up and pressed a button, illuminating the interior of the low-slung Porsche. Reaching for the leather handbag on the passenger-side seat, she searched for the small leather case with her license, opened the glove compartment, removed the vehicle's registration and handed it to the cop.

"Fucking hell," she whispered over and over, her fingers beating a tattoo on the leather-covered steering wheel. If she'd been sober she would've seen his cruiser behind the copse of palm trees and definitely would've slowed down. She'd been speeding to get away from Tyrone Wyatt who'd tried to get her to engage in a ménage à trois after they'd had mind-blowing, drug-induced sex.

"Fucking hell!"

She'd promised her parents—her father in particular—that she would stop driving under the influence, but then he hadn't kept his promises to her, so why should she comply with his? All of her life she'd tried, albeit unsuccessfully, to gain Langston Parker's attention. She'd become a straight-A student because she knew how important education was to a man who, despite completing only one year of college, had become a recording-industry mogul. Then there was her mother: beautiful, talented Grammy-award-winning Karma Ryder-Parker, who'd relinquished the responsibility of raising her daughter to headmistresses and live-in nannies.

Breanna Renee Parker's exile had begun within days of her birth after a psychiatrist had diagnosed Karma with postpartum depression—the symptoms of which she turned off and on at will.

Once Bree turned six her parents enrolled her in a private convent school where classes were taught by nuns in unfashionable black habits that exposed only their hands and faces. And when Mother Superior deemed her too incorrigible, she was banished to a prestigious all-girls European boarding school, returning home for the summers and Christmas, or when it proved advantageous to enhance the image of Langston and Karma Parker as a Hollywood power couple.

The Parkers had spent thirty years perfecting their image, only to have their son announce that he'd become involved with another man. Their shame was compounded when Bree returned to the States, eschewing involvement in her father's company to party all night, sleep away the day then get up to begin the nonstop partying all over again.

In the six months since returning to L.A. she'd joined the ranks of Paris Hilton, Nicole Ritchie, Lindsay Lohan and Britney Spears as Tinseltown's latest "It girl"; she was shadowed relentlessly by paparazzi, while tabloid headlines reported every alleged uninhibited escapade.

Tonight, she'd managed to escape their lenses only because

she'd concealed her dark-brown hair under a short, curly auburn wig, and had replaced her usual designer dress for baggy cargo pants, a hoodie and psychedelic running shoes.

"Is your father Langston Parker?"

Bree was coming down off the most exhilarating high she'd had in years. Her head came around slowly as she tried to focus on the police officer's face. He'd hunkered down outside the driver's-side door.

"Yes."

"You can call him now."

"May I call my brother instead?" She'd changed her mind. If Langston knew she'd been stopped for driving under the influence she'd have to relinquish the keys to the brand-new Porsche. The car, a birthday gift, had come with a laundry list of conditions. Three infractions and she would forfeit the car for a month. Tonight was her third infraction.

"Miss Parker, I don't care who you call, but you're not moving this vehicle." The officer held out his hand. "Give me your keys."

Turning off the ignition, Bree dropped the car keys onto the outstretched palm, then retrieved her cell phone from the compartment between the seats and punched the speed dial. Ryder Parker's phone rang five times before being picked up.

"Ryder, it's Bree," she said quickly.

"Do you have any idea what time it is?"

"No." The single word came out in a sob. "I need you to come get me. A cop won't let me drive."

"Where the hell are you?"

Bree closed her eyes, her head pounding. "Please don't, Ry."

"Where are you, Bree?"

She opened her eyes, staring through the windshield. "I know I'm somewhere in Bel Air, but I can't make out the name of the street. I don't think I'm that far from the house."

"I'll be there as soon as I call a taxi and throw on some clothes."

Bree palmed the tiny phone, then settled back to wait for her brother. Ryder would rave and rant, but she could at least count on him to protect her from their father's celebrated temper. She rested her forehead on the leather-wrapped steering wheel, praying she wouldn't lose the contents of her stomach before she made it home.

She'd turned twenty-three on November fifth, and she didn't know why, but she felt much older. There were times when she'd believed she was living in a parallel universe—one in which she was a child thrust into an adult world, and the other where she'd been born as an adult wishing to retreat into a child's world.

She almost wished she could return to the womb and start life all over again, this time with a different set of parents. She'd grown up believing her parents loved her, though they weren't quite certain how to show that love. Their son was different: Ryder was firstborn, male and heir to a recording company rivaling Atlantic and Columbia Records.

Suddenly Bree felt something damp on the back of her hand. She stared numbly at one drop, then another. Cupping her hands, she held them to her face as blood pooled into her palms and trickled through her fingers. She was hemorrhaging. An icy chill swept throughout her, her body shaking then convulsing.

I'm dying. The realization hit her with the same impact as the white powder that had numbed her brain before taking her beyond herself.

Her hands fell into her lap as she rested her head on the steering wheel. The steady blare of the horn in the stillness of the warm December night sounded like a death knell as she slipped into an abyss of blackness at the same time as the police officer returned to peer through the driver's-side window.

chapter two

"I can't believe you let them take her to a municipal hospital," Karma Parker whispered angrily, glaring at her son. "It's going to be hell getting her out of this place past those piranhas and lookie-loos."

Ryder, lounging gracefully in a chair near the window in Bree's private hospital room, didn't bother to glance at his mother. "I don't believe you! You're more concerned about someone photographing Bree than you are about why she's drinking and drugging."

Large gold-brown eyes, eyes that Ryder had inherited from his mother, darkened with Karma's rising temper. "Don't you dare you talk to me about my child."

Pushing to his feet, Ryder approached his mother. "When has she ever been your child, Mother?" His face twisted into a scowl that distorted his perfectly symmetrical features. "It's always been 'my son' but never 'my daughter.' I can't believe you've waited twenty-three years to finally refer to *my sister* as your child."

Karma combed her fingers through her fashionably cut dark-auburn hair. The embodiment of style and sophistication, she never went out in public without makeup or her hair coiffed.

"You're wrong, Ryder."

"No, I'm not wrong, Mother, and you know it. Bree wasn't

your daughter when she was born, and she's definitely not your daughter now."

He ignored the tears welling up in his mother's eyes. He wasn't moved by them. The last time Karma had resorted to tears was just after he'd taken control of his trust fund. He'd informed his parents that he was resigning as executive vice-president of LP Records and then disclosed his alternative lifestyle.

Karma had broken down, sobbing inconsolably, while Langston had been too shocked to respond. His father didn't have to say anything because his expression said it all—he was ashamed *and* disappointed.

Straightening her shoulders, Karma stared at Ryder. There was something in his voice that garnered her undivided attention. "What aren't you telling me, Ryder?"

"I've told Bree that she can come live with me and Connor for as long as she wants."

Ryder had had long talks with his sister since her return to L.A. He knew she hated living with their parents, and he'd offered his home for as long as she wanted. She'd thanked him for the offer, but had remained noncommittal. He knew her drinking and drugging was a cry for help *and* attention.

Karma took note of her firstborn, her incredibly beautiful golden child. At six-two he was two inches taller than Langston, and he cut a magnificent figure. Broad shoulders, slim hips and graced with a masculine elegance that took some men a lifetime to acquire, Ryder had been born with it. His clear chestnut-brown coloring was the perfect match for his close-cropped auburn hair. He'd been born with shocking strawberry-blond hair that had darkened over time. However, he always wore a cap whenever he spent an inordinate amount of time in the hot southern California sun, because he'd tired of people asking whether he dyed his hair.

"Your father will never permit that."

Ryder shook his head. "It doesn't matter, Mother. Bree can live wherever she wants."

"Lang will disown her," Karma countered, angrily.

"You disowned her the day you brought her home from the hospital. I'll give her whatever she needs."

Karma knew she had to make amends with her son, but didn't know how. She had no way of knowing how much hostility he'd harbored over the years. Even when she believed he'd been the good child, the perfect son, he'd been harboring a deep-rooted resentment of his parents. And he'd waited until he was twenty-five to unleash his venom.

"Please let's wait until your father gets here so we can talk about it together."

"There's nothing to talk about, Mother. When Bree leaves here she's coming home with me."

Bree opened her eyes at the sound of the familiar voices. She didn't remember when she'd been wheeled into the hospital or hooked up to an IV. Once she was conscious an E.R. doctor had informed her that he'd cauterized her nose to stop the bleeding and she'd been given a unit of whole blood.

"It doesn't matter what Daddy says. I'm going to stay with Ryder for a while." Her voice sounded as if it didn't belong to her. It was low and raspy.

Karma walked over to the bed where her daughter lay. Clear liquid flowed from a tube and into her veins. She stared at the flawless dark-brown face, as if she were seeing Breanna for the first time, seeing things she hadn't noticed before.

How, she thought, had she missed her daughter's understated beauty? When had she dyed her dark-brown hair raven-black? The nose she'd always thought too short and pug made her appear much younger than she was. High cheekbones, expressive, round, wide-set eyes and her tall, thin body had made her the favorite model of Yves St. Laurent the year she'd turned seventeen. Would Brenna be lying in a hospital bed if she and Langston hadn't forced their daughter to give up modeling?

Reaching over, Karma placed a hand on her daughter's forehead. It was cool to the touch. "I'm going to ask the doctor when I can take you home."

Bree closed her eyes, unable to meet her mother's gaze. "I told you that I'm not going home with you."

A soft gasp escaped Karma's parted lips. "You intend to live with Ryder and that…?"

"I'm going to stay with Ryder until I decide what I want to do with my life."

"I know what you want to do with your life," Karma spat out.

"I didn't know you were clairvoyant," Bree countered hotly.

Karma froze, her eyes widening at the unexpected quip. "You're competing with the other stupid little Hollywood bitches abusing alcohol and drugs. Do you have any idea what an embarrassment you are, Breanna Parker?"

"I thought Ryder was the family's embarrassment," Bree retorted, pushing into a sitting position. Reaching around her body with one arm, she pulled up a pillow to support her shoulders.

"I'd rather have a gay son than a crackhead for a daughter."

Bree closed her eyes again. "Ry, please get her out of here before I forget she's my mother."

Karma straightened and threw up an arm when Ryder reached for her. "Don't touch me!"

"What the hell is going on in here?" Langston Parker stood in the doorway, resplendent in formal dress. "Please, not everyone answer at once," he continued when encountering deafening silence.

"Ask your wife," Ryder said with no emotion in his voice.

Langston's dark gaze shifted from his son to his wife before lingering on his daughter in the hospital bed. He'd been at a fund-raising event for one of his favorite charities when he'd got a 911 page from his son to say that Breanna had been taken to the hospital, only to arrive to find his family at one another's throats.

Tall and powerfully built, Langston reeked of authoritative control, running his record company like a despot while engendering employee loyalty and respect with his straightforward manner and generous spirit. At fifty-five, Langston had achieved everything he'd ever wanted in life, and now all he wanted was to enjoy the fruits of his hard work. He'd dealt with his son coming out of the closet, but what he hadn't been able to accept was Ryder wanting nothing to do with LP Records because he wanted to be a writer. The shock had precipitated his third heart attack within seven years, leading to a quadruple bypass.

It had taken Langston a year to recover fully from the medical procedure, and during his convalescence he'd promised himself that he wouldn't permit anything or anyone to threaten his family's unity or jeopardize his health.

Walking into the room, he gave his wife a reproachful look. He'd only recently got his daughter back, and no matter what Karma proposed or complained about, he didn't intend to lose her again.

He approached the bed, leaned over and pressed a kiss to Bree's forehead. "What happened?"

Bree stared into the deep-set, intense, dark eyes glowing like polished onyx. She'd always believed her father was the most handsome man alive and she still felt that way. His cropped hair was now salt-and-pepper, and in recent years he'd added a mustache and goatee that enhanced the utter masculinity of his face. She knew he'd waited years for Ryder to take over the reins of LP Records, and when Ryder had told him that he was leaving the company the news had devastated Langston. The thought he'd spent thirty-five years building an empire he would eventually relinquish to those who weren't his flesh and blood rankled.

Bree thought about concocting a story, but changed her mind. Tests had confirmed the cocaine and alcohol in her blood, so lying wasn't an option. Her eyelids fluttered wildly. "Can I talk to you, Daddy? Alone?"

Langston nodded. He turned around. "Ryder, could you please wait outside with your mother. Breanna and I need to talk."

Ryder moved over to Karma and forcibly led her out of the room, closing the door behind them. He raised his eyebrows when she pulled out of his grasp. "Don't push it, Mother," he warned softly. "You've turned Bree against you, and it wouldn't pay for you to be on my shit list, too."

Karma turned her back, swallowing the curses poised on the tip of her tongue. Her children were turning on her! She hadn't wanted this to happen, because while Langston ruled his company with an iron fist, it was she who controlled her family. Her devious mind raced. It was time she came up with a new strategy.

chapter three

Langston settled himself on the side of the bed. "What do you want to tell me, princess?"

Bree averted her gaze. She'd never been able to look directly at Langston Parker when he called her princess, because the moment of tenderness never lasted. In the past he'd talk to her and then give an account of their conversation to Karma, who invariably opposed everything they'd agreed upon. When Langston had promised she could return to the States to enroll in a Los Angeles high school the plan had been thwarted when Karma had said earning a diploma from an elite European finishing school would carry more weight if and when she applied to a U.S. college.

To spite her mother Bree had moved to France, enrolled in the Parsons Paris School of Design and graduated with degrees in Fashion and Fine Arts and Design and Management. Karma had threatened not to pay her tuition and living expenses, but Bree had reminded Karma that it was Langston Parker who'd paid for her education and he didn't care what college she attended as long as she obtained a degree.

"Ryder and I talked about it when I first came home. He's invited me to live with him for a while and I've decided to accept."

A frown appeared between Langston's eyes. "Are you sure that's what you want?"

Bree nodded. "It's what I need, Daddy, it's what I really need. And you can take back the keys to the Porsche if you want."

Langston shook his head in weariness and defeat. "That's all right, Breanna. You can keep the car. After all, it was a gift."

"What good is a gift that comes with restrictions on how I should live my life?"

Picking up her slender hand, Langston cradled it in his much larger one. "You promised me that you'd stop with the drugs."

"And you promised that you'd stop smoking," Bree whispered. "You know your cardiologist warned you about smoking cigarettes and cigars."

"I only had one cigar."

"That's one cigar too many, Daddy. The doctor said you shouldn't—"

"I know what he said," Langston shot back angrily. "I don't need you to lecture me—"

"Then don't lecture me, Daddy," she countered. "That's why I'm giving up the car."

"This is not about a car, Breanna. It's about your life."

"When have you ever concerned yourself with my life? You've seen me more in the past six months than you have in all of my existence. And that's all I've been doing—existing. I go to sleep, get up, eat, go shopping, hang out and then go to sleep to start it all over again."

"Your mother and I have given you the best—"

"You're deluding yourself, Daddy," Bree interrupted angrily, "if that's what you believe. From the age of six I've spent more time sleeping in dorm rooms than in my own bedroom. Each time I was sent to a new school it was to 'turn me into a little lady.' And, whenever I asked Mother why she was sending me away it was because I was naughty."

Langston gave her fingers a gentle squeeze. "You weren't naughty, Breanna."

"What was I, Daddy?" A silence descended until the hush became unbearable.

"What happened to you tonight, Breanna?"

A rush of annoyance swept over Bree. Whenever Langston didn't want to lie, he either shut down completely, or he'd answer her question with his own question. Her anger and rage built until it hurt her chest to breathe.

"I went to a club, hooked up with a guy and went home with him. We drank, did coke and then we had sex, Daddy." Langston's impassive expressive did not change. "Of course, I made certain he used a condom. I didn't know there was another woman hiding in the closet watching us, so when lover boy decided on a threesome I hauled ass. A cop pulled me over and when he found out that I was Langston Parker's daughter he told me to call someone to drive the car instead of arresting me. End of story."

A muscle throbbed noticeably in Langston's jaw. "You 'had sex,' Breanna? You pick up a stranger, go off with him, do drugs and have sex. You're lucky you're lying here in a hospital bed instead of on a slab in the morgue."

She emitted an unladylike snort. "He wasn't a stranger."

"Who is he?"

"Why do you want to know, Daddy?"

"That's none of your business," Langston shot back.

"That's where you're wrong," Bree argued. "Have you forgotten that I'm an adult, and I can do anything I want?"

There came a beat before Langston said, "Have you forgotten who I am, Breanna Renee Parker? The only reason you're not in jail is because you're my daughter. But, if you don't mind being fingerprinted and posing for a mug shot, then tell me again that it's none of my business."

Anxiety gnawed its way through her bravado. Bree knew better than most people that her father didn't issue idle threats.

It wouldn't be so bad if the man she'd slept with hadn't signed onto her father's label, because there wouldn't be much Langston could do aside from issuing a well-intentioned threat that he was to stay away from his daughter.

"Tyrone Wyatt. He gave me cocaine."

The seconds ticked off as two pairs of near-black eyes regarded each other. Langston hadn't realized he'd been holding his breath until he felt the band of constriction around his chest. He'd signed the incredibly talented singer to his label the year before, and within days of his first album dropping it went gold. He knew he couldn't stop Tyrone from sleeping with his daughter, but he would make certain he would never give her drugs again. He closed his eyes and exhaled audibly.

"What are you going to do to him?"

Pushing off the bed, he stood up. "Nothing, other than make certain he never offers you drugs again."

Turning on his heel, Langston walked out of the room and motioned to his driver/bodyguard lounging against a wall in the waiting area. It took him less than a minute to relay his instructions to the man he'd known all of his life. Walter Rockwell was closer to him than his own brothers, who were serving life sentences in a New York maximum-security prison for murder and drug trafficking.

He watched Walter make his way to an area where he could use a cell phone, then turned to his wife and son. "I'm going to find out when Breanna can be discharged."

Karma stood up and approached her husband. "I hope you're not thinking of letting her stay here."

"I'm not moving her unless it's to take her home."

"Dad's right," Ryder said, coming to his feet. "Once Bree's discharged I'll take her home with me."

Karma glared at Ryder. "What if she needs further medical attention?"

Ryder's gaze didn't waver. "I'll hire a nurse to take care of her."

Langston nodded. "That does it," he stated with a finality indicating the discussion was moot.

chapter four

"Are you really going to stay with Ryder?"

Bree continued searching the racks in her walk-in closet for clothes to take with her. She'd left the hospital undetected, dressed in a pair of scrubs and the wig she'd worn to the club, slipping into a taxi that had just dropped off a passenger. She'd directed the driver to take her an area where Ryder waited in her car. He paid the driver and then drove to their parents' house.

"Yes, Mother, I am."

Karma took a step. "I don't want you to go," she said quickly. "I want you to stay here with me."

Bree spun around. It was only eight in the morning, and Karma was dressed as if she were leaving to have lunch at Michael's or the Ivy with her friends. The large green jade studs in her pierced lobes and the matching necklace around her smooth, slender throat were the perfect complement to her tailored raw-silk aubergine pantsuit. Her shoes were black ostrich-skin-and jade-green-suede Louboutin pumps, one of thousands of pairs that lined the shelves of her closet.

"Why, Mother?"

Karma took several steps, stopping only inches from her daughter. She had to admit to herself that Breanna looked wonderful, despite having spent the night in the hospital. Her freshly scrubbed face radiated good health. Human hair extensions made it virtually impossible to detect that she'd added an additional three inches to her chin-length hair. She may have inherited Langston's coloring, but there was no doubt Brenna was her child.

"I need—I want us to..."

Bree was confused. She'd never known her mother to be anything but direct, and couldn't understand her hesitancy. "What exactly do you want?"

Compressing her vermilion-colored lips, Karma paused to compose her thoughts. "I want us to go away together for a few days." Her sultry voice was almost a whisper.

"And do what, Mother?"

"It's been a while since we've done anything together."

"That's because we've *never* done anything together."

Karma took a deep breath. She didn't want to argue with Breanna, because it would only push her further away. "What about last week when we went to have a mani-pedi and our eyebrows threaded?"

Bree turned away, refocusing her attention on the rack holding more than four dozen pairs of jeans. Her love affair with the pants had begun once she'd returned to the States. After twelve years of school uniforms and conservative attire when attending college classes, she'd overindulged on designer jeans. As a fashion and design major she'd been more than critical of the cut and fit of most garments, but regardless of the price tags attached to the denim she'd discovered that she couldn't resist buying just one more pair.

Many of the store personnel who worked in the shops along Rodeo Drive recognized her as soon as she walked in, and those who didn't were more than familiar with Langston Parker's name. She knew she'd caught a lot of people off-guard when she revealed that she was Langston and Karma's daughter, because the stages of her growing up hadn't been splashed in magazines or tabloid family photo-ops. But that all changed when she began club-hopping.

Ryder had received his share of publicity frenzy whenever he was spotted with a different woman. There were nonstop rumors about who would be lucky enough to get the handsome record exec to pop the question.

But unlike Ryder, Bree had no money of her own, relying solely on her father for a weekly allowance. Buying clothes or indulging in personal services hadn't become an obstacle only because she patronized the same boutiques and salons as Karma. Sales clerks merely added her purchases to the accounts Langston had established for his wife.

"You're buggin'. We just happened to show up there at the same time, so don't try and make it appear as if we'd set up the mother-daughter bonding session beforehand. But, if you really want a mother-daughter outing then I'm going to indulge you. If you can clear your calendar next week I'll see if we can hang."

A rush of color darkened Karma's cheeks as she struggled not to scream at her daughter. "I didn't put out a million dollars for a quality education to have you turn around and use ghetto slang."

"*You* put out a million dollars, Mother? I thought it was Daddy's name on the checks, not yours? The only thing you've ever done for me was to keep me away from my father, so you could have him all to yourself. So, please, don't delude yourself into thinking you exiled me to European schools because you wanted me to have a quality education. I could've gotten that right here in California. Now, if you'll excuse me, I'd like to finish packing."

After Karma left the bedroom Bree folded her body down on the upholstered bench in a corner of the expansive closet. Interacting with her mother was not only bothersome, but also tiresome. Ghetto slang, indeed. What would Karma think if her daughter really let loose with the colorful expletives she'd learned from the "nice girls" from the "good families" who'd attended the outrageously overpriced boarding school where a year's tuition plus room and board was comparable to top Ivy League colleges?

The nice girls had also turned her onto drugs. She'd gone from smoking marijuana to snorting cocaine occasionally. And because of the school's no–tolerance-drugs-rule, the students waited until they were on holiday to rush headlong into their clandestine indulgences.

More than anything else in the world Bree wanted to be close to her mother, but Karma's controlling and I-know-what's-best-for-you attitude was smothering. But, as much as she'd tried to please Karma or agreed with her because she didn't want to be labeled a recalcitrant, naughty little girl, it was all for naught. She'd spent so many years trying to be what Karma wanted her to be that she no longer cared what her mother thought of her.

She would keep her promise and indulge her in a mother-daughter bonding get-together. It would permit them time alone to get to know each other better; perhaps some day they'd be able to occupy the same space for more than hour without being at each other's throats.

Pushing off the bench, she walked over to a compartment of drawers to select T-shirts and undergarments. She placed her clothes and personal grooming products in a Louis Vuitton Eole 60 bag. It was one of a quartet in the monogram collection that had been a birthday gift from Karma. Her parents thought that by giving her designer luggage and luxury cars they were demonstrating their affection. They hadn't realized that she didn't want material gifts.

She wanted what they'd given Ryder.

She wanted love.

Fortunately there'd never been any sibling rivalry between Bree and her brother, and because they'd always supported each other she'd rather live with him rather than with her parents.

chapter five

"Good morning, sir. How may I help you?"

"Please ring Mr. Wyatt and let him know that Rock is here to see him."

"Is he expecting you, Mr. Rock?"

"Yes. And, it's just Rock."

The older man, wearing maroon livery, drew himself up straighter, squaring his shoulders. His gaze shifted from the man who'd identified himself as Rock to another man standing several feet behind him. Both were dressed in tailored suits, but there was something sinister about them. They were obviously identical twins. They each had light-brown skin with a spray of freckles over tiny noses, full lips and large bulging eyes the color of rich, dark coffee. They reminded him of pug dogs. He hadn't been able to discern their hair color because they'd shaved their heads.

"Should I announce you as Rock, sir?"

"Yes."

Walter Rockwell's expression didn't change as he swung his gaze away from the doorman of the opulent building where Tyrone Wyatt lived. He'd lied to the man. Tyrone wasn't expecting him, but there was no doubt when he heard the name he would *make* himself available.

He knew Tyrone was at home; he'd called him earlier, hanging up quickly when he'd heard the phone being picked up. After what Langston had told him about Tyrone and his daughter, Rock doubted whether the talented young singer would be up before noon.

"He'll see you, Mr. Rock," the doorman announced, placing the receiver in its cradle. "His apartment number is..." His words trailed off as Rock and his clone headed toward the bank of elevators.

The elevator ascended quickly and at the eighth floor the two men stepped out into a hallway with plush carpeting, fabric wall covering and exquisite mahogany side tables and chairs.

Winston Rockwell moved off to the side as Walter rang the doorbell. A hint of a smile curved his full lips when it gonged like London's Big Ben. The seconds ticked off. He waited for someone to come to the door, then rang again.

"Is that you, Rock?" asked a deep male voice on the other side of the door.

"Yeah, it's me. Open the door, Tyrone."

"Look, man, I'm busy right now. Can you come back later?"

"Open it!"

The door opened. "What the—" Tyrone wasn't given the chance to react before he found himself on his back, the heel of Winston's shoe resting on his throat.

Leaning over the shocked young man, Walter gave him a sinister smile. Tyrone had come to the door with only a condom on his semi-erect penis. "You are a very, very busy boy with the ladies, aren't you?"

Tyrone stared up at Langston Parker's driver. He'd barely exchanged more than ten words with the man since he'd been signed with LP Records, so he couldn't understand why he and his mirror image had barged into his home and were now threatening to crush his windpipe.

"I—I don't know what you're talking about." Reaching up, Tyrone tried pushing the foot off his neck.

"I think you do, Tyrone," Walter countered as he went down on one knee.

"Roni, baby. What are you doing?"

Straightening, Walter turned to see a skinny, pale-skinned young woman with blond extensions, enormous implants and platinum-blond pubic hair cut into the shape of a diamond, standing under the arch to the entryway. He waved his hand. "Go back into the bedroom and wait for *Roni*. We have business with him."

Her round blue eyes widened. "Why is Roni on the floor?"

Winston increased the pressure on his hapless victim's throat. "Get rid of her," he whispered savagely.

Tyrone closed his eyes as he swallowed his rising fear. Had Langston sent his driver to kill him because he'd slept with his daughter? "Go back into the bedroom, Diamond. Please, baby," he pleaded.

The brothers shared a knowing look. Diamond had diamond studs in her ears, belly button, on her toes *and* a large diamond hoop between her legs. Walter waited until Diamond left. Redirecting his attention, he gave Tyrone a placating grin.

"I suppose you're wondering why we're here? Not only were you using drugs, but stupidly you involved the boss's daughter."

"I… I didn't know she… she was LP's kid until she told me," Tyrone stuttered in a hoarse whisper, his eyes filling with tears. The pressure on his throat was excruciating.

Bending, his knees framing Tyrone's head, Walter grasped his wrists, holding them in a savage grip until his fingers were outspread on the marble floor. He nodded to his brother, who took his foot off the singer's throat. A millionth of a second passed before the heel of Winston's shoe came down on Tyrone's left hand. The sound of bones breaking was chilling. A blood-curdling scream rent the air before fading into whimpering moans.

Walter bared his teeth like a rabid dog. "You're lucky that all you'll have is a sore hand. Screw up again and you'll be dropped from the label and it'll be another five years before you'll be able to sign with another," he warned softly. "Get rid of your little lady permanently, and it'll be up to you to make her forget what she saw here." Writhing in pain, Tyrone nodded. "You're a smart kid, so I know you'll come up with something imaginative to tell everyone how you hurt your hand. Mr. Parker will see you in his office tomorrow morning at ten o'clock. Try not to be late." Walter rose to his feet, turned and walked out, Winston following close behind.

Walter and Winston Rockwell shared identical DNA, but that's where the resemblance ended. Walter didn't smoke, drink or swear nor had he cheated on his wife since marrying her twenty-six years earlier. He'd grown up on the streets of Harlem with Langston Parker, watching each other's backs. Winston had joined a street gang, served three years in prison for burglary and, once paroled, became hired muscle for a drug dealer.

Two years ago Winston had called to tell Walter that he was moving to the west coast because he'd tired of New York's long, cold winters. What Walter hadn't known until he met his brother at the airport was that Winston had spent three weeks in the hospital recuperating from multiple gunshot wounds. Winston refused to disclose the circumstances behind his injuries, and Walter didn't press the issue. He allowed him to move into his guesthouse, convinced Langston to put him on his payroll and called upon his "special skills" whenever they were needed.

Supplying drugs to Langston Parker's daughter had proven to be a critical mistake for Tyrone Wyatt, and unfortunately Winston and Walter Rockwell had enforced the consequences for his lapse in judgment.

chapter six

Tyrone was ushered into Langston Parker's private office, his cast-covered left arm resting in a sling. He'd called a cousin after discovering he couldn't move his fingers, pleading with him to take him to a nearby hospital's emergency room. X-rays revealed a broken wrist and two fractured fingers. The attending orthopedist wrote a prescription for pain medication, but he'd had to take twice the prescribed dose to dull the excruciating throbbing. It was only after he'd smoked a blunt that he forgot about the pain, falling asleep until his cousin woke him to tell him that he had to be at LP Records by ten.

He stared at the back of the man whose broad shoulders, tapered waist and slimness belied his age. He, Tyrone Alan Wyatt—aka Tee Y who counted gang members amongst his friends and several family members, and at one time had held a loaded gun to the head of a man who'd challenged his manhood, was terrified of the president of LP Records.

Langston Parker had dispatched the bookend pit bulls to his place to send a message, and yet Tyrone knew if their boss had come then he would've sustained more than a broken wrist. What unnerved him about the man who'd signed him to a two-year, multimillion-dollar recording contract was that the record mogul never raised his voice—not even when issuing a warning or threat. It was as if ice water had replaced the blood in his veins.

* * *

Langston stared out the windows of the twelfth floor of his Century City office building. Seemingly he was transfixed by the traffic moving along Santa Monica Boulevard. He'd spent the night tossing and turning restlessly, and all because of the man standing in his office.

Turning slowly, he fixed his gaze on the platinum-selling recording artist. Tyrone Wyatt was what Langston considered superstar trifecta: he'd been blessed with looks, charm *and* talent. And rumors were swirling around Tinseltown that he was being considered for an acting role in a big-budget film, and that a TV producer had hinted that he wanted him for a new drama series where he'd become a part of an award-winning ensemble cast. He had so much going for him, yet he was about to lose it all because he'd chosen the wrong woman with whom to share his drugs.

Langston waved a hand. "Sit down, Wyatt."

Nodding and forcing what could pass for a smile, Tyrone walked on shaking legs to a nearby chair covered in dark-brown suede, collapsing into it like a rag doll. The combined effects of the painkiller and weed made it virtually impossible for him to maintain his balance and coordination.

"Thank you, Mr. Parker."

Coming around his desk, Langston leaned against it, crossing his arms over the front of his stark white shirt. A dark eyebrow lifted slightly. "What happened to your hand?"

Tyrone closed his eyes for several seconds to clear his thoughts. "As if you don't know," he drawled recklessly.

A slight frown appeared between the older man's eyes. "What did you say?"

Sitting up straighter, Tyrone was suddenly alert. The look on Langston Parker's face was one that didn't bode well for him. "What I meant is that I thought you knew."

"Why would I know?"

"Didn't you ..." His words trailed off when he swallowed the words poised on the tip of his tongue. "I'm sorry, Mr. Parker," he apologized quickly. "I'm not thinking clearly because of...because I'm taking...a painkiller. I fell and broke my wrist," Tyrone said quickly, attempting to cover up his faux pas.

"When did you break it?"

"Last night."

Langston gave Tyrone a long, penetrating look. There was something about the singer's face that reminded him of a young Marvin Gaye. "I have to assume it was after you shared your cocaine with my daughter." Tyrone dropped his head, nodding.

"I also know you tried to coerce my daughter into having sex with you and another woman!" Although Langston hadn't raised his voice, his accusation had the same effect as if he'd shouted it. "Did you think she wouldn't tell me?"

Shock rendered Tyrone motionless *and* speechless. "I...I didn't know she was your daughter until—"

"Until she told you," Langston said, finishing his statement.

Tyrone's heart was beating so fast that he thought he was having a heart attack. "I think I'm going to be sick," he mumbled, covering his mouth with his uninjured hand.

"Be sick on your on time," Langston crooned without a pretense at pity. "You throw up on my chair or rug and you'll clean it up with your tongue." He'd specially ordered the one-of-a-kind hand-knotted rug from Turkey.

Dots of perspiration stood out on Tyrone's forehead as he swallowed back the bile in the back of his throat. *I can't vomit. Not here.* He repeated the refrain over and over until miraculously the frightening moment passed.

"I'm sorry about that."

Langston decided to press his attack. "If word of what you

did last night gets out, then you're going to know firsthand what sorry is."

"It wasn't my idea to have a threesome."

"It wasn't your idea, yet you were ready to become a willing participant."

"I didn't know Diamond was hiding in the closet until after I'd…Breanna and I finished."

Langston shot him a disbelieving look. "You didn't know a woman was in your place? What kind of dumb ass do you take me for, Wyatt? I don't know what kind of kinky games you play, but I'm warning you to leave my daughter out of it, or you'll never work in this town again, and that includes movies and TV. And if you think I'm blowing smoke up your ass then all you have to do is call my bluff."

There was something in Langston's tone that told Tyrone he wasn't bluffing. Langston Parker had moved his three-man operation from New York City to Tinseltown ten years before Tyrone had been born. The record producer had been blessed with an innate gift for recognizing raw singing talent. A consecutive string of hits gave him the respect he sought to compete with the major labels, and five years later his name could be found on every recording, television and motion picture studio executive's guest list. Most of them had invited him because they were more than curious about the little-known music maverick with the Midas touch.

"I know you're not bluffing, Mr. Parker. And I didn't know she was your daughter until she told me. I saw her at the club and I liked what I saw, so that's why I approached her."

Shifting from his position, Langston sat down on the edge of his desk. "You like my daughter?"

A rush of confidence swept over Tyrone as he tried analyzing the shift in the mood of the man who signed his checks. There was no doubt Langston wanted to protect his daughter, but Tyrone wanted to tell the man that Breanna Renee Parker could take care of herself. He'd slept with a lot of girls before and after he'd become a high-profile recording artist, and he wanted to tell Langston that Renee was one of the more memorable ones.

He smiled, the elusive dimple in his right cheek winking attractively. "I like her a lot. I don't how she feels about me, but I'd like to ask her whether she will be my date for the Grammy awards."

The seconds ticked off as Langston glared at the cheeky young man sprawled carelessly on his chair. He failed to understand why most young men sat in their baggy pants with their legs spread apart and their crotches exposed. His mother and grandmother had slapped him upside the head whenever he failed to sit up straight.

"My daughter is at the age where I can't tell her who she should or shouldn't date. But if she agrees to go out with you and I find out that you're offering her shit then I *am* gonna stomp *yo muthafuckin'* brains out." Langston flashed a Cheshire-cat grin. "Do you catch my drift?"

Tyrone sat up straighter, exhaling an inaudible sigh of relief and counting himself blessed that he'd only gotten off with a broken wrist. Langston wasn't just blowing smoke when he'd issued his veiled death threat.

"Yes sir, I understand."

Waving a manicured hand in a gesture of dismissal, Langston straightened and turned his back. "Go home and stay there. Someone will call you to let you know when you're scheduled to go back into the studio."

Tyrone stood up. "When do you think I can begin recording—"

"I don't know," Langston snapped curtly. "I don't want you to leave your place except to see the doctor or if I send for you."

He turned to find an expression of shock freezing Tyrone's features. "Everyone coming and going will be monitored, so I suggest you choose your visitors wisely. I'll let Breanna know that you want to take her to the Grammys, and if she's amenable then she'll contact you."

Bowing as if Langston Parker were royalty, Tyrone smiled and backed out of the office. "Thank you, Mr. Parker."

Waiting until he was alone, Langston walked across the expansive office and closed the door. If smoking and eating rich foods didn't trigger another heart attack in him, then his daughter would.

Tyrone hadn't been completely truthful with his boss. He'd known Diamond was in the closet, watching and waiting for his cue to join him and the woman he hadn't known at the time was Langston Parker's daughter. It would have been the first time he and his secret girlfriend had engaged in a ménage à trois. After getting Renee high and screwing her he'd looked forward to a threesome. Diamond had been so turned on watching him with another woman that she'd done things to him he'd never experienced before.

But on the other hand he hadn't lied when he told Langston that he wanted to escort Breanna to the ceremony where he'd been nominated for six awards. Tyrone was willing to do anything, including begging and groveling, to maintain his recording contract *and* to sleep with Renee again.

After riding the elevator to the lobby, Tyrone walked out to the parking lot where his cousin sat behind the wheel of the late-model Hummer 2 Tyrone had picked up from the dealer earlier that week. Tarik had rolled down the windows and turned the radio up so loud that it could be heard from fifty feet away.

"Turn that shit down!" Within seconds the volume dropped

appreciably as Tyrone climbed up and onto the passenger seat. "Take me home." Leaning back against the leather seat, Tyrone willed his mind blank and the pain in his left hand gone.

chapter seven

Bree finished setting the dining-room table with china, silver and crystal. She'd spent all afternoon cooking in the hope that she would surprise Ryder and his partner with her cooking skills. In addition to language arts, foreign languages, mathematics and science, she and the other girls had been taught culinary arts and social deportment at boarding school. She loved cooking, excelling in French and Italian cuisine. Taking a backward step, she surveyed her handiwork.

It'd taken several calls to half a dozen gourmet shops before she could get one to agree to deliver the items she needed, charging them to her father's credit card. Bree knew she could've had her own credit cards if only she'd conformed to Langston's dictates.

Her financial dilemma would be remedied if she accepted a position with LP Records, but her parents couldn't—or didn't want to—accept that her passion was fashion not music. However, her financial woes would end when she came into her trust fund. She had less than two years—twenty-three months—until she'd be able to control her own destiny.

Glancing at her watch, she noted the time. It was a little after five. Ryder had called to inform her that he was coming home early with the intention of taking her out to dinner. She'd spent the past two nights at his house, but she'd been asleep whenever he and Connor returned home. Most nights they stopped at a twenty-four-hour sports club to work out.

She had mixed feelings when it came to her brother's domestic partner. Bree felt as if he was using her brother, and his display of jealousy and possessiveness was definitely misplaced when it came to her. After all, she was Ryder's sister, not someone vying for his attention, or a romantic liaison.

When Ryder had first disclosed his sexual proclivity, he'd also said that he believed he'd found his soul mate in Connor, who'd been born Willie Clyde Jackson but had legally changed his name to W. Connor Jennings, claiming it sounded more theatrical. As an aspiring actor Connor had spent years taking classes and auditioning for bit parts on soaps and prime-time dramas. At twenty-nine he was still waiting for his big break.

Since he'd hooked up with Ryder Connor had stopped waiting tables and enrolled in advanced acting classes, studied with a celebrated drama coach and worked out at an upscale sports club. In an effort to assist Connor realize his dream, Ryder had assumed the responsibility of supporting him financially.

Bree retreated to the guest wing to shower and change before Ryder and Connor arrived. She'd come to love the views from the expansive windows of the custom-designed Hollywood Hills home. Nearly four thousand square feet of living space made it possible for her to share the house with the two men without any of them running into one another at every turn.

Ryder usually left early for classes at Occidental College where he'd enrolled in their writing program, while Connor slept late, except when he had an audition. His afternoons were filled with acting classes and private lessons with an acting coach.

Her brother's offer to share his living space with Bree presented her with a respite from her critical, controlling mother.

All she had to do was be patient, and the next two years would be over before she knew it.

Bree was standing in the living room when Ryder walked in with Connor. She gave her brother a bright smile. "Welcome home."

Ryder, closing the distance between them, pulled her to his chest and kissed her cheek. "Thank you."

Holding her at arm's length, he studied his sister intently. Her skin was flawless, reminiscent of whipped chocolate mousse. Her eyes were like a doll's, round and slightly slanting at the corners. He'd teased her, saying she could've been the prototype for a black Barbie. Her tiny nose and full, lush mouth gave her the look of a petulant child. And that's what she'd been for as long as he could remember. Breanna was always surly and impudent. Even when he'd cautioned her not to talk back to their mother she refused to heed his warnings. The verbal clashes always ended with Karma as victor and Bree on a jet for a return flight to Switzerland.

"I have a surprise for you," Bree said cheerfully.

Lowering his arms, Ryder lifted a reddish-brown eyebrow. "What is it?"

"I cooked dinner. As soon as you and Connor wash up, I'll begin serving."

"You cook?" he teased, as he reached out to pull the length of hair she'd secured with an elastic band.

Resting a hand over his chest in a gesture reminiscent of silent actors, Connor let out an audible gasp. "Be careful you don't pull out her weave!"

Bree rolled her eyes at the man she'd grown to dislike the more knew about him, successfully biting back the acerbic retort on the tip of her tongue. Forcing a smile that froze before it reached her eyes, she said, "As I said before, I'll begin serving as soon as you wash up." Turning on her heels, she headed in the direction of the kitchen.

Ryder glared at his partner after Bree left the room. "Was that necessary?"

"What are you talking about?" Connor affected a perfected expression of innocence.

Ryder studied the tall handsome man with whom he'd fallen in love. The first time he'd seen the former Willie Clyde Jackson he'd felt as if he'd been struck by a bolt of electricity. What had shocked Ryder most was that he'd never reacted to a man the way he had with Connor. He'd seen himself as heterosexual until he became involved with Connor.

"You didn't have to talk about her hair."

"Well, she is wearing a weave, isn't she?"

"Yes. But, you didn't have to be tactless and mention it," Ryder chided softly.

Frowning, Connor crossed muscular arms over his chest. "I'm not the one wearing dead hair and from what I've heard about your little sister, she's not that thin-skinned."

"What the hell are you talking about?"

"Check out TMZ.com under the topic of 'Naughty Girl,' and you'll know what I'm talking about." Connor winked at Ryder as he made his way across the living room, the rubber soles of his boots leaving black smudges on the pale marble floor. Ryder was an obsessive compulsive when it came to his house. He'd contracted with a cleaning service to come in five days a week to dust and clean what had been dusted and cleaned the day before. Normally Connor would've taken off the boots and left them outside the front door, but right now he didn't care about the priceless floor because he was angry with Ryder for inviting his sister to live with them.

Ryder watched his partner's retreating figure. They would soon celebrate their second anniversary as a couple. He'd met

Connor at a club when both had attended a private party for a Golden Globe-nominated television actress. They'd hung out together for year, while Ryder continued to date women, but everything had changed when he and Connor had shared a bed for the first time. He'd never had a lover as selfless as the aspiring actor; whatever Ryder wanted him to do he did.

They'd discussed at length about making their relationship public, but Connor claimed being labeled a gay actor would limit his roles. After all, at six-one and two hundred and ten pounds of solid muscle, he was the perfect physical specimen as a tough-guy character. His agent had concluded that he had the right "look" for soaps, and was now steering his client in that direction.

Ryder and Connor were seldom seen in public together, and if he was asked about their association Ryder lied, claiming Connor was a cousin who'd moved in with him while he pursued his acting career. The lie was plausible because there was a marked physical resemblance in their height and coloring. Connor was fortunate enough to have inherited Middle Eastern or Caribbean features, and his most marketable talent was for perfecting accents.

Ryder wasn't certain whether the tension between his sister and his lover was real or imagined, and one thing he didn't want to do was take sides. Breanna was his sister, but as long as he was with Connor he felt emotionally connected to him.

He recalled Connor's comment about TMZ.com and made a mental note to check the Internet. It wouldn't be the first time his sister had captured the media's attention with her aberrant behavior. She hadn't been in the States a month when she'd been photographed with her tongue down the throat of a barely legal boy-band singer. And when she'd hooked up with Sierra Bellows and Letisha Walsh they'd become the tripartite embodiment of Hollywood hell-raisers.

After dinner he would check the latest cyberspace gossip, then he would have a serious face-to-face with his sister. She was only twenty-three, and if she didn't curtail her self-destructive behavior then she would become one more statistic in the growing number of young Hollywood celebrities whose lives ended tragically.

chapter eight

Bree busied herself filling water goblets with sparkling water and lighting the tapers in crystal holders. The white wine was chilled, and she'd opened the bottle of merlot to let it breathe. Ryder, a wine aficionado, had a collection of vintage wines spanning thirty years, and he was a familiar figure at wine auctions whenever a rare vintage went on sale.

She dimmed the overhead chandelier and retreated to the gourmet kitchen to bring out the first course: arugula leaves, asparagus spears and bite-size pieces of smoked chicken breast topped with a macadamia-nut dressing and garnished with sprigs of fresh chervil. She'd sliced a baguette and toasted the slices until they were crisp and golden-brown to accompany the salad.

"You fucked up not once, but twice. I don't eat meat and nuts make my face swell."

Bree's head came around quickly. Connor had come into the dining room without making a sound. "What did you say?"

"I said I don't eat meat and I'm allergic to nuts."

She narrowed her eyes. "Not that—*bitch!*" She'd rolled her neck with the expletive. "I'm talking about your saying that I 'fucked up.' "

The muscles in Connor's shoulders bunched up under his black tank top as he took a step. "Who're you calling a bitch, *be-yotch?*"

Bree glared at the man who'd elected not to pass along his

exquisite gene pool to another generation. If he'd been straight, there would've been no doubt that she would've found herself attracted to him. She wasn't remotely fazed by his sexual leaning, but she was enraged because she knew he was using Ryder.

"You—*bitch!*" she spat out. "Anytime a healthy, able-bodied man permits another man to take care of his basic needs then he's nothing more than a bitch. Or, would you prefer that I call you a *punk* bitch!"

Connor rounded the table, stopping suddenly when a plate of salad sailed within inches of his head. His eyes narrowed and hardened when he saw the steak knife in Bree's hand. He smiled. "What do you plan to do with that?"

"I'll gut yo' pimping ass if you take another step."

"I don't think so, bitch," Connor crooned.

"What did you call her?" Ryder asked as he walked into the dining room to find his sister and his lover glaring at each other.

Connor forcibly swallowed his rage. It wouldn't pay for him to alienate Ryder; after all, blood was thicker than water. "She called me a bitch, so I was just returning the favor."

"I don't care what she called you. And, if you ever disrespect my sister again, you better look for someplace else to live."

The fragile rein Connor had on his volatile temper snapped. "I can't believe you're taking her side without hearing me out, Ryder. Everything was perfect until she came. Her being here has changed you. We don't even make love anymore," he continued recklessly. "Is it because you don't want her to hear us? We're consenting adults and—"

"That's enough, Connor," Ryder cautioned softly. "Right now you need to calm down."

"Fuck calming down, Ryder! What if I don't want to calm down?"

"Go for a walk, Connor. I need to talk to my sister."

A full minute passed before Connor swallowed his pride. He knew when he'd been bested. He would go along with Ryder Parker because he didn't have too many options. In fact, he had *no* options. He had no job, no money and he had no intention of joining the hoardes of homeless scratching out a day-to-day existence on the streets of L.A.

"I'm sorry, Breanna."

Bree didn't know whether Connor was sincere, but at least he'd extended the olive branch. "I'm sorry, too, Connor."

Waiting until she was alone with Ryder, she put down the knife and rounded the table and knelt down to pick up the salad.

"Leave it," Ryder ordered, grasping her arm and pulling her forcibly to her feet. He tightened his grip on her upper arm. "Come with me."

She pulled back. "I need to wipe up the olive oil."

"Don't worry about the floor."

Bree knew Ryder was angry. He was talking through clenched teeth. "I'm going back to Bel Air," she announced as they entered the solarium.

Ryder stared at his sister's strained profile. "You don't have to leave." She turned to face him, her expression softening.

"I know I don't, but I want to, Ry. Besides, I promised Mother that I would spend some time with her."

"You're kidding?"

Bree shook her head. "No, I'm not kidding. We've declared a truce. Fragile as it is I'm going to try and keep it."

"When are you leaving?"

"I think it'd be better if I left tonight."

Closing the distance between them, Ryder wrapped his arms around Bree's shoulders, dropping a kiss on her hair. "You don't have to leave tonight. I can always have Connor spend the night in a hotel."

Tilting her head, Bree recognized pain in the gaze fusing with hers. "Don't do that, Ryder. I'm leaving tonight, so you can make peace with Connor."

"Is that really what you want?"

"Yes."

Ryder kissed her forehead. "Are you sure you're going to be all right?"

She winked at him. "When have I not been all right?" Not waiting for a reply, Bree walked out of the solarium, leaving her brother staring at her back. She hadn't planned to return to Bel Air until the end of the week, but the rising tension between her and Connor would force Ryder to choose between her and his lover.

She didn't want him to choose.

She wanted him to see Connor for what he really was.

The former Willie Clyde Jackson was nothing more than a parasite.

chapter nine

Bree dropped her bag on the passenger-side seat, rounded the car and slipped behind the wheel. Reaching into her handbag, she turned on her cell phone, activating the Bluetooth feature. She hadn't turned on the phone in days because she hadn't wanted to talk to anyone.

It would've stayed off indefinitely if she'd stayed with her brother, yet what she'd suspected had come to fruition. Connor didn't like her *and* she didn't like or trust him. If she'd known he had an allergy she would've ground up the macadamias then watched him blow up like a puffer fish.

Connor reminded Bree of her boarding-school roommate: during the week Tara Stevens was the perfect student and tidy roommate; practically monosyllabic. Come the weekend Tara morphed into a femme fatale, making the rounds of the local clubs and attracting older, well-to-do men like bees to honey. Six months before graduation she'd been arrested for solicitation. She'd embraced the world's oldest profession to earn money to maintain her clandestine drug addiction. Although they'd shared a room, Bree had never suspected that Tara was abusing drugs.

Bree thought of Connor as a male whore who'd targeted Ryder just as Tara had targeted the men she'd seduced. What Bree found puzzling was that Ryder hadn't exhibited any signs of being attracted to a same-sex partner until he'd met Willie

Clyde Jackson. He'd always dated women, although none of his liaisons had lasted more than six months, and she was uncertain whether Ryder'd been the one to end them, or whether he was commitment phobic. Not only had Connor moved into Ryder's house, but he'd also gotten him to provide the financial support he needed to pursue his acting career. She knew Connor wouldn't be able to keep up the act, and like Ryder's female partners before him, Connor would eventually be sent packing.

A distinctive chime from her cell indicated she had a text message. Activating the feature, she counted the number of text messages from Letisha and Sierra. There were eight texts from Sierra and six from Letisha. Rather than read the messages, she punched in Sierra's speed dial.

"Why are you blowing up my cell?" Bree asked when Sierra answered.

"Where are you Bree, and thanks for saying hello."

"I'm in Hollywood Hills. Why?"

"You *have* to come to my place."

"Why?"

"Please, Bree, don't start interrogating me over the phone. Just come."

Bree heard the underlying panic in her friend's tone. "Okay."

Ending the call, she slipped on a pair of oversize sunglasses before she started up her car and maneuvered out of the driveway in a burst of speed. She wasn't particularly fond of her stateside friends, but preferred Sierra to Letisha who hadn't attended college, had no intention of enrolling and lived off the money her father doled out to her whenever she went to him with her hand out.

Sierra was different. The daughter of a Japanese-American mother and an African-American father, she'd had dropped out of Stanford in the middle of her junior year when she'd decided she didn't want to become a lawyer like her parents. Her mother had become a prominent divorce attorney for high-profile actors, while her father was head counsel for LP Records. Sierra now attended classes at UCLA as an art history and design major.

Bree left the Sunset exit of the 405 Freeway, turned onto Sunset Boulevard and into the Museum Heights Brentwood neighborhood. She left her car in visitor parking at Sierra's ultra-modern glass-encased condominium.

"What's up with all the nine-one-one texts?" she asked Sierra when she opened the door.

Sierra's large clear brown eyes shimmered with unshed tears when she met Bree's questioning gaze. "You'll have to see for yourself."

Bree followed her friend through a spacious entryway and into a living room decorated with Asian- and African-influenced furnishings. The first time she'd come to Sierra's apartment she'd been taken aback by the meticulously chosen tables, lamps, chairs and accessories, believing the young woman had worked with an interior decorator. When Sierra had told her she'd taken more than a year to select the furniture for her spacious condo Bree knew Sierra had found her passion.

Sierra touched the mouse on her computer work station and what appeared on the large flat monitor paralyzed Bree. An icy chill swept over her at the same time as an exhalation of shock escaped her parted lips. The images were grainy, but she recognized the man and woman rolling around on the king-size bed as sounds of unrestrained moans and groans of sexual ecstasy assaulted her. She closed her eyes, but she couldn't shut out the sound of her own voice when the image of a woman came into camera range. Someone had videotaped her and Tyrone Wyatt having sex, then her pronouncement that she was Langston Parker's daughter.

"No!" she screamed. She was still screaming when her cell phone rang, the sound penetrating the disbelief weaving its way into her brain.

"Bree, your cell is ringing," Sierra shouted.

Her hands were shaking when she reached into her bag to retrieve her phone. Not bothering to look at the display, she put the tiny instrument to her ear. "This is Bree."

"Where are you?" Ryder's voice reverberated in her ear.

"I'm at Sierra's."

"What were you thinking, Bree?"

She closed her eyes, praying that Ryder hadn't seen the video before she could explain what had happened. "What are you talking about?"

"Not only is your sexcapade with Tee Y in living color on the Internet, but why the hell did you have to identify yourself to the world?"

"I swear I didn't know I was being videotaped."

"Hold on, Bree, I have another call coming through. Shit! It's Dad."

"Damn!" she whispered, as she waited for Ryder to come back on the line. Her gaze met Sierra's. "My brother knows, and it's only a matter of time before my father will also know."

"The shit's 'bout to hit the fan," Sierra said. She was more than familiar with her godfather's celebrated temper. It wasn't often that Langston Parker displayed his emotions but when he did everyone found something else to do or somewhere to go.

Bree heard a soft click, then Ryder's voice again. "Dad wants you home now."

She nodded even though her brother couldn't see her. "I'm on my way." Pressing a button, she ended the call and hugged Sierra. "Thanks for the heads-up."

Sierra returned the nod, fear and another emotion clearly

etched on her full, round face. She forced a smile that tilted the corners of her full mouth. "Good luck, girl."

"I need more than luck," Bree whispered under her breath. What she needed was a miracle to extricate herself from her latest dilemma.

chapter ten

Bree downshifted, slowing and maneuvering along the winding Bel Air street. Her eyes widened when she saw them: some were leaning against car bumpers, while others were pacing like large cats at feeding time, and it was obvious that she was the main course. The paparazzi were camped out on the block, waiting for her to put in an appearance.

Right now the only way she would be able to avoid the long-lens cameras was either to join a convent or go into complete seclusion in the Bel Air mansion—two things she hadn't wanted to do. Twelve years of living in castle-like structures with high stone walls, massive iron gates to keep the girls in and boys out, rigid headmistresses and enough inflexible rules and regulations to last two lifetimes had taken its toll in her quest for complete freedom.

She let out a ragged sigh. She'd recovered enough to accept that she couldn't change what was. She'd met a man, gone home with him, shared drugs and sex with him, so she would just have to take her lumps. After all, she and Tyrone were consenting adults, so what the hell was everyone so shook up about?

Sex with Tyrone had been an enjoyable encounter, but his taping their tryst raised her hackles. And posting it on the Internet was his undoing. A hint of a smile touched her mouth. If the photo hounds wanted something for their sleazy tabloids, then she was going to give it to them. Depressing the clutch, she shifted into a higher gear. Her foot hit the gas pedal and the car shot forward in a streak of red, the roar of the powerful engine drowning out the voices of the photographers who were caught off-guard. Reaching up, Bree pressed a button on the remote device attached to the visor and the electronic iron gates shielding the Parker property from intruders swung open smoothly as the Porsche sped through.

Photographers scrambled wildly to focus their cameras, hoping to capture the image of the driver. Only those lounging on the sidewalk near the gates were lucky enough to capture Breanna Parker's profile before the gates closed behind the fast-moving car.

Bree parked about twenty feet away from a six-car garage and made her way into the house through a rear entrance, running into the live-in cook carrying a tray of finger foods. "What's going on, Miss Ileana? Why is there a van parked outside?"

Ileana Serrano gave her employer's daughter a blank stare. What she'd asked was of no concern to the hired help. Langston Parker had come home earlier than usual and locked himself in his library, not emerging until the butler knocked on the door to inform Langston that his visitors had arrived.

She'd worked for the Parkers for seventeen years, and during that time she'd become an American citizen, had learned to mind her business *and* keep her mouth shut. A portion of the money she earned as a cook she gave to her brother to pay for his daughter's college education.

Ileana wasn't going to do or say anything to upset her very orderly existence; she lived in a grand house, had paid health care, free meals and a month's paid vacation.

Lowering her gaze, Ileana stared at the tray of hors d'oeuvres she'd hastily put together when Mrs. Parker had informed her that they were having guests. "You have to ask your father."

"I will." Bree knew she wouldn't be able to get anything out of the cook, or any other household employee.

Walking down a narrow hallway that opened out into a sitting area off the formal living room, Bree saw her mother perched stiffly, legs crossed, on the edge of a silk-covered armchair. Clenched fists, ramrod-straight back and compressed lips said it all: Karma Ryder Parker was tense.

"What's going on, Mother?"

Karma turned her head slowly, as if she feared breaking into millions of tiny pieces. Her eyes flared pain and fire. Her face appeared to crumble in slow motion. "How could you, Breanna?" Her pain spilled over with the trembling query.

Bree went completely still. It was apparent that her mother believed that she'd agreed to be videotaped in bed with a man.

"You think I planned it, don't you? You actually believe I wanted someone to film me in bed with a man?" The tears glistening in Bree's eyes slowly found their way down her cheeks as she bit hard on her lower lip to still its trembling.

Karma blinked once, her heart pounding a runaway rhythm in her chest as a shock flew through her. Seeing the tears reminded her of the only other time she'd ever seen her daughter cry. It had been the day Mother Superior had escorted the six-year-old Bree out of the office to meet the other young girls who were enrolled in the Mount Carmel School for Girls. She'd been expelled at the end of the school year and sent to an all-girls' school twenty kilometers outside Zurich, Switzerland. That time, when she and Langston left Breanna, there were no tears, not even a good-bye. The seven-year-old had walked away without a backward glance, her head held high.

The thing Karma remembered was the vacant look in daughter's eyes as she was led away—an expression she'd never seen again until now. Heaviness settled in her chest making it difficult for her to draw a normal breath. She'd given birth to a healthy, beautiful baby girl and it'd taken her twenty-three years to acknowledge her daughter as her own flesh and blood.

Moving off the chair, she approached Bree and cradled her face between her hands. She saw her tears, felt her trembling. "It's going to be all right, baby. Your daddy and I are going to take care of everything."

Bree felt the warmth from her mother's body, inhaled the perfume that was so intrinsically Karma Parker and she heard the softly spoken words of comfort. The vestiges of resistance and resentment that had festered over the years made her feel uncomfortable. This was a woman she didn't know how to respond to.

Burying her face against Karma's scented neck she closed her eyes and lost herself in the shared moment; mother and daughter were almost as close as they'd been when Karma had carried her unborn child beneath her heart.

"I'm sorry, Mama," Bree sobbed with another rush of tears.

"Hush, baby, don't cry. You don't want your eyes puffy when you're in front of the camera."

Bree went completely still. "What are you talking about?"

Karma lowered her arms and took a step backwards. "Your father has arranged a press conference with a photographer and reporter from *The Insider.* He wants you to give an account of what actually happened before the tabloids fabricate their sordid lies."

"What's this really about, Mother? Is it about damage control or protecting your image?"

A rush of color darkened Karma's face. "This is definitely not about me or your father so it has to be about you, Breanna. I'm not the one who's become tramp of the month!"

"Let's not make things worse than they are with us by being at one another's throats." Bree and Karma turned at the same time to see Langston standing only a few feet away. And from the expression on his face it was apparent he'd overheard their heated exchange.

Walking over to her father, Bree hugged him. "Do I have to talk to a reporter?"

Langston lowered his chin and kissed the top of her head. "Yes." Reaching out he cupped her chin in his hand. "Go upstairs and clean up your face. We'll be waiting for you in the library."

She nodded. "Okay."

Waiting until they were alone, Langston glared at his wife. "When are you ever going to learn that screaming and calling her names doesn't solve anything?"

Karma's eyes narrowed as she struggled to control her rising temper. "Why don't you tell me what the answer is? She's been back six months, and not a week has gone by when she hasn't done something to embarrass us."

Langston smiled at his wife. "Don't be so hard on her, Karma. She's still a young girl."

"She's a full-grown woman, Lang, and much too old to act out like a spoiled child."

Langston extended his hand. "We'll talk about this later. Come with me, darling. In less than half an hour all of this will be behind us."

Karma wanted to believe her husband, but knew all too well that their daughter's acting out was payback—payback for sending her away.

chapter eleven

Bree hesitated for a beat when she met the gazes of those sitting on the leather and suede seating grouping in Langston Parker's office/library. Her parents sat together on a cream suede loveseat. Nathaniel Bellows, Sierra's father and the head of LP Records's legal division sat on a matching chair, while an undernourished-looking photographer stood off to the side checking the room's light with a meter. She didn't recognize the person she assumed was the correspondent from *The Insider,* since she never watched celebrity gossip television.

The hair on the back of her neck stood up as she spotted the last person she thought she'd ever ever see. Sitting on her father's right in a straight-back leather chair was Tyrone Wyatt, his left hand and forearm covered with a cast. Their gazes met, fused for several seconds before Bree glanced away. All of the men stood up, waiting until she took the last remaining chair next to Tyrone before reclaiming their seats.

Langston nodded to Nathaniel. "We're ready." It was the photographer's cue to begin filming.

Nathaniel, a brilliant entertainment attorney with a deep rumbling voice, crossed his legs. As usual, he was impeccably dressed. His features reminded Bree of those she'd seen on African masks, and, with his shaved head gleaming like polished teak, he could have been a model for those sculptors.

"As legal representative for the Parkers, I want to say that this entire interview will be on the record." He and Langston had decided beforehand that informing the entertainment reporter they had nothing to hide would dispel the rumors that Breanna had become a willing participant in taping the sex act. "First of all, I want to say that the very personal and intimate act between Breanna Parker and Tyrone Wyatt should've remained that—personal."

The journalist leaned forward in his chair. "Are you saying it was obtained without their knowledge?"

"That's exactly what I'm saying. When Mr. Wyatt and Miss Parker returned to his home, Mr. Wyatt had no idea that a woman who'd apparently been stalking him for months had gained access to his condo."

The reporter turned to Tyrone. "Are you familiar with the woman?"

There came a beat when Tyrone stared directly at Bree. "No. I'm not familiar with her," he lied smoothly, "but I have seen her around a few of the clubs. I never paid her much attention until she jumped out of my closet."

"Did you know she'd been following you?"

Tyrone lifted his broad shoulders under a midnight-blue silk jacket. "No."

The reporter pressed his attack. "How is it she got into your apartment when you live in a complex with twenty-four-hour concierge?"

Tyrone's mouth thinned and the dimple in his right cheek softened his attractive masculine features. "That's something building security is investigating."

"What about you, Miss Parker? Did you know the young woman hiding in the closet?"

Bree shook her head. "I never saw her before that night."

"How familiar are you with Tyrone Wyatt?"

She and Tyrone stared at each other. "He's under contract with LP Records, so I'm quite familiar with him."

"Are you a couple?"

Bree wanted to tell the reporter that sleeping with someone once did not make them a couple. "I'm not ready to go public with that information," she said instead.

"Why did you feel it was necessary to identify yourself on the tape?"

Bree paused. "When Tee Y's stalker suggested a threesome I felt compelled to tell her who I was." She didn't want to reveal that it was Tyrone who'd whispered in her ear that he had a surprise for her, and, much to her shock, he'd wanted to watch as another woman made love to her.

The reporter took a quick glance at his notes then focused his attention on Breanna. "You've become L.A.'s latest bad girl—"

"Naughty girl," Bree said, interrupting him, with a beguiling smile. "There *is* a difference."

Smiling, he nodded. "Did you sunbathe topless at a poolside party to upstage the guest of honor, because she referred to you as, and I quote, 'a ho?' "

Bree's eyebrows lifted slightly. "With whom am I supposed to be feuding?"

"Sources have reported that you and Raina Hunter had a heated argument after which you took off your top, jumped into the pool and then spent the rest of the party sleeping topless on a chaise to shift attention away from her."

Bree stared directly into the lens of the camera. She'd had words with the talentless starlet, but she wasn't going to admit it on tape. "I'd like to set the record straight that I'm not feuding with Raina or anyone else in L.A. Topless bathing is acceptable in Europe, so it's going to take some time for me to not think and behave like a European."

"How many years did you live in Europe?"

"Sixteen. I was educated there."

"Why Europe and not the States?"

"Why not Europe?" she asked. "The schools I attended are some of the best in the world, and my parents wanted to give me the best."

"Do you agree that it was the best for you?"

Bree chose her words carefully. "At first I didn't, but as I matured I realized I never would've been exposed to so many different cultures and languages if I'd been educated in the States."

"How many languages do you speak?"

"I'm fluent in French, Italian, German and, of course, English."

The reporter turned to Tyrone. "Are you willing to talk about your relationship with Breanna?"

He rested his arm over the back of Breanna's chair as she glanced up to meet his lingering stare; the camera captured the blatant, intimate gesture. "Breanna and I wanted to keep our private lives private, but unfortunately this stalking incident destroyed what we've worked so hard to safeguard."

Bree couldn't stop the smile tilting the corners of her mouth. She had to hand it to Tyrone. He was good—very, very good. In fact, he was the smoothest liar she'd ever met.

The interview continued for another ten minutes and Karma found that she couldn't look away. Her daughter's freshly scrubbed face shimmered with good health, making her look barely out of her teens. Her hair, parted in the middle, was tucked behind her ears. Recessed lighting sparkled off the diamond studs in her pierced lobes. A white man-tailored shirt, jeans and leather mules enhanced her casual, dressed-down look. Even her voice was mesmerizing. The embodiment of poise, she'd answered the reporter's questions intelligently while exhibiting a maturity beyond her years. It was as if the tears Karma had witnessed earlier had never happened.

How was it, she mused, that she actually didn't know Breanna Renee Parker? An unplanned pregnancy, difficult delivery and post-partum depression had left her emotionally empty and unable to nurture her infant daughter.

Karma closed her eyes, praying she'd be able to develop a relationship with Bree before she lost her altogether.

chapter twelve

The interview over, Bree reached for the cell phone tucked into the waistband of her jeans as she leaned closer to Tyrone. "I need to talk to you," she said in a quiet tone.

Tyrone stared at the tall, slender woman who looked nothing like the one who'd introduced herself to him as Renee. When he'd asked whether she had a last name her response had been *Renee is all you need to know.* He'd never suspected that Renee was Breanna Parker, whose father literally and figuratively held his future in his powerful grasp. Aside from her natural dark-skinned beauty, Tyrone admired her confidence *and* sassiness. She'd acted as if she were the platinum-selling artist, while he was nothing more than her lackey. It was only when she'd revealed her full name that he'd understood why: she was the daughter of a Grammy-award winning mother and a record mogul father.

Leaning toward her, he pressed his mouth to Bree's ear. "We can't talk here."

Bree nodded. "Come with me." Reaching for his uninjured hand, she stood up and led Tyrone out of the library and into a room off the kitchen where the household staff took their breaks. She sat on a high stool at a butcher-block table, motioning for him to take the one opposite her. Resting her elbows on the top, she peered closely at the man whose sensual features made her feel things she didn't want to feel, and a shiver of lust had her nether region pulsing. She might not have been forthcoming with her true identity, but that couldn't begin to compare to the subterfuge that he'd obviously concocted.

Tyrone rested his cast-covered hand on the table. He angled his head. "Wazzup, Renee?

Fire flashed behind Bree's eyes. "I should be the one asking you what's up—Tee Y." Tyrone flashed the crooked smile that most women found so endearing.

"With the exception of a fucked-up hand, not much is goin' on."

"I beg to differ with you," Bree countered, her expression impassive.

"What you say?"

A frown appeared between her eyes. "Lose the ebonics, Tyrone. I'm not impressed with affected thug personas."

She was aware that Tyrone Wyatt, unlike so many young rap and hip-hop artists, hadn't chosen a career in music because he viewed it as a means of achieving fame and money, but because it was his passion. He'd grown up in a middle-class Oakland neighborhood as an indulged only child with his widowed schoolteacher mother.

Tensing, Tyrone felt waves of heat eddy up the back of his neck. Within seconds the tremors swept over him and he found it impossible to control his arms and legs. It had been a year since he'd had his last panic attack. The first one had come during his last year of high school, and the accompanying symptoms resembled those of someone experiencing a seizure. He closed his eyes, counting slowly and praying he would be able to slow his heart rate. His right hand was shaking uncontrollably as he raised it to wipe away the moisture dotting his upper lip.

Bree saw the moisture on Tyrone's face, heard his labored breathing and she forced herself not to panic. Scrambling off the stool, she went over to him, her arms going around his waist.

"Are you all right?" He nodded, but she knew he was lying to her. She managed to ease him off the stool to lie on the floor. His eyes were rolling back in his head. "I'm going to get help."

Tyrone lay on the cool terracotta tiles, awash in sweat and shame. Breanna had seen what he'd shown only a few—complete helplessness. Not even when Langston Parker dispatched his enforcers to teach him a lesson had he felt *this* vulnerable. He wasn't certain how long he lay on the floor, but he'd recovered and was sitting up when Breanna returned with her father.

Langston went down on one knee. "Are you all right, son?"

Tyrone swallowed, finding the reflex painful as he tried relieving the dryness in his constricted throat. "I think so," he whispered.

Anchoring a hand under the younger man's shoulder, Langston pulled him to his feet. "What happened?"

Tyrone swayed slightly before regaining his balance. "I think it was a reaction to the pain medication I took earlier." Tyrone had told yet another lie. He'd lied more since meeting Breanna than he had in years. Yet there was no way he was going to admit to anyone—especially Langston Parker—that he suffered from panic attacks; rumors were circulating among those in the hip-hop community that he was "soft." Other rappers claimed his songs lacked the hard-core lyrics so pervasive throughout the genre, and if word got out that he had a panic disorder then there was no doubt he'd be labeled a bitch.

Langston frowned. "Stop taking them." It was the second time he'd witnessed Tyrone sick. "Do you want me to call a doctor?"

"No, thank you. I'll be all right in a few minutes."

"Are you sure?" Bree asked.

Tyrone forced a smile. "Yes."

Despite his predicament, he couldn't stop reliving sleeping with Bree. He'd lost count of the number of women he'd slept with since signing on with LP Records, but there was something about the way they'd connected in and out of bed that made Bree unforgettable.

There was silence for a moment and then Bree said, "We'll talk again when you're feeling better."

"What if I call you tomorrow?"

"No, I'll call you."

Tyrone didn't want to argue with Bree, not with her father watching him as if he was a piece of offal that he wanted rid of. As much as he didn't want to acknowledge it, Langston Parker had saved his ass *and* his career when Nathaniel Bellows had briefed him on the questions from the entertainment reporter. He was told that the footage would be edited and when shown to the viewing public Tyrone Wyatt and Breanna Parker would be seen as unwitting victims of an obsessive stalker.

Langston's dark gaze shifted from his client to his daughter and then back again. There was something impalpable going on between them—something he wasn't able to discern. Something his grandmother had said came to mind: *If whatever it was didn't come out in the wash then it was certain to come out in the rinse.* He'd lived long enough to know that patience was a virtue, and for him patience was never in short supply.

"Rock is waiting outside to take you home."

Tyrone curbed the urge to genuflect. He would go home and stay there as ordered. He'd gotten a reprieve, and if things had gone the other way he knew the record producer would've eviscerated him.

"Good night, Mr. Parker." He nodded to Bree. "Good night, Breanna."

He felt two pairs of eyes boring into his back as he walked out of the mansion and into the cool, fragrant L.A. night where Walter Rockwell waited to drive him home.

chapter thirteen

Bree took a deep breath, and held it for several seconds before letting it out slowly. Tyrone's reaction to his pain medication had thwarted her attempt to get answers from him. She wanted to know who the woman was who'd hidden in the closet, whose idea had it been to tape them and who'd uploaded the tape onto the Internet.

She looked at her father, unable to read his closed expression. Langston was as much a stranger to her as she was to him. "Thank you, Daddy."

Langston nodded. "Just don't get caught up in something like this again." That said, he turned on his heels and walked away.

For the tiniest fraction of time, she went completely still, startled by his warning. Did he actually believe she'd orchestrated someone taping her while having sex? Did he think she needed that kind of negative attention? What she couldn't believe was that it was the second time Langston had uttered the same warning.

Yes—there were occasions when she'd drunk too much, smoked weed or snorted coke and then attempted to drive, but the truth was she didn't sleep around. She'd plead guilty to abusing booze and drugs, but she was not a slut.

Bree used a staircase at the rear of the house to avoid talking to her mother. Karma, stylishly dressed and coiffed, had sat through the televised interview, like the consummate actress she was, her expression holding enough concern and pain to make her a candidate for mother of the year. But inwardly Bree knew Karma was seething with rage and contempt. She would talk to her mother, but not tonight.

Walking into her suite of rooms, Bree closed and locked the door behind her. Making her way through an expansive sitting area, she entered the bathroom and filled the garden tub with water and scented bath salts. She stripped off her clothes, leaving them on a nearby chair and sank into the warm lavender-infused water. Sighing audibly, she rested her head on a bath pillow, closing her eyes and recounting what had taken place in her father's office/library.

Tyrone wasn't the first man she'd slept with since returning to the States. She'd lost her virginity at fifteen to her much-older French ski instructor. Her lessons had ended abruptly when she told him she was pregnant; he'd calmly revealed that he was a married man with three children, he wasn't going to leave his wife and he couldn't afford to support another child.

She'd placed a call to her parents telling them of her dilemma, and they'd flown to Switzerland the following day. In less than a week she was granted a leave of absence from her school. She went to stay at a convent in Brussels until she delivered her child. Langston, with Nathaniel Bellows's assistance had arranged for a childless American couple to adopt the baby. Bree was a week past her sixteenth birthday when, after twenty-two hours in labor, she delivered a healthy baby girl. Her parents flew back to the States with her father's warning imprinted on her brain: *Don't get caught up in something like this again.* She'd heeded his warning, and had a doctor insert an IUD as protection.

Bree returned to school the following year and threw herself into her studies in earnest, graduating third in a class of thirty-four. Her best friend had told everyone that Bree had come down with mononucleosis and she didn't confirm or deny the malady. However, the fact remained that she'd become an unwed teenage mother.

The water had cooled and the bubbles were gone when she stepped out of the tub, wrapping a bath sheet around her body. In a few short hours she had gone from preparing dinner for her brother and his partner to seeing images of herself on the Internet writhing on a bed with a superstar performer and participating in a rehearsed impromptu interview orchestrated to salvage what little of her so-called good reputation remained.

She wasn't one to instigate trouble yet it seemed to follow as if she were a magnet.

Bree had settled into bed, her back supported by several pillows, and her journal resting on her knees when her cell phone rang. Taking a quick glance at the display, she picked up the tiny instrument.

"Hello, Ryder."

"How was the interview?"

"You knew about the interview?"

"I just got off the phone with Dad."

"It went okay," she admitted.

"If it went okay, then why do I hear doom and gloom in your voice?"

Bree closed her eyes. "It's going to take me a while to get over everyone seeing Tee Y screwing his boss's daughter."

"What if you and your hip-hop boyfriend—"

"He's not my boyfriend!"

"He may not be your boyfriend, but if the two of you are seen together publicly, then it would silence the gossips if word gets out that you were a one-night stand for him."

"Once you see the interview you'll believe that we *are* a couple."

"Do you like him, Bree?"

What, she mused, did her brother want her to say? That sleeping with Tyrone had been an incredible experience? "I could get to like him."

"Would you like some brotherly advice?"

Bree smiled. "What's that?"

"Go out with him for a couple of months, while doing the whole red-carpet scenario, and if it doesn't work out then you make a clean break and move on. And keep in mind that you don't have to sleep with him again if you don't want to."

But I do want to sleep with him, she thought. She wanted to uncover whether Tyrone was *that* good. "I think I'm going to take your advice."

"Good."

"How's Connor?"

"He's okay."

"I'm sorry about—"

"Forget it, Bree. Connor's good."

"Thanks for letting me hang out with you for a couple of days."

"There's no need to thank me, Bree. Any time you want to hang out here, just let yourself in. You have keys."

She nodded. Not only had her brother opened his home to her, but he'd also given her a set of keys. "You're a saint, Ryder Parker."

"If you knew what Connor and I do with each other you wouldn't say that—"

"Hold up, brother. That's a little too much information."

"On that note, I'm going to hang up. Good night, baby sis."

"Good night, bro."

Bree ended the call, took note of the time on the cell phone and then placed it on the bedside table. The night felt thousands of hours old although it was only minutes before ten.

Closing her journal, she put it on the table and turned off the lamp. All she wanted was to sleep and forget that she'd been publicly humiliated.

She lay in the darkened room reliving the images flickering across Sierra's computer monitor. After a while, the images faded as sleep crept over her, bringing with it a comforting peace.

chapter fourteen

Bree wended her way down a long hallway that led to another wing of the Mediterranean-style house where Karma, when at home, spent the majority of her time. She walked into the space that her mother had set up as her study. Heavy, dark Spanish-inspired furnishings dominated the expansive area, southeast exposure flooding the beautiful room with sunlight.

Sitting on a silk-covered armchair near the door, she waited for her mother to finish dictating a letter to a woman who was the personification of efficiency. Judi Cramer, a petite middle-aged woman with short steel-gray hair and piercing gray eyes, was the last of a steady stream of assistants Karma had employed over the past decade. Not only had Judi survived the mandatory three-month probationary period, she'd recently celebrated her fourth year as Karma Parker's personal assistant.

Judi guarded Karma's privacy with the same tenacity as the Secret Service, and Bree acknowledged the woman with a barely perceptible nod when she turned to see who'd entered her boss's inner sanctum.

As the wife of a prominent businessman Karma's days and nights were filled with board meetings, charitable and political fund-raisers, lunch dates with three other women who went by the sobriquet "the wild bunch," and standing weekly appointments at an exclusive Beverly Hills salon for a manicure, pedicure, hairdo and facial.

Karma glanced up over the frames of her reading glasses, meeting Bree's gaze, only her eyes expressing surprise; recent Botox injections had immobilized the muscles in her face. Her words flowed as she continued dictating a letter to a consortium of small businesses, thanking them for their generous contribution to purchase Christmas toys for needy children.

Bree closed her eyes so she wouldn't see her mother's frozen, supercilious expression. What she wanted really to do was put her fingers in her ears to shut out the facetious, saccharine gratitude dripping from her lips like warm honey.

She opened her eyes, staring at the woman who'd given birth to her, a woman she called mother but to whom couldn't relate. The persona Karma Ryder-Parker presented to the world wasn't the same woman who'd born a daughter, then unceremoniously shut her out of her life. That Karma watched every morsel she put into her mouth, had her plastic surgeon on speed dial and flew to Paris and Milan twice a year to view the coming season's haute couture.

"Breanna, darling, do you need me right now, or can it wait until later?"

Bree rolled her eyes at her mother. "Have you made a decision as to where you want us to go?"

"Yes. I believe Catalina Island would be the perfect getaway."

"When are we leaving?"

"I don't have anything on my calendar until Christmas Eve, so I thought perhaps we could leave tomorrow and stay a couple of days. What do you think?"

"It's okay."

"It's okay?" Karma repeated.

"It sounds wonderful, Mother," Bree said, forcing herself to sound enthusiastic.

"It's going to be wonderful," Karma said confidently. "After I finish with my correspondence, if you want, we can do lunch."

Bree stood up. "I can't. I have to meet someone. I'll be home in time for dinner." Karma sat down to dinner every night at seven, with or without her husband, with or without her children.

Karma nodded when she wanted to smile. "Ryder has promised to come tonight, so it'll be the first time in weeks that we'll all eat together."

"Is he bringing company?"

"No. He said that his *friend* has a prior engagement."

"That's too bad." *Now, who's being facetious?* Bree mused.

"It is," Karma crooned.

The two women shared a knowing look. It was the first time they'd agreed on something, signaling a beginning and the possibility that they weren't as different as they'd believed they were.

chapter fifteen

Bree didn't want to have lunch with her mother. She wanted to talk. She returned to her bedroom and dialed the number of Langston's private line at the record company, smiling when she heard his voice. His executive assistant only answered his private calls when he wasn't in the office.

"How's my favorite girl?"

"I thought Mother was your favorite girl?"

Langston laughed softly. "Your mother hasn't been a girl in a very long time."

"Don't let her hear you say that," Bree warned, smiling.

"She'd be the first to admit it. I had the accountant add up what I've paid out to her plastic surgeon over the years, and it's enough to put his kid through medical school."

"Damn!"

"Ditto," Langston said. "But I know you didn't call me to talk about your mother."

"You're right, Daddy. I need Tyrone Wyatt's number."

There came a pregnant pause from Langston. "Why?"

"I need to talk to him."

"Right now I'd prefer if you didn't have any contact with Wyatt."

"I have to, Daddy. I need to find out what he knows about the tape."

"I'm going to have someone look into it."

A warning voice whispered in Bree's head that whatever her father uncovered wouldn't bode well for Tyrone. "Please hold off, Daddy, until I talk to him."

"What makes you think he'll be truthful with you?"

"He wants to talk."

"Did he tell you that?"

"Yes."

A heavy sigh came through the earpiece. "Okay. I'll tell my man to hold off for now."

Bree's smile was dazzling. "Thanks, Daddy. Now, will you please give me his number?" Langston granted her request, giving her numbers to Tyrone's cell *and* his home.

"How are you getting to his place? When I left the house this morning I spotted a couple of photographers hanging out at the foot of the hill."

"I plan to call a taxi."

"Don't bother," Langston said. "I'll send Rock over to pick you up."

"Thanks again, Daddy."

"No problem, sweet baby girl."

A rush of tears filled Bree's eyes as she rang off. She didn't know why, but her father's endearments always brought her to tears. All of her life she'd wanted to be daddy's little girl, yet Karma had come between them with her displays of jealousy and feigned bouts of depression. But now, at twenty-three, she was much too old to be any man's "sweet baby girl."

Tyrone stood in the doorway in his bare feet waiting as Breanna Parker stepped out of the elevator. Minutes after her call, he'd gotten out of bed, showered and pulled on a T-shirt and walking shorts. The instant he'd heard her voice, his mood, as dark and gloomy as the rainy day, brightened. She'd asked if he was busy and he wanted to say that, thanks to her father, he was on lockdown *and* unofficial house arrest, but he admitted to wanting to see her again.

With the exception of Tarik, who brought him food from takeout restaurants, he hadn't had any other visitors. And because he only had the use of one hand he'd loaned the Hummer to Tarik, who had the audacity to complain about how much he had to spend to gas up the vehicle.

If he'd had to sustain a broken hand, then he was grateful it wasn't his right hand. At least he could shower, feed and dress himself, albeit very slowly, which provided him a modicum of independence.

His face split into a wide grin with *Renee*'s approach. Everyone called her Bree or Breanna, but to him she would always be Renee. Today she looked different—yet again dressed entirely in black: baseball cap, jeans, riding boots and a three-quarter-length raincoat. Her eyes were hidden behind a pair of oversized sunglasses.

Brushing past Tyrone, Bree walked through the entryway and into a living room decorated in chrome and glass and black and white leather. The first time she'd come to the condo she hadn't taken notice of the furnishings. The space looked sterile, reminding her of the furniture in Karma's plastic surgeon's waiting room. What she did remember was the circular wrought-iron staircase leading up to the bedrooms.

The heat from Tyrone's body seeped into hers when he came to stand behind her. He smelled of soap and his body's natural masculine scent, a scent she remembered even when she hadn't remembered every aspect of his face. When she'd walked into her father's library and seen him there her heart had stopped momentarily, only to kick into a higher gear making her feel lightheaded. His physical pull on her was as powerful as the moon on the ocean; she helpless to resist the intangible force.

"Please sit down, Breanna." Waiting until she sat on a loveseat, he took the one facing her. "Would you like something to drink?"

Taking off her glasses, Bree shook her head. "No thank you." Raising her chin, she gave him a direct stare. "I came here for two things—to get my underwear before it ends up on eBay and to get the truth from you."

"Your panties are upstairs."

"What about the truth?" Bree knew she had to get Tyrone to tell her everything about that night.

"I said all I'm going to say to that reporter."

A heavy silence filled the space as Bree glared at the arrogant young man who refused to accept blame for what had become an embarrassment not only to her but to her family. "I haven't said all that needs to be said," she said cryptically.

For a fraction of a moment, Tyrone went completely still, stunned by the softly spoken veiled threat. "You don't know what you're talking about."

Bree pushed to her feet. "I may have been high, but I wasn't so high I don't remember you telling me that you had a surprise for me. Instead of popping out of a cake, your surprise came out of your closet. Tell me, whose idea was it to tape us—yours or Goldilocks?"

"I had nothing to do with the taping. And I hope you're not threatening me."

Tyrone Wyatt had taken enough intimidation from the Parkers. Langston was one thing because he'd changed Tyrone's life for the better. However, a woman getting in his face was something he refused to put up with.

Not only was he frustrated, he was coming down off a high after taking three pills followed by a joint from the last of his weed supply. The pills, which should've lasted him ten days, he had taken in three.

"I don't have to threaten you. I'm merely issuing a warning." Bree slipped on her sunglasses, her delicate jaw tightening as she successfully swallowed the curses she wanted to spew at Tyrone. "Go get my underwear," she ordered.

Tyrone's right hand tightened into a fist. If Breanna had been any other woman but Langston's daughter he would've hit her. He gave her a lingering glare then headed toward the staircase.

Bree paced back and forth in front of a picture window as Tyrone climbed the staircase. She'd come to see Tyrone as much to protect him as to get answers. He was an incredible talent and what he didn't know was that Langston Parker had ended the careers of others signed to his label with a scrawl of his signature.

Reaching for her cell phone, she dialed her father's private line for the second time that day. His phone rang six times before going to voice-mail. It was apparent both her father and his assistant were out. "Daddy, this Bree. I'm leaving Tee Y's place now. Call me back on my cell when you get this message."

Tyrone stopped on the last stair, listening to Breanna as she held a phone to her ear. She hadn't lied when she said she'd come to warn him. But he had to ask himself who was she seeking to protect him from? It had to be Langston or she never would've come to him.

"I'll tell you whatever it is you want to know."

Bree had just completed her message to her father when she realized Tyrone had come back. Turning, she saw fear in his gaze and heard a note of imperceptible pleading in his voice.

Bree held out her hand for the scrap of black silk. Tyrone tossed her her thong panty and she stuffed it into her handbag. She returned to the loveseat and sat. "Talk, Tyrone, and please don't leave anything out."

chapter sixteen

Staring at his bare legs and feet, Tyrone took a breath. "I lied when I said I didn't know Diamond."

"Her name is Diamond?"

Tyrone's head came up, meeting her incredulous stare. "That's her stage name. She's an exotic dancer."

"How did you meet her?"

"She'd come to an after-party in Atlanta. We kicked it a few times. The next city on the tour was Miami, and she showed up there, too. She told me that she used to work in some of the clubs outside Atlantic City but had to leave because she was the only eyewitness to a pimp who'd beaten a hooker to death because she owed him money."

"You hooked up with a hooker?"

"Exotic dancer."

Bree rolled her eyes. "A rose by any other name still has thorns. Is she still dancing?"

"No."

"Is she working?"

"No."

"You're taking care of her." Bree's query was a statement.

He nodded. "She had a tough childhood, so I thought I'd help her out. I told her she could stay here, but she didn't want anyone to know she was living with me."

Bree rolled her eyes again, unable to believe he could be *that* gullible. There was no doubt the girl was a hooker and Tyrone Wyatt aka Tee Y had become her latest mark.

"Whose idea was it to videotape us?"

Suddenly Tyrone's expression grew hard, resentful. "It had to have been hers. Diamond and I had agreed beforehand that if brought someone home we'd have a threesome."

"Are you saying that she took the pictures without your permission?"

"I may have lied about not knowing her, but I'm not lying when I say that I'd never agree to being photographed while having sex."

"When did she upload the tape to the Internet?"

"It was after I told her that she couldn't live with me any longer."

Bree and Tyrone stared at each other, seconds ticking off into a full minute. "You were set up, Tyrone," she finally said in a quiet voice. "Diamond had you thinking with the head between your legs instead of the one between your ears, and you fell right into her trap. That girl is nothing but trouble and it's best that she's gone."

"Hooking up with her was a mistake. Can I make it up to you?"

Bree forced a slight smile. "Maybe." Rising, she adjusted the shoulder strap of her handbag. "I'll be in touch," she said in parting and walked across the living room to the door. She opened and closed it softly behind her, leaving Tyrone motionless, staring at rivulets of rain sluicing down the wall-to-wall, floor-to-ceiling windows.

chapter seventeen

Bree smiled at Walter Rockwell as he held open the rear door to the stretch Mercedes Benz. Her meeting with Tyrone had taken less than half an hour.

"Thank you, Uncle Rock."

Walter's penetrating gaze swept over his goddaughter. She didn't look any different than she had before she went to see Tyrone Wyatt. When Langston had told him to drive Bree to the singer's condominium, he'd thought his lifelong friend had lost his mind, but although he was closer to Langston than to his own twin, he knew enough not to question his motives.

He got in behind the wheel, started up the limo and then peered up into the rearview mirror. Bree had closed her eyes while resting her head against the back of the leather seat. "Are you all right?"

Her eyes opened. "I'm okay."

Rock didn't believe her. "Your father gave me the afternoon off. Would you like me to drive you somewhere?"

Bree managed a tired smile. "No, thank you. Please take me home."

She wanted to go home and stay there—for a very long time. If it were possible she would remain cloistered behind the thick abode walls and electronic gates until her twenty-fifth birthday.

She'd returned to the States believing she would have the same independence she'd had in Paris. When she'd moved into the furnished one-bedroom flat along the Left Bank Bree had been suddenly faced with the realization that she was totally responsible for her day-to-day existence. No one would prepare her meals, wash her clothes or provide lodging as they had at the boarding school.

Langston cabled money to her Parisian bank account at the beginning of each month to cover her living expenses. The first month she'd spent it with wild abandon, eating all her meals at cafés and restaurants and going to jazz clubs several nights a week. The third week had found her completely broke. She would've starved if not for a baguette, half a pound of cheese and two bottles of wine. Too embarrassed and proud to ask her classmates to loan her enough euros to tide her over until her father replenished her account, she divided her larder into portions that kept starvation at bay until a call from the bank gave her the news she'd anxiously awaited.

That frightening ordeal taught her to set up a budget and keep to it. After paying her rent, she went shopping to fill her pantry, prepared lunch to eat in between classes and curtailed her nighttime social escapades to one night each week. There were men—much older men—who offered to take care of her needs, but the offer always came with a caveat: they wanted to share her bed.

Bree waited until her senior year to become involved with a fellow student. Kahlil stayed over at her flat during the week and she lived with him at his on the weekend. Her relationship with Kahlil was easygoing, comfortable. There was no need for declarations of love or promises of a happily-ever-after, because he was engaged to marry a girl from his native country.

They were students, living in a foreign country and they both loved fashion. What Bree shared with Kahlil wasn't based on sex but on companionship and male protection. Whenever she lay in bed with him, her body pressed to his, she'd pretend he was hers—totally hers to love forever. And, she did learn to love him—his patience, gentleness and his ability to make her laugh at life and herself. He'd teased her, saying that she was nothing more than a poor little rich girl who'd chosen to live among the commoners in a drafty flat because she felt the need to rebel against capitalism. No matter how many times she tried to convince him that she wasn't a socialist, he refused to believe her.

Kahlil returned to Morocco to marry and join an uncle's textile business, while she'd come back to the States to pursue a career in fashion design, unaware that Langston had created a position for her at the record company. The proverbial shit hit the fan once she informed him that she had no intention of working for LP Records. Her father retaliated by cutting off her allowance, but Bree overcame the obstacle of being cash-poor by using her mother's accounts. Whenever she needed money to hang out she went to Ryder. He usually gave her whatever cash he had on hand. Knowing she could go to Ryder made her two-year wait tolerable.

The chiming of her cell disturbed the quietness inside the uber-luxury sedan. Reaching into her handbag she answered the call without looking at the display. "This is Bree."

"There was something else I didn't say to you."

Sitting up straighter, Bree stared at the partition between her and Walter Rockwell. Her godfather did double duty as Langston's chauffeur and bodyguard, and it was a rare occasion when he didn't carry the licensed automatic he concealed in a shoulder holster. Even during the sweltering L.A. summer heat he wore a jacket.

"What is it, Tyrone?" Her tone was one of unadulterated boredom, while her heart beat a rapid tattoo against her ribs. Every time she relived making love with Tyrone her body betrayed her.

"I'd like to know if you'd come to the Grammy Awards with me."

Her mouth opened and closed several times before she said, "What?"

"I'd like you to be my date for the awards."

"You must be smoking crack, Ty—"

"I already asked your father," he said, cutting her off.

"My father can't speak for me," Bree retorted angrily.

"That's what he said."

"When did he say that?"

"It was the day he asked that I come to his office to talk about you and me."

"What did he say when you asked him?"

"He said he can't tell you who you can or can't date. And he also said that if I offered you *shit* again that I could forget about a singing career."

Bree smiled. "That sounds like my father. It isn't often that he has to threaten someone."

Tyrone's warm laughter came through the tiny earpiece. "I suppose I'd become the exception. Back to why I called. Will you go with me?"

"Let me think about it."

"What's there to think about, beautiful?"

"Dial down the bull, Tyrone. As I said, I'll let you know."

"Thanks, Bree. At least you didn't say no."

"I don't want you to forget that I could say no."

"I'll keep that in mind."

"You do that," she said, ending the call.

Bree knew that if she continued her conversation with Tyrone, she would give in to the sensual magnetism that radiated from him like waves of heat. Whether he was wearing a tailored suit and his trademark hat with the turned-up brim perched on his head at a cocky angle, or wearing next to nothing, at six-six, two-hundred-ten-pound, twenty-four-year-old Tyrone Wyatt had become the media's latest sex symbol. He was the complete package: looks, brains, talent and sex.

Bree thought about what Ryder had said about she and Tyrone being seen in public together to offset some of the rumors about their alleged relationship. She'd agreed to take her brother's advice. She also needed to tread carefully in order not to get caught up in another scandal.

chapter eighteen

Bree didn't understand why her mother wanted her family to eat together when there was hardly any conversation until after dessert was served. Karma claimed it interfered with digestion to talk while eating.

Bree caught Ryder's gaze across the table as she swallowed a slice of fork-tender meat. Ileana had outdone herself when she'd prepared a scrumptious dinner of pink peppercorn rack of lamb, buttered green beans and roasted Yukon Gold potatoes. Ryder had arrived with two bottles of wines—red and white—from his private stock.

"What courses are you taking next semester?" Bree asked her brother.

Putting down his knife and fork, Ryder pressed a damask napkin to his mouth. "I signed up for Women of Words and American Short-Story Writers."

"Ryder, darling, you know we don't discuss business over dinner," Karma chastised sweetly.

Langston, having drained his wineglass, set it down and glared his wife. "Karma, I don't understand you."

"What is there not to understand, Lang?"

"You complain that as a family we don't get together enough, and now, when we're all here, you don't want anyone to talk."

His words, though spoken softly, held an edge of steel, which was more than familiar to Karma. There had never been a need for Langston to raise his voice at his wife or his children. Anyone who knew Langston Parker knew that he always spoke his mind.

"Those sound like interesting courses, son," he continued without taking a breath.

"I'm really looking forward to the one on short-story writers," Ryder replied, smiling. It was the first time that his father had broached the subject of his returning to college.

Langston refilled his glass with merlot. "What kind of writing do you want to do?"

Ryder's features became more animated than his family had seen in months. His decision to leave LP Records to pursue a career as a writer had been a source of contention between himself and his parents. Langston considered his actions traitorous, while Karma blamed his defection on Connor.

"Right now I'm leaning toward literary magazines. But, eventually I'd like to get into publishing."

"Which type of publishing?" Bree asked.

"It'll probably be book publishing. I'm not sure whether it'll be fiction or nonfiction."

"Why didn't you tell us years ago that you wanted to be a writer?" Karma asked, joining the conversation for the first time.

A swollen silence filled the dining room as the four occupants regarded one another intently. Ryder laced his fingers together. "At the risk of sounding self-absorbed, I didn't want to say anything because I didn't want to lose my trust."

Langston closed his eyes and inhaled a deep breath. When he opened his eyes they were filled with pain. "Did you really think I would retaliate and disinherit you because you did something I didn't agree with?"

"I didn't want to risk it, Dad."

A flash of anger replaced the hurt as Langston glared at his son. "When have you known me to take revenge on my family—my children in particular? You've disappointed me, Ryder, as has Breanna with her immature behavior, but I'd never withhold what I've promised you. The trusts were set up as irrevocable, which means whether I'm dead or alive the funds are available within twenty-four hours following your twenty-fifth birthday. The monies, including earned interest, are exempt as community property in a divorce proceeding, so if your domestic partner decides to sue for palimony, then I suggest you tell him that he's assed-out. I say all of this to let you know that you still could've been with LP Records, and I would've permitted you to rearrange your schedule to accommodate you taking classes."

Ryder stared down at the food on his plate. "I didn't know that, Dad."

"That's because you didn't trust me enough to come to me and tell me your plans. My father didn't live to see me become a man, but if he had there wouldn't have been anything I wouldn't have run past him."

Ryder managed to look contrite. "You're right," he conceded, "but I saw how you ran your company and how the employees reacted whenever you walked by or called them into your office. You scared the living shit out of them."

Langston's gaze narrowed. "Do I scare the living shit out of you, Ryder?"

"Lang, please," Karma pleaded.

"Stay out of this, Karma," he warned. "I have more respect for Breanna, because she told me straight up that she wasn't coming to work for LP Records. Not only is she the one with the business background, but it also looks like she's the one with the balls."

Pushing back his chair, Ryder rose to his feet. Tension covered the room like a shroud, tightening until there was only the sound of measured breathing. A flush of color had darkened Ryder's face as a muscle danced spasmodically in his jaw.

"Thank you, Father, for letting me know exactly how you feel about me." He nodded to Karma. "It's not going to work, Mother. We'll never be the family you want us to be." Rounding the table, he leaned over and kissed Bree's cheek. "Call me."

Reaching up, she held his hand. "Love you, bro."

He kissed her again. "Love you back, sis."

Waiting until Ryder walked out of the room, Bree glared at her mother, then her father. "Why can't you accept that he's not going to be what you want him to be? He wants to be a writer, not a record producer. He's involved with a man, which means he's never going to father children to carry on the Parker line. Why can't you be happy for him because he's doing what makes him happy?"

"He's so confused," Karma crooned.

"Oh, please," Bree said, sneering. "Ryder's confused while I'm fucked-up."

Langston's fist hit the table with a dull thud. "Watch your mouth, Breanna."

Anger and the need to lash out at her parents for the ongoing pain they caused Ryder because of his lifestyle choice made Bree reckless. "You should tell your wife to watch her mouth, because I'm only repeating what she said to me."

Langston pounded the table again. "Enough!"

Standing quickly, she almost tipped over her chair. "Daddy, why do you always take her side? Even when you know she's wrong you side with her. What makes her better than us?" Turning on her heels, she raced out of the room, ignoring her mother and father as they called out to her to stay.

What she'd hoped would become an easygoing family dinner had turned into a personal attack on Ryder. She'd memorized the Ten Commandments and the one that always stuck in her head was: Honor thy father and thy mother: that thy days may be long upon the land which the Lord thy God giveth thee.

She lost count of the number of times she'd gotten on her knees to pray that her mother would come and take her home. The prayers had stopped when she'd developed unattractive calluses on her knees from kneeling on the stone floor.

It'd been Ryder, not Karma or Langston who'd called her every weekend. And it was Ryder who sent her cards with funny pictures and even funnier messages to lift her sagging spirits whenever she cried during their telephone conversations.

Bree wanted to live with Ryder until she was financially independent, but hadn't wanted to come between him and his partner. She'd promised Karma that she would accompany her to Catalina Island and she would. Spending several days alone with her mother would either bring them together or cause an irreparable rift that would last an eternity.

chapter nineteen

Karma reined in her temper, swallowed her rage and chose her words carefully. It wouldn't pay for her to blow up at Langston when he was in a bad mood. He'd come home scowling, monosyllabic, and when she'd asked him what was wrong his response had resembled a grunt.

"Did you have to be so hard on Ryder, Lang?"

Langston glared at his wife over the rim of his wineglass. "In case you haven't noticed, *your* son is a grown-ass man. He's soft, Karma, because you've turned him into a mama's boy. And, why are you asking me about Ryder when it's Breanna you should be more concerned with."

Pinpoints of heat stung Karma's cheeks. "You told me you were going to take care of pulling that awful video from the Internet."

Setting down his glass, Langston touched his napkin to his mouth. "I did take care of it and it's been pulled. But I'd also expected you to ask me about it."

Karma's eyelids fluttered wildly. "I'd told myself that if I didn't talk about it, then I wouldn't have to relive the whole sordid episode." She blinked back tears. "Lang, darling, what are we going to do with her?"

Langston saw the look of distress marring his wife's beautiful face. He'd met the former Carmen Rodriquez when she was only fifteen, and had found himself instantly enthralled with her beauty, talent and hunger for success. He married her two days after she'd celebrated her eighteenth birthday and she'd made him a father for the first time two weeks before her nineteenth birthday.

"You're going to have to love, support and protect her, Karma."

"I'm trying, Lang. That's why I suggested a mother-daughter getaway weekend."

"That's a start, sweetheart." Langston covered a yawn with his hand. "I'm going to take a shower and turn in early tonight. I'll try and wait up for you."

Karma knew whenever Langston turned in early he wanted to make love to her. The frequency with which they made love had decreased appreciably after her husband's heart surgery, yet, whenever they did have sex she found it more than satisfying.

"Don't wait up for me, darling. I'm not certain when I'm coming to bed."

Langston Parker's coal-black eyes widened in a face the color of polished mahogany. "Are you having an affair?" He'd never known Karma not to join him when he readied himself for bed.

Karma found breathing difficult as she replayed her husband's accusation over and over in her head. Not once since she'd married Langston had she ever looked at another man. The truth was that he was and had been the only man in her life. She'd had a few schoolgirl crushes, one or two pretend boyfriends, yet none had ever touched her, seen her naked, or gone so far as to make love to her. It wasn't until after she'd exchanged vows with Langston that she'd offered him her love, her innocence and her future.

"I can't believe you'd ask me that," she whispered, her voice trembling.

Resting his elbows on the table, Langston angled his salt-and-pepper head. "We always retire for bed together."

"I need to sign a few more Christmas cards and then finish packing."

"I thought you were packed."

"Not completely. I still have to pack my toiletries and feminine items. My period hasn't been regular, so I'm not certain when it's coming."

Langston smiled. "Maybe you're pregnant," he teased. "I wouldn't mind hearing the patter of little feet around the house."

Karma sucked her teeth, while at the same time rolling her eyes at her husband. She knew Langston hadn't wanted her to get her tubes tied after she'd had Bree, but he'd agreed when her doctor had stated that another pregnancy would exacerbate her depression.

A scowl distorted her delicate features. "You're crazy as hell, Langston Ashley Parker. Even if I hadn't had my tubes tied I wouldn't have another baby at my age."

"A lot of women are still giving birth in their forties," Langston said, smiling.

"Oh, not this forty-five-year-old woman, Lang. And, if by some crazy fluke I got pregnant I'd abort—"

"Stop it! Please don't say it, Karma."

She saw the pain in the dark eyes staring intently at her, heard the pain in his voice. Langston's first wife had had two abortions during their short-lived marriage because she'd been sleeping with her husband and another man at the same time, and hadn't known whose child she was carrying. "I'm sorry, darling. You know I don't believe in abortion. The only patter of little feet we should hear would be our grandchildren's."

"I don't know when that's going to happen, sweetheart," Langston said, sighing.

Rising from her chair, Karma rounded the table to sit on her husband's lap. "Maybe Bree will surprise us one of these days when she decides to settle down."

Reaching up, Langston combed his fingers through the soft curls on the nape of his wife's neck. "Don't hold your breath." He pressed a kiss to her ear. "Come to bed with me, baby."

"To do what, darling?" she teased.

"I want to show the most beautiful woman in the world how much I love her."

Karma rested a hand over his heart. "Are you sure you feel all right?" She'd found herself holding back her passion once she and Langston had resumed sexual relations for fear of his heart condition.

"If I have to check out while in the saddle, then I'm certain I'll die a happy man."

"Hush!" she admonished. "Don't talk foolish. You're going to live a very long time, Langston."

Shifting slightly, Langston covered Karma's mouth with his. "There are times when you talk too much, baby." Easing her off his lap, he stood up. Holding her hand in a firm grip, he led her out of the dining room, down a hallway to a rear staircase leading to the second floor.

Karma leaned against her husband as much for physical support as emotional reinforcement. Not a day had passed since she'd become Mrs. Langston Parker that Karma hadn't told her husband that she loved him.. She knew she was a good wife, but she hadn't been a very good mother. But she hoped that would change tomorrow. She had only two uninterrupted days with Bree to offset the alienation that had existed for twenty-three years.

chapter twenty

Bree slept during the drive from Los Angeles to Newport Beach, waking only when her mother shook her gently to let her know they'd arrived in time to board the ferry to take them to Catalina Island.

After leaving the dinner table the night before, she'd retreated to her bedroom and called Sierra to ask whether she wanted to hang out together. Sierra's cell had been turned off, and Bree had decided not to leave a voice-mail message. She did consider calling Letisha Walsh but had quickly changed her mind. Bree preferred her own company to dealing with Letisha's whining. She'd sat up most of the night watching classic black-and-white movies not so much for their storylines but for the fashions. Dawn had brightened the sky when she'd finally fallen asleep, only to be awakened by her mother telling her that their driver was waiting to drive them to Long Beach for the ferry ride to Avalon on Catalina Island.

Bree hadn't had to pack because she'd done it days before. Showered and wearing baggy sweatpants and a matching shirt, well-worn running shoes, and a painter's cap pulled low over her brow, and with a pair of sunglasses covering her puffy eyes, she was hardly recognizable as the woman whose amorous exhibition had been fodder for the media's rumor gristmill.

Settling down in a chair next to her mother, Bree gave her a sidelong glance. "You look nice this morning."

Karma, casually dressed in a pair of mango-colored silk slacks, a white silk tunic top with trumpet sleeves and variegated pastel fabric-covered pumps looked absolutely ravishing. Her eyes and rich mocha-hued skin were literally glowing. She also wore a straw-colored wide-brimmed hat to protect her face from the damaging rays of the California sun. At forty-five, her few gray hairs were quickly covered with a rinse that matched her natural dark-auburn hair. Thanks to Botox injections there were no telltale frown or laugh lines to mar her flawless complexion.

Her daughter's compliment caught Karma completely off-guard. Recovering quickly, she gave her a rare smile. "Thank you, Bree."

Closing her eyes, Bree smiled before quickly smothering a yawn. "You're welcome, Mother."

"You must have been up very late, because when I came into your bedroom this morning the television was still on."

"It must have been some time after four before I fell asleep, because I did see the beginning to *To Kill a Mockingbird.*

"Even though I never saw the film I loved the book," Karma admitted.

The ferryboat, carrying less than half its capacity, pulled away from the dock; passengers standing at the rail stared at the churning waters of San Pedro Channel. The sky was a startling blue with only a few puffy clouds, the morning temperatures in the low seventies and Bree experienced a sense of freedom on the water that she never felt on dry land. A cool breeze coming off the water feathered over her face. Taking a trans-atlantic cruise was at the top of her to-do list once she was solvent.

Karma's disclosure that she'd read a modern American classic shocked Bree because she never saw her mother with a book. Magazines and supermarket tabloids were her reading choices, not books, unlike Langston whose library was packed tightly with titles from every subject and genre.

"Mother, why didn't you go to college?" she asked Karma.

A moment of silence followed Bree's query. "I don't know. I married your father right out of high school and less than a year later I became a mother."

"Had you planned to go to college before you met Daddy?"

"Once I met your father it was as if I couldn't think straight. I was only fifteen when I came face-to-face with him for the first time. I was the lead singer and youngest of a girl group trying to break into the music business. All of us were either working part-time while going to school, or holding down two jobs to pay our manager to set us up at a Manhattan recording studio to cut a demo. Meanwhile we were writing songs and taking turns rehearsing in one another's apartments. After we'd given our manager enough money to pay for five hours of studio time he disappeared."

"What did you do?"

"There wasn't much we could do. The other girls gave up their dreams but I'd held on to mine. I'd read somewhere about Langston Parker signing new singing talent, so I wrote him a letter telling about our manager running out on us with our money, and that he only had to give us five minutes to prove that we were legitimate. He wrote back, saying he liked my spunk and if I called his assistant he would set up an appointment to see us."

Bree sat up straighter, shocked and intrigued by Karma's willingness to talk about her past. Whenever she'd asked her mother about her childhood she'd become mute. Not only was Karma a mystery to her daughter, but she was also an anomaly among those in her social circle. Langston had jealously guarded her singing career, keeping her out of the spotlight, which added to her mystique. She'd won an armful of awards at seventeen, married Langston at eighteen, and then abruptly quit the business.

"What happened?"

"One girl opted out, another had gotten engaged and her boyfriend didn't want her in the group and the third found out that she was pregnant, so she had to drop out. When I told my mother about what I'd done she told me to audition as a single act. She, my aunt and grandmother went with me to the audition and three months later I had a contract.

"I'd become the label's first female artist and Langston banked everything he had up to that point on my success. It took a year to find the right songs for my range and pitch, and another six months to complete the album. I came out of the chute on fire. Seven of the ten cuts went gold within of weeks of their release. I won a Grammy for Best New Artist, Best Female R&B Vocal Performer, Best R&B Song and Lang earned his first Non-Classical Producer of the Year."

"Were you dating Daddy during this time?"

Karma emitted an audible sigh as she crossed her arms over her chest in a protective gesture. "When I met your father he was married to another woman."

Bree leaned forward, her gaze narrowing. "*You* dated a married man?"

A wave of deep color crept up Karma's neck to her face. "I was a virgin when I married your father."

"I didn't ask whether you were sleeping with him."

Karma shook her head. "I didn't share a bed with Lang until our wedding night," she countered haughtily. "Your father married a girl from his neighborhood, but what he didn't know was that she'd continued to sleep with an old boyfriend even when married. She got pregnant, but didn't know whose baby she was carrying, so she decided to abort. When your father discovered that she'd had two abortions he filed for divorce."

"How long were they married?"

"Two years."

Bree listened intently as Karma disclosed her uneventful first pregnancy that was followed by postpartum depression lasting several weeks. "Ryder had turned three when Lang and I decided to have another baby. I got pregnant again, but went into premature labor at the beginning of the last trimester." Karma closed her eyes to stem the tears pricking the backs of her eyelids. When she opened them they were shimmering with unshed moisture. "It was a girl. She was stillborn."

"Mama, I didn't know," Bree whispered, reaching over and grasping her mother's ice-cold fingers. It was the first time since she'd been a little girl that she'd called Karma *Mama.*

Karma gave her a brittle smile. "Once the doctor told me that I'd lost my baby I began crying and couldn't stop. I couldn't sleep, barely ate and totally ignored Ryder. I was diagnosed with postpartum depression. After three months Lang hired a nurse to care for Ryder. The poor child didn't understand why his mother refused to get out of bed to play with him.

"Six months later Lang flew his mother from New York to L.A. to look after Ryder while he and I took a cruise to Hawaii. What had begun as a ten-day vacation became a month-long convalescence. We spent most of our time either in bed or on the beach. It became the honeymoon I'd always dreamed of. Despite taking precautions I discovered I was pregnant again. I went into an emotional decline where I had recurring dreams of dead infants. They were so vivid that I stayed awake all night, becoming an insomniac. That's when I began taking sleeping pills."

Bree withdrew her hand. "Why didn't you tell me this before?"

Karma stared straight ahead. "I didn't want anyone to know my life had been ravaged with mental illness, and if I didn't take my medication I couldn't get out of bed or function normally."

Her mother's rationalization as to why she'd alienated her daughter settled in Bree's chest like a heavy stone. "You're not unique, Mother. Most of the girls I went to school with took prescription medication from their mother's purses when they weren't looking. We're not living in the dark ages where mentally ill people are locked away in asylums. You were sick and you got help."

"But, that still doesn't explain why I had to send you away, Breanna."

"Why did you send me away, Mother?"

"It was to save you."

"Save me from what?"

"It's not from what, but whom."

"Did someone want to hurt me?"

"Yes, baby. *I* wanted to hurt you." Karma's voice was barely a whisper. "I'd entertained thoughts of smothering you while you slept, because I felt that baby girls were better off dead. Luckily I told Lang and he had me evaluated by a psychiatrist. Even after I was on medication he still didn't trust me around you. That's when he decided to send you to a boarding school. It wasn't as if he didn't love you, but he did it to save you from me."

Bree's expression was one of horror and dismay. All of these years she'd thought that her mother didn't want her around to compete for Langston Parker's attention, believed she'd turned her depression off and on at will. She'd also believed Karma was jealous of her when in fact she was suffering from a mental illness where she'd entertained murdering her own child. She remembered a newspaper account of a mother who'd drowned her babies because she hadn't been able to cope with pervasive postpartum depression.

"Are you still taking medication?"

Nodding, Karma said, "I have to. My mood swings exacerbated after you were born and eventually I had to take Thorazine. Now I'm taking something where I don't feel like a zombie all the time. But, whenever I come off my meds I have an episode."

"Did you ever have an episode when you were a girl?"

"No," Karma admitted.

It was Bree's turn to fight tears. "I can't believe that it's taken you seventeen years to tell me why I was sent away, why you never hugged me or even attempted to kiss me. Even when I came home during school breaks or on holiday you never treated me as if you loved me or wanted me around."

"I loved you—"

"You love Ryder, Mother."

"I love you, too, Bree. Please, baby, give me a chance to make it up to you."

Bree glared at Karma. "Why should I, Mother?"

"Because I'm asking, that's why. If you want me to beg, then I'll beg."

"No, Mother. Please don't do that." She'd never begged Karma for anything—not even when she'd wanted to. Besides, begging denoted weakness, and she'd never known Karma to exhibit a modicum of weakness. Nodding, she said, "Okay, Mother. I'll give you a chance. We can begin with this weekend."

Karma whispered a silent prayer of gratitude. It wasn't that she didn't love Breanna, it was just that she didn't know her.

chapter twenty-one

Bree returned to Bel Air with a new look and a new attitude. Karma's idea of a bonding weekend was an exclusive luxury spa treatment following by a beauty makeover. European exfoliating facial, hot stones, full-body massage and seaweed wrap did wonders for Bree's mind and body. She'd spent hours in a stylist's chair, removing tracks of hair extensions, followed by a process that lifted the dye and restored her hair's natural color. The talented stylist had cut her chemically straightened hair into a style with a wisp of bangs feathering over her forehead while dark-brown blunt-cut strands with subtle reddish highlights swayed gently under her jaw.

She had no idea Karma was so much fun to be around; they shared a queen-size bed, watched movies, read to each other from their favorite entertainment magazines and talked for hours as if on a sleepover. Bree was given a glimpse of the woman her father had fallen in love with and married. Karma always made certain to take her antidepressant medication before retiring for bed, and within half an hour she would be sleeping soundly.

The first evening after their return to Bel Air, Bree saw light shining from under the door to Langston's library and knocked lightly. "Daddy, are you busy?"

"Come on in, Bree."

She opened the door and was surprised to find Tyrone Wyatt

rising to his feet. An expression of surprise filled his eyes until he quickly shuttered his gaze. "Hello, Tyrone." Bree waved to her father. "I'm sorry, Daddy. I didn't know you had company. I'll come back later."

Standing, Langston beckoned to her. "Please stay, Bree. I was just talking to Tyrone about his future."

Walking into the room, she sat down beside Tyrone as she had the night of their televised interview. "What about your future?" she asked him.

Tyrone and Langston shared a glance. "The police found her," Langston said quietly.

"Found who?" Bree's gaze shifted between the two men.

Langston exhaled an audible breath. "Diamond. She was found in a crack house several miles from the Vegas strip. An unofficial police report states that she died of a drug overdose."

Unconsciously, Bree made the sign of the cross, while at the same time trying to analyze Tyrone's reaction to the news that his former girlfriend was dead. "What's going to happen now, Tyrone?"

He gave her a direct stare. "Your father has given me six weeks to finish recording my next album before I'm scheduled to fly up to Vancouver the first week in March to begin filming exterior—"

"You got the part?" Bree interrupted, her voice rising in excitement.

Grinning broadly, Tyrone nodded. "Yes. My agent called me this morning with the news. I just dropped by to tell your father."

"Congratulations. I'm really happy for you."

"Thanks. I still can't believe that I'm going to be on the same movie set as Will Smith."

Langston cleared his throat. Tyrone and his daughter were staring at each other as if there wasn't another person present. "Tyrone's mother's driving down from Oakland for the Christmas break and I invited her and Tyrone to come to our Christmas Day open house."

Bree blinked as if coming out of a trance. "That's nice, Daddy."

"You don't have to sound so disappointed," Langston teased.

Pinpoints of heat stung her cheeks. She couldn't believe they'd segued from the news that Diamond had been found dead to the topic of the upcoming Christmas festivities with all the emotion they'd used to flick away an annoying insect.

"I'm—I'm not disappointed. In fact, it's very nice that you've invited her." Bree pushed to her feet, Tyrone rising with her. "I need to unpack, so I'll leave you gentlemen to your business."

Tyrone reached out with his uninjured hand, stopping Bree's retreat. "I'd like to talk to you about something."

She looked up at him through her lashes. Why, she mused, hadn't she realized how much taller he was than she? She was five-nine, and most men, other than basketball players, didn't tower over her.

Pushing back his chair, Langston walked around his desk. "You can talk to her here." He clapped a hand on Tyrone's shoulder. "Congratulations again on your first film."

Tyrone flashed a dimpled smile. "Thank you, Mr. Parker. Waiting until they were alone, he ran his fingers over Bree's freshly relaxed hair. "You look incredible."

"You want to talk to me about the way I look?"

"What ever happened to 'Thank you, Tyrone'?"

"Thank you, Tyrone," Bree mimicked.

He leaned closer. "You're welcome, beautiful. I need to talk about us."

"What about us, Tee Y?" A small smile lifted the corners of her mouth. She knew Tyrone was flirting with her, and she liked it—liked it a lot. "Why are you acting as if Diamond never existed? After all, she was a human being."

"I'm not responsible for what happened to Diamond. I tried

to get her to give up crack, but she wouldn't listen. I didn't kill her, drugs did."

"What is it you want to ask me?"

"Will you permit me to take you out?"

"You want to date me?"

"Umm-hmm."

"Why me, Tyrone, when you have hordes of women lining up to *date* you."

"I don't date."

Bree knew Tyrone had spoken the truth. The air of mystery surrounding Tyrone Wyatt was increased by the fact that he was never seen with the same woman more than twice. He'd been hyped as the elusive sex symbol with the velvet voice. His face had appeared on the covers of teen and entertainment magazines, and his image emblazoned on the covers of *Vibe* and *Rolling Stone* had validated his status as a recording-artist superstar.

"I know," she countered. "You just shack up with homeless exotic dancers."

A scowl distorted his good looks. "That's over, and you shouldn't speak ill of the dead."

"I'm truly sorry about Diamond, Tyrone. I know you were very fond of her."

"You're wrong, Breanna. Diamond wasn't my girlfriend or even close to being my woman. Whenever I needed sex she was there for me."

"Have you forgotten that you also had sex with me?"

"We made love, Breanna. What I felt when I was with you was very different than what I had with Diamond."

"Of course it was different. You were screwing your boss's daughter."

His frown deepened. "When I met you I had no idea you were LP's daughter, *Renee*."

Bree angled her head. She wanted to see Tyrone again but

there was no way she was going to make it *that* easy for him. "*If* you'd known I was LP's daughter would you have arranged to have a third person in your bed?"

"No."

"How often do you have a ménage à trois?"

"Would you believe me if I said that would have been the first time?"

"No. Why should I believe you?"

"If Diamond were here she would tell you that I'm not lying." Tyrone hadn't had a threesome with Diamond and another woman, but it wouldn't have been his first time if Breanna had been a willing participant. His libido always went into overdrive whenever he saw two women together and he usually was able to bring both to climax before ejaculating.

"The threesome was her idea?" Tyrone nodded. "Do you always do what a *hooker* tells you to do?"

The seconds ticked off while Tyrone regarded Langston Parker's daughter. She was hard and unrelenting. Even before he'd discovered who she was he'd found himself enthralled with her. There was something about her face that drew him to her like a moth to a flame. He wasn't certain whether it was the arrogant tilt of her chin, her mesmerizing dark eyes, or the aloofness radiating from her like radioactive waves.

"There's always the first time for everything," he said, after what appeared to be an interminable pause; in reality it was only seconds. Much to Tyrone's surprise Bree seemed amused by his response. "You think that's funny?"

Bree sobered. "No, Tyrone. I just didn't expect you to admit it, that's all." She smiled again. "I'll go out with you. *If* or *when* I decide I want to sleep with you again there will *never* be a third person in the bedroom or you'll rue the day you ever met me."

A lump formed in Tyrone's throat as he swallowed the expletives he yearned to throw in her face. He wasn't the least bit afraid of Breanna Parker. It was her father's warning that struck fear in his heart: *If she agrees to go out with you and I find out that you're still offering her shit then I'm going to stomp your fucking brains out.*

Langston Parker's warning wasn't just a warning; it was a death threat.

Unlike many high-profile performers Tyrone didn't travel with bodyguards or an entourage. Most times he kept a low profile, only rarely frequenting the more popular L.A. nightspots, following his publicist's advice that he remain out of the spotlight. The exception was celebrity-award and fund-raising events. His limited public access made it virtually impossible for him to meet women, yet that hadn't become a problem because whenever he needed a physical release Diamond was more than willing to take care of that.

After the damning video had been uploaded to YouTube his publicist had called to say that he, his agent and his manager had had a video conference call with Langston who had reassured them he would take care of everything. And he had.

However, Breanna Parker was what Diamond could never hope to be: the total package. Breanna was blessed with an exotic, smoldering, dark, sexy beauty matched only by her intelligence. And despite the rumors around Hollywood about the so-called feud between her and Raina Hunter, Breanna was black Hollywood royalty, whereas he still had to prove that his first CD had been more than a stroke of luck. Very few recording artists were blessed with the longevity of Tina Turner, Prince, the Rolling Stones, Madonna; even fewer went on to have successful acting careers.

"It will never happen again."

"It will never happen again with *me,*" Bree drawled arrogantly.

Smiling, Tyrone nodded. "You're so right," he whispered. The head of LP Records had changed his life with a single telephone call and a relationship with the record mogul's daughter was what he needed to boost his acting career. He moved closer, dipped his head and pressed a kiss along the column of her soft, scented neck.

"I'll call you later."

"Call me tomorrow."

He winked at her. "Tomorrow it is."

Bree stared at Tyrone as he walked out of the room. The weekend had been filled with pleasant surprises. She and Karma had related to each other as mother and daughter for the first time *and* she looked forward to going out with Tyrone Wyatt.

Diamond's life had ended tragically, reminding Bree of the risks associated with substance abuse. Getting high had helped her to forget the countless nights she'd cried herself to sleep six thousand miles from home, and the times she'd forced herself to smile instead of weeping when she'd been the only student whose parents hadn't come to visit during parents' week.

Only once had her parents come—the time she'd placed the overseas call after she'd gotten herself into a *situation.* They hadn't hesitated, flying to Switzerland to take her to Belgium to protect not only her reputation, but also theirs.

It'd taken years, but Bree had finally realized that nothing was more important to the Parkers than image. It had only taken one telephone call from Langston Parker to have the damning video pulled from the Internet.

Again, he had salvaged his own reputation, as well as those of his daughter and his most bankable artist. Whoever had coined the phrase *money talks* was indeed a genius.

chapter twenty-two

Bree slipped out of the house through a side door. Walking along a slate path, she made her way to the pool. Strategically placed flood lamps lit up the pool area, reflecting off the turquoise and lapis mosaic tiles and turning them into sparkling jewels. She settled herself on a webbed lounger and closed her eyes. It hadn't taken more than a few hours for her to conclude that she was bored—bored from the incessant chatter, bored with the plastic people who laughed a little too loud and openly flirted with other people's spouses. Bree reminded herself that she lived in Hollywood, a place where fantasy and reality merge, making it virtually impossible to discern one from the other.

She took a deep breath, inhaling the aroma of damp earth and blooming night flowers. Although Christmas Day had dawned with overcast skies and a forecast of precipitation, the rain had held off until early evening. A brief downpour had washed away the fog and the skies had turned a vivid gold-orange with the setting sun.

The entire household had slept late after a Christmas Eve dinner, followed by the family tradition of opening gifts. Ryder had come, sans Connor who'd flown to Texas to spend a week with his Houston relatives. Earlier that day Bree had exchanged the last of her euros for U.S. currency before going on a whirlwind last-minute shopping spree.

She spent less than an hour in two Beverly Hills boutiques, purchasing a cashmere Hermès shawl for Karma and a Louis Vuitton desk agenda cover and calendar for Langston and Sabane computer case for Ryder. With the last ninety dollars to her name, she bought herself a gift of half a dozen cloth-bound journals. Instead of her favored plaids, she'd opted for several paisleys, a pinstripe, tweed and hound's-tooth.

Bree had carefully hoarded her prized euros from the monthly allowance Langston deposited into her account when she lived in Paris. Finding herself completely without funds her first month in the City of Lights had honed her survival skills: spend some, save some. However, the sense of loss she'd felt when exchanging the euros was short-lived, because unlike past Christmases this one wouldn't find her counting down the days to having to leave her country of birth.

She'd come home this time to stay, and having money was no longer important, because she didn't have to concern herself with rent, food or the other little incidentals that made her life less stressful. Bree planned to return to Europe for either business or on holiday, but it would be at her discretion and not her parents.

"Oh, there you are. Look who I found."

Bree swallowed a groan. Try as she might, she didn't want to talk to Letisha Walsh. When Letisha walked in with her mother, who was apparently under the influence, it had gotten so quiet that one could hear a rat piss on cotton. Ever since Letisha's father had remarried, the second Mrs. Walsh had come to the open house with LP Records's Director of Marketing. There came a collective sigh of relief when Karma took Letisha aside and told her to take her mother home after she'd called her much younger replacement a "cheap home-wrecking bitch."

Bree sat up to find Letisha leading a man toward her.

Swinging her legs over the side of the lounger, she came to her feet. Her pulse raced as she stared at the tall figure in a dark suit and white shirt open at the throat. Smiling broadly, she extended both hands. It was close to ten, and she'd thought that he wasn't coming.

Tyrone Wyatt looked so shockingly handsome that she found it hard to draw a breath. "Merry Christmas, Tyrone," she crooned.

Tyrone, ignoring Bree's proffered hands, slid an arm around her waist, pulling her close to his body. He heard her soft gasp of surprise, felt the increase in her breathing and inhaled the sweet, feminine scent that was inherently Breanna Parker's. And it was not for the first time that he was looking forward to hooking up with his boss's daughter. He really liked her.

Dipping his head, he brushed a kiss over her parted lips. "Merry Christmas, Bree. I would've been here sooner, but my mother got caught up with my cousins. She's inside with your mother and after what I told her about you she's quite anxious to meet you." Turning, he glanced over his shoulder at Letisha. "I'd like to have a few words with Bree—in private," he added when Letisha, with wide eyes, stared trancelike.

A slight frown marred Letisha's thin, angular face in its frame of profusion of braided hair extensions. First, she'd been told to take her mother home, and now she was being ceremoniously dismissed by Tyrone Wyatt, who not only acted like he owned the Bel Air mansion but like he was hosting the party.

Seeing Letisha's crestfallen expression, Bree hoped the young woman wasn't going to have a meltdown, as she did occasionally when things didn't go her way. It was enough that she'd become an object of scorn when she brought her intoxicated mother to an event she hadn't been invited to.

"It's all right, Tyrone. Tisha's my girl."

Tyrone frowned. "I don't want her to hear what I have to say to you," he said through clenched teeth.

Bree's frown matched his. "Perhaps you didn't hear me—"

"I heard you, Breanna," Tyrone shot back, his voice rising slightly. "You were the one who said you don't want a third person in our bed, and I don't want a third person in our business."

Leaning closer, she rested a hand on his shoulder. "Don't get ahead of yourself, Tyrone. We haven't even begun seeing each other and already you're trying to tell me what I should or shouldn't do."

Tyrone went completely still. He'd underestimated Breanna Parker. What was he thinking? Why would she be any less controlling than her powerful father? If he hoped to make it in Hollywood as a crossover performer, then he knew he had to play by Bree's rules. If not, then his climb to the top would take a lot longer than he'd planned.

Most people thought they knew him. To the public he presented as a talented musician who played every instrument in the orchestra, composed lyrics and sang his own songs. Low-key in manner and conservative in dress, he'd become somewhat of an outsider in the world of hip-hop and R&B. He hadn't flaunted his newfound wealth and popularity, preferring instead to assume a mantle of mystique and elusiveness. Although his publicist had arranged for a number of interviews, the media still hounded him because they always wanted to know *more.*

"I'm sorry," he said with enough contrition to make him believe he actually was genuinely sorry for his remark. "I wanted to ask you whether you'd bring in the New Year with me."

Bree's eyebrows lifted. "What do you have in mind?"

He smiled. "I was thinking of throwing something small at my place."

"How small is small?"

"No more than a dozen folks. I'll order in, we can put on some music and toast the New Year away from the spotlight."

What Tyrone didn't know was that he'd gone up several cool points with Bree. The furor surrounding their sex video had just begun to wane, and if she was going to be with Tyrone, then it was to their advantage to maintain a low profile. She wanted to stay away from the prying eyes of the paparazzi until the Grammy awards.

It took her less than thirty seconds to make up her mind. "Okay."

Tyrone's dimpled smile was enchanting. "You can invite whoever you want."

"I'm going to ask Tisha and my other girlfriend Sierra."

Tyrone threw a disapproving glance at Letisha who appeared to be hanging on to their every word. "Not a problem. My mom isn't going back to Oakland for a couple of days, so do you think we can get together after she leaves?"

Bree remembered that Tyrone's mother was a teacher, which meant she was on school recess until after January first. "Instead of me hanging out at your place, I'll come by and pick you up and we'll hang here."

Tyrone flashed his dimpled smile. "That's sounds good to me. Now, are you ready to meet Lynda Wyatt?"

Why did Tyrone make it sound as if she was going to meet her future mother-in-law for the first time? A chill shook her, raising goose bumps on her exposed flesh. When she'd been on the massage table, completely relaxed, fantasies of being married to Tyrone had drifted into her consciousness. As soon as they had entered her head, she'd dismissed them. But, now they were back.

Could she, she wondered, marry Tyrone and become the mother of his children?

Yes, whispered a silent voice.

What she didn't want to think about was falling in love. She'd done that once, with disastrous results, and it wasn't something she looked forward to repeating.

chapter twenty-three

"Are you certain you don't want me to come up with you?" Walter Rockwell asked Bree as he handed her a wicker basket filled with foodstuffs from a Beverly Hills gourmet market.

Bree smiled at her father's driver. He'd made himself available to her for several days while Langston and Karma had gone to Palm Springs with two other couples. They'd planned to remain at the desert resort to golf and ring in the New Year.

"I'm quite certain, Uncle Rock." Walter Rockwell wasn't her uncle, but he was her father's lifelong friend and her godfather. He'd whispered to her on more occasions than she could count that if anyone attempted to hurt her, then they had to answer to him. She'd never known him to raise his voice, but there was something about him that radiated a latent danger that was almost palpable. Not only was he Langston's driver but also his bodyguard, for he carried a concealed weapon on his person at all times. The first time she'd seen the semiautomatic handgun she'd stared at it, transfixed until Walter explained that he carried the licensed firearm to protect her and her family from those wishing them harm. When she'd asked who would want to harm her or her family Walter had given her a vague answer, which had managed to satisfy her childish curiosity.

Walter nodded. "Call me when you're ready to come home."

"It may be late, Uncle Rock. I could always call a taxi."

A slight frown appeared between Walter's bulging eyes.

"I don't care if it's three in the morning. I want you to call me, Breanna."

It was Bree's turn to nod. Walter Rockwell had never shortened her name. She was aware that Langston had given his driver explicit instructions to monitor her whereabouts, and that meant driving her wherever she wanted to go despite Bree having the Porsche at her disposal.

Taking a step, she pressed a kiss to his smooth, moist cheek. "I'll call you."

Bree hoisted the wicker hamper, pressing it to her chest as she made her way to where a doorman stood at the ready to open the door leading into the luxury building.

Tyrone stood next to Bree, his uninjured arm around her waist as he watched her add a handful of herbs to a pot of simmering garlic-infused tomato sauce with bite-size pieces of sausage, spareribs and meatballs. The aromas filling his kitchen had him salivating.

"Who taught you to cook like this?" he asked.

When Bree had asked about his favorite cuisine and he'd told her Italian, he'd expected her to boil spaghetti and serve it with store-bought sauce and frozen meatballs. She'd surprised him when she'd unloaded a picnic hamper filled with freshly made linguine, plum tomatoes, Romano and parmesan cheese, loaves of fresh and day-old Italian bread and packets of fresh, fragrant herbs.

Smiling, Bree stirred freshly chopped basil into the rich thick sauce. "I learned in school."

"Cooking school?"

"No. Twice a year the headmistress invited different chefs to come to the school for an intensive two-week course covering every aspect of cooking from baking, braising and sautéing to presentation. It was a course in which I excelled."

Reaching for a teaspoon, she spooned a small portion of sauce from the pot, holding it out to Tyrone. "Tell if you like it."

Opening his mouth, Tyrone licked the sauce off the spoon, his expression mirroring shock and surprise. "Da-a-amn!" he drawled. "That's really good."

Using her forefinger, Bree wiped a dot of sauce from his upper lip. "I made enough to last you at least a couple of weeks. You can store the sauce in the freezer in plastic containers, and then take out what you want."

"What about the pasta?"

Bree rolled her eyes at him before going back to stirring the pot. "I saw boxed spaghetti in your—"

"How am I going to cook it with one hand?" Tyrone asked, cutting her off.

"The same way you shave, shower and get dressed. Luckily it's your left hand that's out of commission right now."

"I haven't turned on the stove since I broke my wrist."

"Aren't you eating?"

"Yeah, I'm eating, but only what my cousin brings me, or when I order in."

Bree stared up at Tyrone, feeling as if she were drowning in the liquid depths of his dark-brown eyes. "What do you want, Tyrone?"

"I want you to come over every day and cook for me."

She was hard-pressed not to laugh in his face. "Why don't you call an agency and hire a cook?"

Tyrone blinked once, his expression impassive. "I don't like strangers hanging out in my place."

Bree wanted to remind him that Diamond had once been a stranger but held her tongue. "I'm not coming over and cooking for you, because to me that's playing house."

He smiled. "I wouldn't mind playing house with you."

"I don't play house, Tyrone." After her relationship with

Kahlil she'd promised herself she would never live with a man again. The exception would be her husband.

"What if we were married?" Reaching up, Tyrone tugged at a curl falling over her moist forehead. Bree had styled her hair in a mass of tiny curls that gave her the appearance of a delicate black doll.

Bree swatted at his hand. "We're not married, so the topic is moot."

"Would you marry me, baby?"

The sounds of measured breathing and the soft popping from the simmering sauce were magnified in the ensuing silence as Bree and Tyrone regarded each other. The seconds ticked off until a full minute had passed before Bree broke their stunned entrancement. There was something in the man's expression that said he was just as shocked by the query as she was.

Tyrone knew he'd surprised Bree with his proposal, but that was exactly what he'd wanted to do. The smug expression and attitude of supreme confidence and entitlement she flaunted were no longer evident. If he hadn't had a hidden agenda, Tyrone would've laughed in her face.

Bree recovered smoothly, flashing a smile parents usually reserved for children who'd accomplished a task without their assistance. "I can't marry you."

"You can't, or you won't?"

"I can't," she repeated.

"Why not?"

"I don't love you."

Taking a step, Tyrone pulled her into the circle of a loose embrace. "Didn't Tina sing about 'What's Love Got to Do With It'?"

"It may be a second-hand emotion to you and Ms. Turner, but love is very important to me," Bree countered.

"And it is to me, too," Tyrone crooned, his mouth inches from hers. "I like you, Breanna Parker."

Tilting her chin, Bree met his gaze. "You like sleeping with me."

"Wrong, baby. I *love* sleeping with you."

Her eyebrows lifted slightly. "Aren't you confusing love with lust?"

He shook his head. "No, Bree. I'm well aware of the differences between the two." Tyrone brushed his mouth over her parted lips. "Give me a chance to prove to you that what we have isn't all about sex?" His gaze met and fused with the round-eyed stare of the woman who unknowingly had challenged not only his superstar status, but also his manhood.

"How do you propose to do that, Tyrone Wyatt?"

"I'm going to be *myself,* Breanna Parker. I'm going to be the man your father didn't drop from his label because I swore to him that I'd never give his daughter drugs again. I'm going to live up to my promise to my mother that all she had to sacrifice in order to give me private music lessons and pay for my college expenses wasn't in vain.

"I also want you to know that I'm not some thug using music as a means of escaping the ghetto. I don't need a steady trail of ass to validate my masculinity, and neither do I need ice and platinum draped around my neck, in my ears or around my wrists to announce that I've arrived. I've learned to enjoy myself without always being in the spotlight. My goal is to be taken as a serious recording artist and actor and..." His words trailed off.

"And you won't be taken seriously if you hook up with a chickenhead," Bree said perceptively, completing his statement. "That's why you decided to keep Diamond in the closet. Sorry about the pun," she added.

Tyrone shook his head at the same time he pressed the pad of his thumb over her lips. "You're such a naughty girl."

Her smile was dazzling. “That’s what they call me.” Within seconds she sobered. “You think being with me will enhance your image.”

“What you’re not is a chickenhead.”

“That’s not what I asked you, Tee Y.”

“No, Breanna,” he said after a noticeable pause, “Tee Y doesn’t need you or any woman to boost his image. What I want is a normal social life without the drama.”

Bree shifted her attention back to the pot, covering it with a lid. “You’re too late for that. Have you forgotten about our videotaped sexcapade?”

“That’s behind us.”

The words were barely out of her mouth when Tyrone moved closer, trapping her between his body and the stove. She closed her eyes, biting down on her lower lip to stop its trembling when she felt the solid bulge pulsing against her bottom. Then, without warning, her body betrayed her as the hidden place between her legs throbbed with a pleasurable pain as foreign to her as the desire she felt for this man who had the power to seduce her without uttering a word. But she didn’t intend to fall into bed with Tyrone again just because lust was flowing through her like red-hot lava.

“May I make a suggestion?” she whispered.

Tyrone trailed light kisses along the column of Bree’s scented neck, lingering on her nape. She’d exchanged her silk blouse for one of his white dress shirts that looked incredibly sexy on her slender figure. He wanted her so much that he feared exploding in his jeans.

“What is it, baby?” he whispered back.

“Use your good hand and go take care of your hard-on.”

Tyrone went completely still, replaying her suggestion in his head. “You did not just say that.”

Bree giggled softly. “Yes, I did.”

"I think we're going to have a lot of fun together."

Resting the back of her head on Tyrone's shoulder, Bree peered up at him. "I think you're right."

chapter twenty-four

Tyrone came down the staircase, slowing his descent when he encountered near-darkness. Bree had dimmed the recessed lights in the living/dining area, lit dozens of white candles in varying sizes and positioned vases and ceramic pots of white flowers throughout the entryway. Warming trays and stacks of white-and-black pinstripe dishes were set on corresponding solid, striped and checkered black-and-white tablecloths and runners. The pattern was repeated in napkins and helium-filled balloons. His gaze shifted from the banquet table to the woman adjusting the vase of long-stemmed white roses on a living room side table.

"Beautiful."

Bree turned to find Tyrone standing only a few feet behind her. She hadn't heard him when he'd come into the living room. "You like it?"

He nodded as he approached her. "I love it." Pulling her to his length, he kissed her coiffed hair. "How did I get so lucky and fall in love with someone like you?"

Bree pushed gently against Tyrone's chest. Instead of the glow she'd thought she would feel when a man professed his love for her, she felt absolutely nothing. Perhaps because men had told her that they loved her—usually in the throes of passion—that she'd become all too cynical about the four-letter word. She didn't want to hear Tyrone say he loved her;

she wanted him to show her love. Her mother had declared that she loved her, while ignoring her tears and pleas as a flight attendant escorted her to a jet awaiting takeoff. Although Karma had explained why she had to send her to Europe, it would take time for Bree to accept her mother's mental illness.

"You look very nice," she said, deftly shifting the topic of conversation away from her. In keeping with the black-and-white color scheme, Tyrone wore a lightweight black linen suit with a finely woven white linen shirt. The beginnings of a mustache and goatee outlined the perfection of his generous masculine mouth.

"Not as nice as you, beautiful." A frown distorted his handsome features. "What if we cancel tonight's party?"

"What are you talking about?"

Tyrone's frown vanished as quickly as it had formed. "I really don't want to beat the hell out of some of my boys who decide to hit on you tonight."

Bree opened, closed her mouth and then opened it again before saying, "You couldn't do a damn thing with one hand."

He fisted his right hand. "I use it to choke my chicken. Well," Tyrone drawled when Bree averted her gaze, "what did you expect me to do when my balls were so hard they could be used as black golf balls?"

"Tyrone!"

"Don't 'Tyrone' me, Breanna. Me no get *punany* in two weeks," he drawled in a musical Caribbean accent.

Smiling, Bree patted his smooth cheek. "My heart bleeds for you."

Tyrone winked at her. She was ravishing in a knee-length unadorned little black dress with capped sleeves and a scooped neckline. She'd pushed her professionally groomed feet into a pair of strappy stilettos that added nearly four inches to her impressive height. With her coiffed hair and expertly applied makeup she was perfect.

"You're hard, Breanna."

She made an attractive moue, bringing his gaze to linger on her lips, to which she'd applied a soft shade of cinnamon-hued lip gloss. "I thought I was naughty."

"You're that, too."

He and Breanna had spent most of the week together at his place. She'd continued to surprise him with her culinary skills, while he'd tried everything in his arsenal of seduction to get her into bed. They had shared his bed but only to talk. He'd told her about growing up in Oakland and his short-lived fascination with a local gang, openly admitting that Lynda Wyatt's decision to relocate to a more upscale neighborhood had saved him from prison and/or the morgue.

Breanna was less forthcoming when she glossed over attending the Swiss boarding/finishing school where most of her classmates were from elite European families. One of her roommates had been the daughter of an Austrian diplomat, and another the granddaughter of a South African diamond mogul. In addition to academics, the young women were taught how to set up a household and hire the necessary staff to keep it functioning efficiently. Her social training was evident whenever she set the table before they sat down to eat. If it'd been up to him he would've eaten off his lap or a tray in the space off the living room where he'd set up a home theater.

Even when Diamond had lived with him they never ate together. A knowing smile crinkled the skin around his eyes. Will had Jada Pinkett-Smith, and with time and patience Bree would become Breanna Parker-Wyatt.

Bree and Tyrone slipped into the role of hosts as if they'd done it together countless times. They greeted and introduced their respective guests, offering each a welcoming cocktail of sparkling white wine and fruit juices with fresh raspberries.

Music played softly from speakers concealed throughout the bi-level condo as the young twenty-something crowd mixed, mingled, drank and sampled hors d'oeuvres and crudités. The varied menu included bite-size chipotle baby back ribs, caviar-topped toast points, spicy shrimp crostini, spicy pork empanaditas with a chunky avocado relish, minted feta-and-pine-nut filo rolls with lemon aioli, sushi, steamed pork and beef wonton, spicy buffalo wings and jumbo shrimp with a variety of dipping sauces.

Half an hour before midnight, Sierra sided up to Bree and gushed, "You and your boyfriend know how to throw a party."

Pinpoints of heat pricked Bree's cheeks. "Is that what you believe? That Tyrone's my boyfriend?"

Brushing the wisp of bangs off her forehead, Sierra nodded. "Yes. You can tell me to mind my business, but I'm going to say it anyway." She paused to take a breath. "Half the world knows that you slept with Tee Y, and the other half will find out soon enough. Also the two of you are hosting a party as if it's something you've done before. And, I'm able to see what you won't or can't see."

"What's that?"

Sierra smiled, the corners of her eyes crinkling attractively with the gesture. "The way Tyrone looks at you. The man's got it bad."

"He's moving too quickly," Bree blurted out before she could censor herself.

"What's he doing, Bree?"

"He's mentioned marriage."

Sierra tucked strands of coal-black, blunt-cut hair behind her ears. "You're kidding me?"

"I wish I was."

"Why do you sound as if you were just sentenced to life in prison without the possibility of parole? Tyrone Wyatt just happens to be the hottest thing to hit town since Denzel Washington." She shook her head. "Most brothers who've made it go around having babies with every woman who'll open their legs for them and you get one who's willing to commit!"

"Commit after sleeping together once? I think it's just a ploy to get me into bed again."

"Men don't have to propose marriage to get a woman to sleep with them."

"It's different with Tyrone and me."

"And, why's that?"

"Don't forget that my business was on display for half the world because of him," Bree spat out angrily.

"But didn't he deny knowing that nasty ho who was stalking him?"

"Yes, but…."

Bree stopped herself before she told Sierra that Tyrone had lied about knowing Diamond; that in fact she'd lived with him. What she didn't understand was his reluctance to let someone clean his apartment, yet he hadn't hesitated cohabitating with a stripper. But, then again, he did admit that he used Diamond solely for sex, and Bree doubted whether Diamond would've gone public about what she knew about the very private Tyrone Wyatt, because who would take the word of a teenage hooker against a supposedly squeaky-clean superstar recording artist?

"What, Bree?"

"I'd feel a lot more comfortable if he just slowed down a bit. I'm not used to a man coming on so strongly."

"Is he good?" Sierra asked.

Bree frowned. "What do you mean?"

A slight flush suffused Sierra's gold-brown complexion. "Is he good in bed?"

Heat flared in Bree's face again. "He's incredible." There was no mistaking the awe in her voice.

"Girl, what's wrong with you? You'd better get some, and while you're at it get some for me."

Bree knew that Sierra had broken off with her current boyfriend because their relationship interfered with her studies. "I'll see what I can do."

Sierra sucked her teeth. "Don't see, just do it."

"Are you sure?"

"Yes, I'm sure." Sierra gave her a wink and sauntered off toward the bar.

Bree stared at her retreating back, then decided to search for Tyrone. She wanted to be by his side when the countdown for the New Year started.

chapter twenty-five

Bree leaned into the hard planes of Tyrone's body as his arm tightened around her waist. Tilting her head, she breathed in his wine-scented breath before his mouth covered hers. She hadn't realized it, but she'd been waiting for his kiss, for the moment when she'd be able to relive the passion they'd shared what now seemed so long ago.

The sexual tension between Bree and Tyrone was so strong that it was nearly palpable. She wanted him, wanted him as much as she wanted to continue to exist.

"Happy New Year!" she whispered, her voice low, throaty.

Easing back, Tyrone stared at Bree from under hooded lids. "Is it really?"

She smiled, her teeth showing whitely in her dark face. "It's going to be, Tee Y."

His smile matched hers. "That sounds like a promise to me."

Bree nodded. "It is. We're going to have fun, Tee, lots and lots of fun."

Tyrone's gaze moved slowly over her face before lingering on her moist, parted lips. "I'm going to make you the happiest woman in the world."

Bree closed her eyes, wanting to believe Tyrone, praying that she could believe him. She'd believed Francois when he'd whispered that he loved her, her innocence and her childish passion. He'd loved her *and* his wife, a woman he'd vowed to honor and protect, forsaking all others, for as long as he lived. Francois—who'd professed to be unable to father children had gotten her pregnant. Francois—the erudite, sophisticated ski instructor whose lovemaking she'd craved as an addict craves a drug, but who in the end had wounded her more than her parents' abandonment.

Her relationship with Kahlil had been different because he'd been forthcoming about his arranged marriage. He was the only man, other than Ryder, that she'd trusted.

She placed her fingertips over Tyrone's lips. "Don't say it, Tyrone, just do it."

A slow smile flitted over Tyrone's face, reaching his eyes. "Okay."

Bree stood with Tyrone as he closed and locked the door behind the last of their departing guests. "At last," they drawled in unison.

"I thought they'd never leave," she said in a quiet voice.

Tyrone placed his palm against her cheek. "I don't think they had much of a choice once you started cleaning up."

"Rather than be rude and tell them to go home, I figured they'd get the message once I put the food away and closed down the bar. Right now, all I want is a firm bed and a warm shower, but not necessarily in that order."

"You go on up and I'll finish down here."

"Are you sure you don't want me to help you?"

He kissed her forehead. "I'm very sure."

Bree glanced around the entryway. The candles lining the tables in the entryway were sputtering and going out. "Don't forget to put out all the candles."

Tyrone saluted her with his good hand. "Consider it done."

She brushed a kiss over his mouth. "I think you're going to be a good boyfriend."

"I'm going to be an incredible boyfriend," he crooned.

Bree offered him a smile. “We’ll see.”

Leaning against him for support, she leaned over, slipped off her stilettos, cradling them to her chest. The muscles in her calves were tight from standing on her feet for hours. Within minutes of the clock striking midnight the tempo of the music had changed, becoming more upbeat. Despite being the hostess she’d found herself dancing instead of seeing to their guests’ needs.

She’d planned to spend the night with Tyrone because she would have been all alone at the Bel Air mansion. All of the household staff had made arrangements for their own New Year’s Eve celebration. Come January second everything would return to normal; she wondered whether when she returned home she too would be the same Breanna.

Bree stirred but didn’t open her eyes when she felt the warmth of the body pressed to hers. “Hey,” she slurred.

Resting his cast-covered arm over her hip, Tyrone kissed the nape of her neck. He smiled in the darkness. Breanna hadn’t wrapped her head in a silk scarf like so many girls who didn’t want him to play in their hair and ruin their “do.” The most he wanted a woman to wear to bed was a nightgown, and he usually divested them of the annoying garment as soon as he could.

He kissed Bree again, rising slightly and alternating kissing and licking her bared shoulder. “You smell and taste so good, baby.”

Bree moaned under the onslaught of Tyrone’s tongue. She’d fallen asleep waiting for him to join her in bed, but now the vestiges of fatigue claiming her mind and body fled when he moved over her, pressing her back to the mattress.

“Tyrone.” His name came out in a fevered whisper as the heat from his sexual onslaught intensified. She wanted him, the itch intensifying until she found that she couldn’t remain still or unaffected.

"What is it baby?"

"I want—"

"What do you want?" was Tyrone's strangled query. He found it hard to draw a normal breath as his erection grew harder, longer, making him feel as if he was coming out of his skin.

"You, you," she repeated. "I want you—*now!*"

He released her, reaching for a condom in the drawer of the bedside table. Using his teeth, he ripped open the packet and withdrew the latex sheath, hindered by the broken wrist.

"I'll help you," Bree suggested, as Tyrone failed in his first attempt to put on the condom. Her hands faltered, but she was finally able to do it. What she didn't want was a repeat of her liaison with Francois.

"Lie on your right side, Bree. I can't put any pressure on my left arm."

Bree smiled. "What if I get on top?"

"That'll work." He lay on his back, arms outstretched, welcoming her as she lay between his legs. The brush of her pelvis against his thigh was his undoing. Reaching for his penis, he pushed it between her thighs. "Help me out, baby."

Straddling her soon-to-be lover, Bree lowered her body until Tyrone's hard length disappeared into her, inch by delicious inch. She lost track of everything going on around her as she lost herself in the sensuous smell and heat of the man who took her beyond herself. She rode him like a woman possessed, sliding up and down, around and around, setting her own pace as she concentrated on taking the pleasure of sharing her body with a man.

Nothing mattered. Not the guttural sounds coming from Tyrone's throat, not the aroma of sweat mingling with her perfume or the distinctive scent of unadulterated sex. Her nipples hardened like tiny pebbles when she rubbed her breasts against his chest as she tried to get even closer.

Then, without warning, it happened. The flutters grew stronger and stronger, her movements quicker and quicker. Clutching the pillow beneath Tyrone's head, she closed her eyes, giving in to the explosive orgasm that left her heart pounding painfully against her ribs.

Tyrone caught Bree around the waist, holding her captive as he met her in a savage thrusting, flesh met flesh with all the ferocity, pounding and slapping of leather gloves in a winner-take-all boxing match. Her screams of ecstasy heated him as he released his own passion in a flood tide of desire that made him feel as if he'd breathed his last breath. Now he knew what it meant to experience *le petit mort.*

Usually he liked being in control in bed, but unknowingly Breanna Parker had changed him. A new year had come, and with it a promise of incredible things. He and Bree were perfect in bed. Now, all that remained was for them to become the perfect couple out of bed.

chapter twenty-six

The driver opened the rear door and Tyrone stepped out, resplendent in a tailored suit, matching black silk T-shirt and Italian slip-ons. The flash of bulbs was blinding when he extended a hand to assist Bree exiting the limo. He felt her fingers tremble slightly before he tightened his grip, pulling her gently to her feet. He hadn't believed she could improve on perfection, yet she had. Tiny curls danced around her face as if they'd taken on a life of their own when she ducked her head. The simple black sheath dress skimming her slender curves exposed her toned arms and shoulders, the hem ending several inches above her knees to display her long shapely legs in a pair of silk-covered black stilettos. He knew they made a striking couple when he registered the gasps of surprise and awe from the onlookers hoping to catch a glimpse of Tinseltown's elite as they were escorted inside the popular club.

"Tee Y, over here!" screamed a childlike voice.

"We love you, Tee!" chorused two others.

"I want to marry you, Tee!" shouted another, this one masculine.

He turned and smiled at the group of screaming and crying young girls. Tyrone raised his cast-covered hand in an acknowledging salute at the same time as his right arm went around Bree's waist. He'd learned early on in his career never to ignore his adoring fans, unlike some of his peers who went out of their way to be rude to the very people who'd made them who they were.

"Marry me, Tee!" screamed a young woman as she broke away from the crowd. She would have tackled him if a member of the club's security team hadn't planted his body firmly between them.

Smiling he said loudly, "I can't baby, because this beautiful woman on my arm has agreed to become Mrs. Tyrone Wyatt."

An instant hush fell over the assembled fans, leaving only the sounds of intermittent gasps and movement from photographers jockeying for space to get a shot of the supposedly engaged couple.

Bree missed a step, causing Tyrone to stop abruptly when she plowed into his back. "Are you crazy?" she whispered angrily.

Dipping his head, he smiled down at her distressed expression. "Yeah, baby. I'm crazy about you."

A young woman holding a microphone stepped in front of Bree and Tyrone and shoved it under her nose. "When's the wedding?"

"We haven't set a date." Bree, knowing the woman was waiting for an answer, said the first thing that came to mind, because all she wanted to do was get inside the club, away from the screaming fans and photographers who reminded her of a pride of lions stalking their prey. Moving closer to Tyrone, she whispered, "Get me the hell inside."

There was something in the mood of this crowd that made her anxious. The crazed expressions and the aggressive shoving and screaming went beyond celebrity worship. Once inside the club, which was quickly filling up with media and studio personnel, Bree reached for a glass of champagne from the tray of a passing waiter and took a sip. The liquid cooled her throat before settling and warming her chest. *What the hell have I gotten myself into?* she thought as she took another swallow.

Bree liked spending time with Tyrone, but she wasn't ready for marriage. She'd only been back in the States a little more than six months, had managed a modicum of independence and, at twenty-three, she wasn't ready to commit or settle down with one man. If her life had been different, then she would've considered Tyrone Wyatt as a life partner. After all, her mother had married when she was eighteen, had become a mother at nineteen and had recently celebrated her twenty-seventh wedding anniversary.

Tyrone professed to have fallen in love with her when he had first seen her at the crowded club. What she'd told him was that he was intrigued by a stranger who'd initially rebuffed his advances, and his ego wouldn't let him accept that a woman didn't want to have anything to do with the very popular Tee Y. She'd stopped short of admitting that she'd gone home with him to find out what his hype was all about.

"Yo, Tee Y!" boomed a loud voice over ear-shattering decibels of music. "Over here!"

Tyrone spied his publicist huddled close to the reporter who'd asked about his wedding date. "Let me handle this, Bree." She rolled her eyes at him. "Don't worry, baby—"

"I'm *not* worried." Going on tiptoe, she said close to his ear, "I don't intend to play this little game much longer."

"You won't have to."

If everything went according to his plan, then Tyrone could expect to marry Breanna Parker before he left the States to go on location to begin shooting in Canada. What Bree didn't know was that the men and women screaming his name outside the club had been paid to do just that. Struggling acting students would agree to anything to make extra money. And his publicist had alerted the reporter that he and Bree would be attending the birthday party.

Holding firmly on to Bree's free hand, Tyrone flashed his

dimpled smile at Marvin, his publicist. Marvin's nerdy appearance and demeanor were deceptive foils for what Tyrone had come to realize was truly a brilliant mind. The man's perceptive ability was without peer. The reporter turned and walked in the opposite direction at their approach.

"Hey, Marv, Tyrone crooned. "This is the woman I've been telling you about. Bree, this is my publicist Marvin Werner. Marv, Breanna Parker."

Bree smiled at the short, slightly built man. He was prematurely balding with oversized round glasses on a pale face—his pallor was totally incongruous in southern California, and Bree wondered if he ever went outside during daylight hours.

"It's a pleasure meeting you, Mr. Werner."

Marvin widened his eyes appreciably behind the lenses of his horn-rims when he found himself staring numbly at Breanna Parker. Her dulcet voice was mesmerizing. He was more than familiar with Langston Parker, had read about the antics of his club-hopping, partying daughter, but hadn't had the pleasure of seeing her in person, or close up; what he saw he liked. Physically she was the perfect female counterpart for his most promising client. Tyrone had revealed that she'd had a European boarding-school education and spoke several languages. His client had chosen well. Langston Parker's daughter's flawless dark beauty, slender body and intelligence along with her father's wealth were certain to give Tyrone Wyatt A-list status.

"I can assure you, Miss Parker, that I'm the one honored to meet you."

"Tyrone told me that you're his publicist." Marvin nodded. Bree wondered what kind of a marketing genius the man was when he'd promoted Tyrone as a performer obsessed with his privacy, yet a crazed fan had been able to breach the sanctity of his home to photograph him in an intimate encounter with a woman. The tabloids had all carried Werner's prepared statement when he went into full throttle to dispel the rumors that his client had been a willing participant in the infamous ménage à trois sexcapade.

"I'm his publicist and somewhat of a surrogate father. I only want the best for Tyrone."

Bree smiled. "That makes two of us."

Tyrone, placing an arm around Bree's waist, winked at Marvin. "I'm sorry to end this, but I want Bree to meet the film's director."

Marvin waved his hands. "Go, go and circulate. I'm only going to hang out here for another half an hour, because I have an appointment to meet with another client later on tonight."

Tyrone barely gave Bree time to mouth the appropriate good-byes before she came face-to-face with a man whose films were beyond spectacular. She was mute when Tyrone introduced her as the woman with whom he wanted to spend the rest of his life. Those standing close enough to overhear his pronouncement immediately interpreted it as a marriage proposal.

She managed to parry their questions with a silly smile that froze her features and noncommittal responses. She moved like an automaton, finally murmuring to Tyrone that she had a headache and wanted to leave. His expression registered genuine disappointment, but she was past caring about his feelings or his status as an actor.

chapter twenty-seven

"Will you please tell me what happened back there?" Bree screamed at Tyrone when they were seated in the back of the limo.

Reaching for Bree, Tyrone pulled her into the circle of his embrace. "Baby, don't," he crooned softly.

"Don't you dare 'baby' me, Tyrone Wyatt. I'm willing to bet my trust fund that rumors of our fake-ass engagement will be all over L.A. before sunrise."

Tyrone went completely still when he heard Bree mention *trust fund.* Knowing she wouldn't have to rely solely on him for financial support made marriage to her even more attractive. Although he didn't need her money, she also didn't need his.

"Look baby—I mean, Bree, I said what I said to keep up the lie we began during the interview." He paused. "Not that I want it to be a lie."

It was Bree's turn to go completely still, as if she'd been hit with a sharp object. "I don't want to believe that you're taking the lie that serious."

"Why shouldn't I, Bree? You're the first woman I've been able to get along with—in and out of bed."

"Is that supposed to make me feel good, Tyrone?"

"No. It's just the truth."

Tyrone hadn't lied to Bree. He'd been with women who were good in bed, like Diamond, yet who couldn't complete a simple sentence using the correct verb tense if their very lives depended upon it. Then there were the ones who were intellectually challenging and stimulating, but who viewed sex as something abhorrent.

"And you think that would make for a good marriage?"

He smiled. "Of course it would."

"What about love? How does that figure into your prerequisite for a good marriage?"

"It's a priority. I don't have to concern myself with that because I'm already in love with you."

He'd lied about being in love with Bree. What Tyrone loved was the fact that she was Langston Parker's daughter. The respect he'd held for the man who'd changed his life with a stroke of his pen had evaporated when Walter Rockwell and his bookend twin had assaulted him. His respect for *and* fear of the head of LP Records now bordered on loathing, a loathing so strong that it had become a virulent disease eating him alive—from the inside out.

Bree blinked as if coming out of trance. Tyrone had professed to love her so many times that she wanted to believe him. But, she still couldn't bring herself to trust him completely. "What do you want from me?"

Cradling the back of her head, he pressed a kiss to her forehead. "Marry me, Breanna Parker."

Recoiling in panicked shock, Bree pushed against Tyrone's shoulder, staring at him as if she were a deer caught in the blinding glare of headlight. "You're serious, aren't you?"

"Of course I'm serious."

She shook her head. "No, Tyrone. I can't."

"Why not, Breanna?"

"We don't know each other."

Tyrone smiled in the vehicle's cloaking darkness as the driver maneuvered slowly out of the parking lot to avoid colliding with paparazzi lurking in the shadows. "We can have a long engagement, and that will give us time to know each other."

"How long is long, Tyrone?"

"Six months." He would've said three months, but he knew Bree still had reservations about him moving so quickly with their whirlwind relationship. If they'd met early the year before, then they would've been a couple making the rounds at the Screen Actors Guild, Golden Globe, Grammy and Academy awards. Being elusive had enhanced his image, but it also stifled him socially. If he'd been any other twenty-six-year-old, multi-platinum recording artist, he would've found himself fighting off women throwing their panties at him. He'd gone along with his manager's and publicist's carefully mapped-out career initiative, but when he'd complained to Marvin that he was tired of being a recluse, the man's answer had been *Marry Bree Parker and salvage what's left of your good-guy reputation.*

"Six months!" Bree repeated, her voice rising slightly. "That's not long at all."

"It's a lot longer than some Hollywood marriages I've read about. You may not love me now, but I'm going to do everything I can to make you love me as much as I love you." He kissed her forehead. "Let me love and take care of you, Breanna."

Bree felt like weeping as she struggled with her swirling emotions. She'd changed and her life had changed from the moment she'd agreed to go home with Tee Y. Something about him had piqued her curiosity, and now she recognized what it was. He was persistent—driven, and he'd just uttered the words she'd wanted to hear from Francois and Kahlil. She'd chosen to give her innocence to a married man and had slept with a man who was a willing participant in an arranged marriage, while the man holding her to his heart wanted her to become a part of his life and future.

Maybe it was better that she wasn't in love with Tyrone, because if they split up then she would be able to walk away without the emotional upheaval she'd encountered with the other men from her past.

Marrying Tyrone would give her the total independence she craved. And, he was right about their compatibility in and out of bed. A cynical smile twisted her mouth. Women the world over were lusting after Tyrone Wyatt and she was balking at his marriage proposal.

"Okay, Tyrone."

"Okay what, Bree?"

Looping her arms under his shoulders, she leaned into him. "Let's get married."

Pushing up the sleeve of his jacket, Tyrone peered at the luminous numbers on his watch. "Do you think it's too late to call your folks and give them the good news?"

Bree breathed a kiss under his ear. "I think it would go a lot better if we stop by the house."

"Are you sure?"

She nodded, smiling. "I'm very sure. I want to see the look on my mother's face when I tell her that she's about to become a mother of the bride." Easing out of Tyrone's embrace, she opened the partition separating the back seat from the driver. "Please turn around and take us to Bel Air." She gave him the address, then settled back against the leather seat and into her fiancé's protective embrace.

Karma was the picture of elegance and grace as she perched on the edge of a silk-covered chair, her gaze darting between her daughter and the young man who'd asked for their blessings for their upcoming nuptials. The announcement didn't seem to shock Langston, because he'd gone over to the bar to uncork a bottle of champagne from the wet bar.

"Isn't this rather sudden?" she asked, regaining her voice.

Bree smiled. "It is, but we're not getting married until June."

Karma blew out a breath at the same time she pressed her palms together. "At least you're giving me time to plan a wedding. You two are planning to have a wedding, aren't you?"

Bree and Tyrone shared a smile. "Yes."

Karma affected what could pass for a smile. "Wonderful. Tyrone, your mother and I will have to get together to compile a list of guests, then Bree and I have to shop for gowns. I'm somewhat partial to Amsale and Wang because of their understated simplicity," she said, counting off on her fingers. "We also have to decide where you want the ceremony, whether it should be private, or accessible to the—"

"Please, Karma," Langston said quietly as he returned with a tray of flutes filled with champagne. Recessed lights shimmered off the silver in his close-cropped hair. Like his wife, he'd slipped on a robe over his pajamas. "The kids just decided they were going to marry tonight, so I doubt whether they've had time to make plans for what they'd like to have."

Karma managed to roll her eyes at her husband before reaching for a flute. "Tyrone, do you plan on giving my daughter an engagement ring?"

Tyrone took a flute and handed it to Bree before taking one for himself. "Yes, ma'am. We're going to Rodeo Drive tomorrow."

Karma pressed a hand to her chest over a carnelian-red silk kimono. "Forget Cartier, Tiffany and Van Cleef & Arpels. I don't want my friends to talk about my daughter getting her ring from a flea market."

"Mother! Tiffany's, Arpel's and Cartier are hardly what would be considered flea markets," Bree retorted, unable to believe that her mother had just upped the snob gauge.

Waving a hand in a gesture of dismissal, Karma continued

as if her daughter hadn't spoken, "I'll call my personal jeweler and he'll design something that will be uniquely you, darling. What do you think, Tyrone?"

"That sounds wonderful, ma'am."

"Please stop calling me ma'am. I am not *that* old."

Tyrone struggled not to laugh. "What do you want me to call you?"

"Karma will do."

Langston wagged a finger at Tyrone. "I'm still going to be Mr. Parker as long as you're signed to LP Records."

That will only be until the end of my contract, Tyrone mused. He'd majored in music because it came to him as easily as breathing. However, when he'd stepped onto the stage to audition for the movie role he knew he'd found his true gift. He knew all of his lines, and even before he'd opened his mouth he'd morphed into character. His two-year contract with LP Records mandated he give them one CD a year and tour for several months, and that left him plenty of time to perfect his acting techniques.

Tyrone nodded. "I understand, sir."

Langston raised his flute. "I'd like to propose a toast to my daughter and future son-in-law. May your lives be filled with love, happiness and above all—trust."

"Hear, hear," came a chorus from the others.

The distinctive ring of crystal stemware echoed throughout the room as the two couples shared smiles.

chapter twenty-eight

February 10—Last night Tyrone and I officially announced our engagement. I'm practically living at his condo. The paparazzi have set up camp not far from my parents' place, hoping to catch a glimpse of us coming or going. I've stopped driving the Porsche because it's too conspicuous. However, our roles have changed because I'm the one seeking to avoid publicity, while Tyrone claims to be tired of being a recluse. Right now I'm not certain which one is the real Tee Y—the publicity seeker or the temperamental solitary musician who spends hours at the piano composing music and writing lyrics. It is when he's at the studio or retreats to the smaller bedroom that he's set up as his music room, that I feel completely alone. These are the times when I either call a taxi or Uncle Rock to take me to Bel Air. The first time I left without letting Tyrone know he went ballistic, then spent the next hour saying he was sorry because he'd thought something had happened to me. I didn't tell him that if he hadn't apologized then I would've ended the engagement. I don't want to remind Tyrone that he will become my husband, because I already have a father.

I've asked Sierra to be my maid of honor and Letisha an attendant. Tyrone asked his college roommate to be his best man and a cousin a groomsman. Daddy has arranged for Lynda Wyatt to fly in from Oakland one weekend each month so she and Mother can plan what Karma Ryder-Parker claims will be the wedding of the season. I'm trying not to get caught up in the hysteria, because if I find myself fighting with my mother then I'll elope.

I like Tyrone, but I'm still not in love with him. There are times when I wonder if I'm actually able to love a man. At twenty-six Tyrone knows exactly what he wants from life and at twenty-three I'm still uncertain. I'll marry Tyrone, play house for a couple of years, then when I come into my trust I'll begin shopping my designs. I haven't told Tyrone I plan to set up my own design firm because I don't want to hear from him about how hard it will be to break into fashion.

What I refuse to do is deal with anyone or anything toxic.

"Over here, Breanna!"

Turning to glance over her shoulder at the entertainment reporter shouting her name, Bree gave her a half smile.

"Who are you wearing?"

She hesitated, forcing Tyrone to slow his pace as they made their way along the red carpet. It was the first time since they'd announced their engagement that she and Tyrone had been seen together in public, and they'd chosen the Grammy Awards to officially come out as a couple.

Her red silk-chiffon dress with narrow straps, revealing décolletage and ruffled skirt ending at her knees flattered every curve of her tall, slim body. The shimmering crimson highlighted the gold undertones in her dark brown skin. Softly curled hair brushed off her face and expertly applied makeup showed off her flawless complexion and balanced features to their best advantage. Her vermilion-colored lips parted in a warm smile.

"The dress is Zac Posen." Bree glanced down at her silk

organza floral pumps. "The shoes are Dolce and Gabbana and my clutch is Miu Miu."

"What about your jewelry?"

"The earrings are my mother's." Karma had loaned her a pair of pear-shaped ruby-and-diamond earrings.

The reporter gestured to Bree's left hand. "Aren't you going to mention the ring?"

Pulling her left hand from the crook of Tyrone's arm, she extended it. "The ring is from Tyrone Wyatt." She and Tyrone shared a smile. The three-carat cushion-cut center stone flanked by another carat of round-cut diamonds along the shoulders of the ring gave off blue-white sparks under the glow of strategically placed flood lamps.

The reporter moved closer to Tyrone. "When's the big day, Tee Y?"

Tyrone shifted for the many cameras trained on him, flashing a practiced sensual grin. "Not soon enough," he said, noncommittally.

He and Bree had set a date, but had agreed not to disclose it. If it had been up to him he would've married her before shooting began. But, that wasn't going to happen because his future mother-in-law wanted nothing short of a Hollywood extravaganza, which he hoped wouldn't turn into a spectacle with a cast of thousands.

However, what he'd prayed for had materialized. He was the multi-platinum-selling singer, yet photographers and reporters were more focused on Bree. Tyrone hadn't known when he spotted the interesting-looking woman in the club that he was about to hook up with Breanna Renee Parker—a beautiful swan who laid golden eggs.

The fashionably dressed reporter leaned in closer, flirting shamelessly with the R&B singing sensation. "Who are *you* wearing tonight?"

"The suit is Armani." Bree had convinced him not to wear his trademark hat with the upturned brim. He looped his left arm around his fiancée's waist. "Let's go in, baby," he said, sotto voce.

Tyrone wanted to go inside the Staples Center and unwind before the ceremonies began. The week before his orthopedist had removed the cast, X-rayed his hand, and then referred him to a hand therapist. Earlier that afternoon the therapist had manipulated and massaged his wrist and fingers until he had to clench his teeth to keep from embarrassing himself. After each session he usually returned home and swallowed a painkiller, but today had been the exception because he wanted to be alert.

He escorted Bree to her seat next to her parents, kissed her passionately then walked down two rows and took his assigned seat. His pulse rate kicked into a higher gear when he recognized performers he'd grown up listening to, some who'd been inducted into the Rock and Roll Hall of Fame and younger singers who would one day be referred to as legends.

Since he'd been bitten by the acting bug Tyrone had all but given up on a recording career. He'd told his agent that he didn't plan on exercising his recording contract option to resign with LP Records, because he'd wanted to concentrate on acting. The entertainment attorney had warned him about being premature, but the altercation with Langston's enforcers was instrumental in his not wanting to remain with the label. And, the clause that he would have to wait five years before signing with another label fitted into his plan to seek out another career.

Bree lost count of the number of Grammy after-parties she attended with Tyrone and her parents. She carried one of the three gramophone-inspired likenesses her fiancé had been awarded. He'd won as Best New Artist, Best Male R&B Vocal

Performer and Best R&B Song, which he'd written during his first year in college. He was touted as the most talented and innovative singer-songwriter since Stevie Wonder.

Her attempt to remain out of the spotlight because it was Tee Y's night was thwarted; reporters appeared more interested in his love life than in the fact that the recording industry was honoring him for his musical talent.

It was after three in the morning when Walter Rockwell drove them all back to Bel Air. Bree would sleep in her bedroom for the first time in weeks, while Tyrone was assigned to a bedroom in the guest wing. She'd cleansed her face of makeup, showered and the last thought to run through her mind before exhaustion claimed her was that she was just like her mother; she would also marry a man in the music business.

chapter twenty-nine

Bree sat up in bed, her back supported by three pillows and her journal perched on her knees. She'd had her hair styled, her face professionally made up and all that remained was getting into her wedding underwear and gown. She opened the book to a blank page.

June 19—Today is my wedding day, but the mood in the house would be a lot better if Mother and I were speaking. I've opposed everything she wanted, and had to repeatedly remind her that I'm the one getting married. My dress isn't Wang or Amsale, but an Elie Saab. It is a beaded sheath with a natural waist, squared neckline, spaghetti straps and a court train in a shimmering ivory. Mother wants me to wear a veil, but I decided to tuck a spray of white rosebuds and pearls into my hair, which I had styled in a chignon on the nape of my neck. I'm going for stark simplicity, because I've never been one for Cinderella-style ball gowns.

Mother even opposed the colors I've chosen for my attendants, but she got her wish when Sierra and Letisha chose long, slender chiffon gowns featuring a gathered bodice, ivory ribbon sash and a floral appliquéd detailed back by Vera Wang. Sierra is wearing a flattering jade green and Letisha's a lighter sea-foam-hued green.

The constant arguing has taken its toll on my nerves, so this past week I've stayed in my room, making certain to lock the door. If it's not dress designers, then it is whether to have a religious or civil ceremony, type of flowers, souvenirs or the cake filling. Mother believes because she's paying for everything that I have to bend to her will. My doubts about marrying Tyrone have been put to rest. Right about now I'd marry a rank stranger if it meant complete emancipation. She wanted the wedding and reception aboard a yacht, but Tyrone ruled against it because he is prone to seasickness. Her next choice was the Beverly Hills Four Seasons Hotel. Disappointed when told she couldn't be accommodated, Mother elected to hold it at the house. In the end she's come to accept this because it means more control over wedding crashers.

I'm to be married at five and a sit-down reception dinner on the lawn will follow at six. Two bands and a DJ will provide music throughout the night. Tee and I will stay at the El Dorado on the Sea of Cortés for our honeymoon. We'll be there for four days, because he is scheduled to perform at an Atlanta charity benefit concert next Saturday. We plan to take another honeymoon before the end of the year.

Pushing back the French cuff on his dress shirt, Tyrone glanced at his wedding gift from Bree—a Domenico Vacca timepiece with an alligator band and diamond bezel showing five time zones. He'd lost track of the number of times he'd checked the time since five o'clock. It was now five twenty-five, and his bride was late for her wedding. He could understand her being late if the ceremony was being held at a church, but not here on the sprawling Bel Air property where one hundred-fifty guests had begun assembling at four for pre-ceremony champagne and caviar.

They'd argued the night before after the rehearsal dinner, and when Bree had changed from a chatty, nervous bride-to-be into a sullen, surly woman who wouldn't speak or even give him a glance he'd been faced with the possibility that he would be left standing at the altar. And because he and the judge had been under the gauzy canopy waiting for Langston Parker to lead his daughter down a white carpet for almost a half hour, Tyrone believed his greatest fear was going to manifest itself. Just when his life couldn't have been better, it was about to be torn asunder if his fiancée became a runaway bride.

His first movie role was nothing short of perfection. He'd arrived at the set on time, in character, hadn't dropped a single line and the on-screen chemistry between himself and Will Smith was mesmerizing. Within days of wrapping the film there were rumors that the film's director was looking at other properties in which to use Tyrone's charismatic cinematic talent. The feedback from the editing crew was that the camera loved him.

The melodious strains of a Bach fugue played by a string quartet segued into the familiar strains of Mendelssohn's "Wedding March." Tyrone stood up straighter as everyone rose from organza-covered chairs. He hadn't realized that he'd been holding his breath until he felt lightheaded. His heart was beating with the speed of a hummingbird's wings.

Please. No, said a silent voice. He prayed he wouldn't have a panic attack—not on his wedding day, not with friends, family and the media personnel as invited guests. Tyrone closed his eyes, inhaling and exhaling in deep measured breaths. It was over as quickly as it'd begun. He opened his eyes, smiling when his college roommate escorted Sierra down the carpet, followed by Tarik with Letisha. The gardenias in the bridal attendants' hair matched those in their bouquets;

streamers of white and green ribbons flowed to the hem of their gowns. Diamond lapel pins, his gift to the men in the wedding party, had replaced the ubiquitous boutonnières.

His smile faded when he stared at Bree as if seeing her for the first time. How had he missed her weight loss and the haunted look in her eyes? He knew the answers before the questions formed in his mind. He'd neglected her. It'd taken a month, working twelve to sixteen hours a day, to complete his second CD, and if he hadn't written and arranged all of the songs it would've taken twice that long.

He'd left LP Records, going directly to LAX for a flight to Vancouver. After two weeks of filming in below-freezing weather, he'd returned to the States, but his reunion with Bree was short-lived. She'd come down with the flu and her doctor recommended complete bed rest. By the time she recovered he was at the studio shooting interior scenes. His total on-screen time was estimated to be about eighteen minutes, but to Tyrone it seemed like eighteen thousand. His face would appear on the screen, name in the credits and he was now a card-carrying member of the Screen Actors Guild.

Noting her ethereal beauty reminded Tyrone that he and Bree would only have four uninterrupted days together before he was scheduled to perform at a charity benefit for special needs children.

Blinking as if coming out of a trace, he nodded to Langston when he placed Bree's hand in his. Her eyes appeared abnormally large when she met his gaze. "I've waited all my life for this moment," he whispered passionately.

Bree nodded. She didn't trust herself to speak, because she feared dissolving into tears. When Langston had come to escort her out of the house she'd panicked, telling her father that she was too young to get married and that she didn't believe she could be a good wife. Langston had waited until she finished her impassioned tirade, then told her if she didn't want to marry Tyrone, she didn't have to and that he would support whatever decision she made.

He'd cradled her to his heart, revealing his own reluctance in marrying Karma. But had gone through with his promise to make her his wife, and the day they'd celebrated their first wedding anniversary Langston knew that he wanted to spend the rest of his life with Karma as his life partner. Her father's explanation calmed Bree's fears and when Karma came into the bedroom to check on her, she'd asked her mother to repair her makeup. Traces of tears were covered up, and when she picked up her bouquet of white roses, lily of the valley and freesia, Bree was ready to change her name and her life.

A tentative smile trembled over her soft lips. "And I'm ready, darling."

A hush settled over the property as Breanna Renee Parker and Tyrone Nicholas Wyatt exchanged vows and rings. The judge's pronouncement of them as husband and wife was drowned by the deafening sound of a helicopter hovering above the property. Langston stood up, signaling his head of security to take care of the obtrusive intrusion. Bree and Tyrone traversed the white carpet together and stood in a receiving line greeting their guests before the helicopter banked to the left and disappeared from view.

The newlyweds posed for photos for family members and exclusive ones that were to be sold to *People* magazine with the money donated to their favorite charities. Her apprehension about marrying vanishing, Bree became a part of the frivolity; she sampled the exquisite dishes prepared by a celebrity chef who'd gotten his big break when Langston had had him cater a pre-Grammy party when the struggling cook was trying to break into the business. She drank two glasses of champagne before refusing a third. She wanted to be sober when she slept with Tyrone for the first time as his wife.

The merriment continued in earnest after Bree and Tyrone danced together as husband and wife, after they'd cut the cake and well into the night when they boarded a private jet for a short flight to the Mexican Riviera.

It felt as if they'd just taken off when the sleek aircraft touched down on Cabo San Lucas. They whisked through Customs and were driven to a villa belonging to one of Langston's golf buddies at the private residential community.

A clock in a bedroom of the Spanish-style house chimed the hour and Bree and Tyrone undressed each other without turning on a lamp. It was exactly midnight. She couldn't remember the last time they'd made love. She'd moved back to Bel Air when Tyrone had returned to the studio to work on his next CD.

She'd found it ironic that she saw more of him when they weren't engaged, but after announcing their upcoming nuptials they'd practically stopped sleeping together. Her imagination had run away with her and she'd thought he was sleeping with another woman, but when she confronted him with her suspicions he vehemently denied it, while sheepishly admitting to masturbating to relieve himself.

The light from a full moon cast an eerie glow throughout the sparsely decorated space as Bree tried making out her husband's expression in the diffused light. His labored breathing and jutting erection aroused her; the area between her legs throbbed with a desire so intense that the gush of wetness bathing her core trickled down her inner thighs.

Tyrone pulled his wife against his body, one hand going between her legs and holding her captive. "Damn, baby, your shit is so juicy." Lowering his head, he caught the sensitive skin covering her neck between his teeth. "Are you going to give me some of your juice?"

Eyes closed, throat bared, Bree emitted a growl when his teeth nipped her. "Yes."

That was the last word she uttered before she found herself in bed, on her back as Tyrone pushed his hard flesh into her without even a pretense of foreplay. His thrusts quickened, slamming into her body like a battering ram. The sounds that came from his throat frightened more than excited her, the grunts escalating with each forceful thrust. It ended quickly, with him growling like a wounded beast when he ejaculated inside her.

Bree pounded his back when his full weight wouldn't permit her to move or breathe. "Get up, Tyrone. You're crushing me."

Lifting his head, Tyrone glared down at the woman who wore his ring and had taken his name. "I'm not finished."

"Yes, you are. You just came inside me."

Tyrone moved his hips at the same time he felt his penis stir again. Diamond had been an incredible teacher and he an apt pupil. She'd taught him how to stop climaxing, which permitted him to make love to a woman for hours.

"I only gave you a little bit. There's a lot more."

It was later—much later when Bree managed to crawl out of bed and make it to the bathroom to fill the Jacuzzi with warm water to ease her sore, battered body. Moisture dotted her face and curled her hair as she sat in the dark crying without making a sound. Her wedding night was one she would never forget. Tyrone's selfish, brutal lovemaking had bordered on rape. When she'd told him that he was hurting her he'd continued to pound her tender flesh. And when she told him to stop, he'd placed a hand over her mouth to stifle her protests.

In the end she'd willed her mind blank and waited for him to finish his assault not only on her body, but also on her mind and heart. When she finally climbed out of the tub, she'd reached a decision: she was going to annul her marriage. It would be done, quickly, quietly. They'd signed a prenuptial, so that eliminated a fight over money or property, despite California's community property law. She didn't blame Tyrone as much as she blamed herself. She'd known who he was, yet she'd ignored all of the signs and permitted herself to be taken in by his declaration of love.

She'd called her parents when as a teenager she'd found herself in trouble, but that was the past. Now at twenty-three she was too old to call Mother and Daddy to resolve a situation which she'd chosen willingly.

Tyrone Wyatt would soon find out that, unlike Diamond, Bree Langston didn't have to tolerate his cruelty or his insensitivity.

chapter thirty

"What are you doing out here?"

Bree opened her eyes to find Tyrone hunkered down beside the chaise where she'd spent her wedding night. She couldn't believe he would have the nerve to question her after sexually abusing her.

Her eyes narrowed. "You have the audacity to ask me that after what you did to me?"

Tyrone frowned. "What the hell are you talking about?"

Sitting up, she swung her legs over the cushioned lounge chair. The heat of the rising sun had warmed the terracotta tiles under her bare feet. "You don't remember raping me?"

Tyrone's eyebrows shot up in surprise. "I did *what?*"

"You raped me, Tyrone Wyatt," Bree spat out, her voice low, angry. An expression of confusion swept over her husband's handsome face with her acerbic accusation. "You raped me, not once, but twice. Even when I told you to stop you didn't." Bree shrank when Tyrone reached out to touch her face. "Don't you dare touch me," she warned between clenched teeth.

"I…I don't believe this. I…can't believe you'd accused me of raping you," he stammered.

"What can't you believe, my dear husband? That you're a sadist?"

"But I wouldn't hurt you, baby. You are my wife."

Bree stared at Tyrone, disbelief freezing her features. "You don't remember what you did to me?"

"No."

She wanted to believe him, but couldn't—not when it hurt just to move her legs. Her pelvis was on fire. "I'd believe you if you were drunk, but you weren't, Tyrone."

Tyrone closed his eyes, knowing what he was going to tell his wife would probably jeopardize his marriage and his relationship with his father-in-law. "I was high."

"You were high?" The query came out in a whisper.

He nodded. "I took a hit of coke before we left."

"That's bullshit, Tyrone! The first night we slept together we both snorted and you didn't rape me."

Running his hand over his face, Tyrone shook his head. "I don't know what happened, baby. I guess it was the coke and the ecstasy that made me a little crazy."

"You took ecstasy, too?"

"Look, baby—"

"Don't fuckin' 'baby' me, Tyrone Wyatt!" Spittle had formed at the corners of Bree's mouth. "You promised me that you were going to stop using."

Tyrone's temper flared. "Don't get it twisted, Bree. I didn't promise you shit! I promised your father that I wouldn't give you drugs again. And I haven't."

Moving gingerly, Bree tightened the belt of her wrap around her waist as she stood up. "If you have to get high to make love to me, then we're done."

"What do you mean we're done?"

"We can either live together for a year and not share a bed or…"

"Or what?" There was an edge to his voice.

"Or I'll contact a lawyer to have our marriage annulled as soon as we get back."

Tyrone realized his bride hadn't issued an idle threat, however, truly, he couldn't remember his wedding night. It was as if he'd blacked out and wakened up totally oblivious to what had happened.

Had he had a panic attack?

Was his blackout triggered by his drug cocktail?

Were the symptoms of his panic attacks exacerbated by drug use?

"I swear, Breanna, I don't remember what happened last night. I love you. You're my wife, and I would cut off an arm rather than hurt you."

She rolled her eyes. "Start slicing, because you did." Walking slowly, she made her way into the bedroom.

Tyrone sank down to the chaise Bree had vacated. He hadn't been married twenty-four hours and already his marriage was in the toilet. He'd managed to snag the daughter of a record mogul, basked in the spotlight of a carefully orchestrated courtship, an engagement that had ended in a multimillion-dollar wedding extravaganza. He couldn't afford to taint his star-power image with innuendos that his failed marriage put his sexuality in question. But that paled when he recalled Langston Parker's threat that he would stomp his brains out.

Bree's ultimatum that they live together for a year without sharing a bed was branded into his brain, and his hatred for her father had just spilled over to his daughter. He'd confessed to Bree that he loved her when in reality he hated her: hated that she'd ruined his secret hookup with Diamond, hated that his very existence was predicated on a laundry list of dos and don'ts.

Within seconds his angst vanished when he realized that his wife hadn't said he couldn't sleep with other women. After all, if she wasn't giving him any, then he would take his pleasure wherever he could. Once he and Bree had announced their engagement he hadn't slept with another woman, and whenever they were apart he masturbated while viewing porn to assuage his high sex drive.

His hands fisted as he felt the rush of blood harden his penis. *"Fuck you, bitch!"* he whispered as he searched through the opening of his boxers to grab his erection. Right there, under the rising Mexican sun, he closed his eyes and jerked off until he deliberately ejaculated on the cushion, much like an animal marking his territory.

"Are you certain you don't want any wine, darling?" Karma asked as she refilled her glass with the pale liquid.

"I'm quite certain, Mother. I'm good with the water."

Karma's gaze narrowed as she gave her daughter her full attention. Her relationship with Bree had changed. They'd made a habit of sharing lunch or dinner at least once a week, and whenever Tyrone was out of town they met more often.

"You've lost weight." She'd purposely tempered her tone as to not sound accusatory.

Nodding, Bree smiled. "I'll probably lose a little more before I start gaining weight."

Karma went completely still. "What aren't you telling me?"

"I'm pregnant." Bree knew her announcement had surprised her mother because Karma looked as if she'd been hit by a jolt of electricity.

Hands trembling and her eyes filling with unshed tears, Karma rose slowly and rounded the small table on the screened-in back patio. She extended her arms as Bree pushed back her chair to come to her feet. The two women embraced, tears mingling as they wept.

"Oh, darling, I'm so happy for you."

Bree cried harder. Her mother had shed tears of joy, while hers were bittersweet. When she should've been happy, she felt as if her heart were breaking. She'd married Tyrone believing he would protect her, that she would come to love him as much as he professed loving her and that they, like her parents, would grow old together. How, she agonized, how was she going to bring a child into a world where his or her parents were living a lie?

Sniffling, she managed a sad smile. "Thank you, Mother."

"When are you due?"

"Early March."

Karma dropped her arms, reached for a napkin, blotting the moisture on her cheeks. "I'm going to warn you now that I'm going to spoil my grandson or daughter. I want it to be the best-dressed baby in southern California."

Bree swiped at her own tears. "Mother, please don't."

"I hope you don't intend to tell me how to relate to my grandchild. *Abuela* will give her *nieta* or *nieto* whatever they want or need."

Shock upon shock slapped at Bree. She had never heard her mother speak Spanish. In fact, she didn't even know that she spoke the language. Karma's pronunciation was flawless.

She retook her seat and took a long swallow of water, staring over the rim of her glass at Karma as if seeing her for the first time. "Where did you learn Spanish?"

Karma sat down across from her daughter, aware that she'd made a serious faux pas. Ever since she'd reinvented Carmen Luz-Maria Rodriquez she'd never her let her new persona as Karma Ryder-Parker slip. Either she was getting old, or she'd tired of the lies.

"I grew up speaking Spanish before I learned English."

Bree closed her eyes. She wasn't the only Parker with a secret. She opened her eyes and affected a smile. "If you don't feel comfortable telling me, then I'll respect your right to privacy."

"You have a right to know, now that you're going to have a

child who will ask questions for which you may not have answers," Karma said in a hushed tone.

"Does Daddy know?"

Karma nodded. "Yes."

"What about Ryder?"

"He knows, but I made him swear never to tell anyone."

Bree wanted to laugh, but the subject wasn't comedic. "Do I have to swear, too?"

"No, Bree. Just as we've concealed the fact that you were an unmarried teenage mother I trust you not to reveal what I'm going to tell you."

"You can be such a bitch, Mother," Bree retorted.

"Why, thank you, darling," Karma drawled sweetly. Her voice and expression changed when she opened her mouth to tell her daughter about her past.

chapter thirty-one

"I was born Carmen Luz-Maria Rodriquez in New York City's *El Barrio* or Spanish Harlem," Karma began in a voice that was barely above a whisper. "Today they call it East Harlem. My mother was sitting on the stoop of her building when she caught the eye of a young red-haired beat cop. She said he came down the block every day at the same time for several weeks before getting up enough nerve to ask her name."

Bree listened, transfixed as the former Carmen Luz-Maria told of the clandestine affair between her mother and the married New York City police officer. He had fathered four children with his wife and become a father for a fifth time when Bree's maternal grandmother told him that she was carrying his child.

Although Colin Ryder couldn't divorce his devoutly Catholic wife to marry his pregnant mistress, he did the next best thing—he set his lover up in an apartment in a three-family house in Brooklyn owned by the father of a fellow officer. However, the fairy tale ended when Colin was fatally shot while attempting to stop a bank robbery.

"I was two when my supposedly widowed mother, wearing the wedding ring Colin had given her when they'd fabricated a pretend ceremony, moved back with my grandmother and two aunts who'd come from Puerto Rico to live with us.

Whenever someone in the neighborhood asked about my deceased father they were told he'd died in an auto accident."

"When did you become Karma Ryder?" Bree asked.

"It was your father's idea that I change my name, because he didn't think he would be able to sell my image as a Puerto Rican R&R singer. I changed Carmen to Karma and Rodriquez to Ryder."

Bree smiled. "I always wondered where you'd gotten your red hair."

"Colin's hair was so bright it looked orange."

"What about your mother and aunts?"

"What about them?" Karma asked.

"How did they react to you denying your Latina roots?"

"After I explained the business, they understood. Once they began complaining about the long, cold New York winters I gave my mother enough money to build a house in Rio Piedras. Unfortunately, Mother passed away a year after she moved in, and my *abuela* grieved herself to death a year later after burying her daughter."

"What about your aunts?"

"Both are alive, in their nineties and will probably outlive both of us."

"When was the last time you saw them?"

"I spent a month with them just before you returned from Europe. It's the only time I'm able to speak Spanish without censoring myself."

A sly grin parted Bree's lips. "How do you feel when you overhear your Spanish-speaking employees talk about you?"

Karma rolled her eyes. "I really don't care if they do or don't like me. In fact, I don't *want* them to like me. What I won't tolerate is them repeating gossip. Have you thought about moving out of the condo and into a house now that you're going to have a child?" she asked, deftly changing the topic.

Bree thought about her mother's query, wondering how much she should tell Karma about her marriage. She'd given Tyrone a year, but that was before she'd discovered that she was carrying his child. He'd grown up without his father, and he'd talked about how much he missed all the things a son should've shared with his father.

"That's something I'm going to have to discuss with Tyrone."

Karma peered closely at her daughter. "How are things between you and your husband?"

"Things are going well," Bree lied smoothly. They were going well because Tyrone was touring. And what she hated was the pretense that all was well, that they were so very much in love with each other.

"Are you sure, darling?"

Bree gave her mother a direct stare. "Of course I'm sure. Why?"

"You seem so sad, distracted."

She forced a brittle smile. "It's the baby."

"Does Tyrone know he's going to become a daddy?"

Bree shook her head. "Not yet. I want to wait until he's finished touring because he doesn't need any distractions."

"When is he coming back?"

"He's scheduled to return on the twenty-sixth. What are you thinking about, Mother?" she asked when Karma gave her a too-bright smile.

"If you can get clearance from your ob-gyn, I'd like to take you to Puerto Rico so you can meet your great-aunts."

"He says it'll be safe to travel up until my eighth month."

Karma's eyes sparkled like newly minted pennies. "Does this mean you're going with me?"

"Yes, Mother, I'm going with you."

Bree would agree to go or do anything with her mother if it meant not having to hang out in the condo where sleeping, taking her meals on the balcony overlooking the ocean and reading made one day run into the next.

Karma reached for her cell phone. "I'll tell Judi to cancel all of my appointments for the next two weeks. We'll have to go to the salon before we go, and, of course, do a little shopping. I want you to look your best when you meet your Titi Elena, Titi Olga and *primos.*"

Bree's eyes narrowed. "How many cousins, Mother?" She didn't want to believe that her mother was living a double life, denying her Latina heritage. It might have been necessary when she'd first broken into the recording business, but as Mrs. Langston Parker she should've flaunted her Puerto Rican roots.

Karma waved a manicured hand. "There are too many to count."

"I can't believe you sent me to Europe to live with strangers when you could've sent me to live with relatives in Puerto Rico."

"I did what I thought what was best for you given my state of mind, Breanna. We can't go back in time and change the past, so I suggest we move forward."

Bree gave her mother a long, penetrating stare. "You're right," she said softly. She smothered a yawn with her hand. "I'm sorry about that. I can hardly keep my eyes open."

"It's the baby that's making you feel tired," Karma said sagely. "Why don't you go and lie down? If you're still fatigued when you get up, then we'll put off shopping, unless…"

"Unless what, Mother?" There was a look in Karma's eyes that said she was hiding something.

"Unless you'd rather we go shopping in San Juan? There's a little boutique in San Juan Viejo that's carries the most exquisite one-of-a-kind outfits."

Within seconds Bree's fatigue miraculously vanished. "Is it possible for us to leave today?"

Karma tried and failed to lift her eyebrows. "Do you really want to go today?"

"Yes, Mother. I don't even have to go back home to pack. I'll use the things I left here." She still hadn't moved all of her clothes to her husband's condo, because he didn't have enough closet space.

"If that's the case, then I'll call Lang and have him ready the jet for us."

"Do you think Daddy would want to come with us?"

Karma shook her head. "I don't think so. He's been involved in negotiations to sign a young girl he wants to market as an R&B and Country crossover."

Bree stood up. "I'm going to throw a few things in a bag before I lie down. As soon as everything's ready, please wake me up." She made her way to her old bedroom, smiling. Not only was she going away, but she was going to meet relatives she never knew she had. Not only did she have Puerto Rican roots, but Irish also. What else, she pondered, was the former Carmen Luz-Maria Rodriquez-Parker hiding?

chapter thirty-two

"Do you want another *chuleta,* Breanna?"

Bree smiled across the table at her aunt. "No, *gracias,* Titi Olga. I'm good."

And, she was good—in fact very, very good. Juicy, inch-thick pork chops with lingering hints of sweet orange tantalized her palate, the perfect accompaniment to yellow rice flavored with the *sofrito* she'd made under the watchful gaze of her aunts. Pink beans with an accompanying avocado salad helped to assuage the pangs of hunger which assaulted her when she least expected it.

She was seven weeks along and there was no doubt she was eating for two. The first time she'd found herself pregnant she didn't remember noticing the fatigue or the hunger after her first trimester. What Bree could not forget was the pain that had signaled the onset of labor—pain that seemed to tear her in two. It was only after she'd been in labor for almost a day that the doctor at the small private Brussels hospital administered an injection that hastened delivery.

Bree had heard her baby cry, but she wasn't permitted to see her as the nurses took her into another room. She'd become hysterical because, in a moment of madness, she'd changed her mind and wanted to keep her baby. But, it had been too late. An American couple had come to Europe to claim her baby.

Olga smiled and a network of tiny lines fanned out around

her alert dark eyes. "When are we going to meet your very handsome husband, Breanna?" Karma had sent her a wedding photograph.

"I'm not sure, Titi. As a singer he does a lot of traveling."

"He shouldn't be traveling now that his *esposa* is with child," Olga chided.

"He doesn't know that he's going to be a father," Karma said in Spanish.

Elena, the younger of the two sisters and the one with an overabundance of dry wit, sucked her teeth. "Is it not his child?"

"Of course it is his child," Bree and Karma said in unison.

"Then, why doesn't he know?" Elena asked. Tall and slender with a snow-white curly braid that reached her waist and ecru skin, the former seamstress, like her sister Olga, had never married.

"My daughter wants to wait until he's finished with his tour to tell him," Karma said, again in Spanish.

Elena glared at Karma. "Carmen, I'm certain your daughter can speak for herself."

A deep flush suffused Karma's tanned skin. Whereas in California her face was always shielded from the sun, on the island she became a Puerto Rican in every sense of the word, enjoying the sun, lapsing easily into speaking Spanish and her body language and gestures becoming more Latin.

"*Mami* is right," Bree said, testing her Spanish. "I want to wait for my husband to finish with his tour before I tell him," she continued in English. "He doesn't need any distractions when people are paying a lot of money to see him perform."

"He has a lot of money, no?" Olga asked.

Bree smiled. "*Sí,* Titi. He has a lot of money."

Elena pressed her palms together. "Good for you. A man with no money will bring you nothing but excuses. That's why I did not marry. There was a boy who asked my *papi* for my hand in marriage, but I refused to marry him because he did not want to work to buy a house for us. He said there was nothing wrong with living with his mother."

Olga nodded. "His mother was a *bruja!*"

Bree's eyes grew wide. "Was she really a witch, Titi?"

"No," Elena said, deadpan, "she was a bitch!"

There came a moment of silence before the four women burst into laughter.

Bree helped clear the table and stack the dishes in the dishwasher before returning to the shaded loggia to collapse in a recliner where she slept for hours under hanging baskets filled with fragrant blooming orchids in every variety and color. Karma woke her at nightfall to tell her to go to bed, where she fell asleep to the distinctive *ko-kee,* the sound made by the coqui—a small frog that had become the official mascot of Puerto Rico.

Bree sat in a chair in the master bedroom waiting for her husband. She'd moved all of her clothes and personal items out of the beachfront condo when the rumors were confirmed that Raina Hunter had been spotted at several of Tee Y's live concerts. Photographs showed them in a passionate embrace in the parking lot of a St. Louis restaurant. Tyrone denied having anything to do with Raina, said that they'd just run into each other, but Bree knew he'd lied. He'd lied about loving her, raping her on their wedding night, and he'd lied about Diamond. And, what else, she mused, had he lied about? Well, it no longer mattered because their marriage was over. She'd only come back to the condo to tell him that to his face *and* to let him know that she was carrying his child.

What she refused to do was discuss her marriage with her parents. Langston was practically monosyllabic while Karma ranted and called Raina 'a talentless *puta*' who knew exactly what she was doing when she kissed Tyrone with photographers in attendance.

Bree's cell phone vibrated and she answered the call. It was from Walter Rockwell. Her godfather had offered to come upstairs with her, but she'd told him to wait for her. What she had to tell her soon-to-be ex-husband wouldn't take more than five minutes.

"He's on his way up."

"Is he alone?"

"Yes."

"Thanks, Uncle Rock." She didn't want an audience when she told Tyrone Wyatt their marriage was over.

Tyrone noted the changes the moment he opened the door and dropped his bags. A flowering plant and a crystal vase filled with an assortment of wilted roses. Petals littered the tabletop. Bree had called and left several texts for him, but it was only earlier that morning, before boarding a flight from Detroit, that he'd retrieved his e-mail messages. She'd called to tell him that she was going to Puerto Rico with her mother. He didn't know why she'd bothered to check in with him because their marriage was nothing more than a sham.

She could go anywhere with anyone she wished, and that also applied to him. Tee Y was his own man, and he'd proven that during the six-city tour. He'd slept with a different woman every night, and a few times he'd had more than one. It was just a coincidence that he'd run into Raina Hunter, but the press had had a field day, posting photos of them hugging and exchanging a friendly kiss.

As soon as the photos were made public, Tyrone called Langston to tell him that there was nothing going on between him and the actress—that she'd come to his concert without his knowledge and she was leaving the restaurant at the same time his driver had maneuvered into the parking lot.

He was glad to be home. He wanted to sleep in his own bed, shower in his own bathroom and sit on the balcony overlooking the ocean and commune with nature. He tossed his keys on the table and emptied his pockets of change and left it beside the keys.

Tyrone saw more changes—a trio of delicate bowls on a side table. He'd paid a professional a lot of money to decorate his home exactly the way he wanted it. Candles and flowers were all right for social gatherings, but he didn't want some crystal doodads cluttering up his place or collecting dust. He took the stairs two at a time while unbuttoning his shirt. Taking long strides, he walked into his bedroom, coming face-to-face with the last person he expected to see.

The last time Bree had been in his bedroom was the day following their wedding when she'd moved her clothes and personal items into the guest bedroom. It'd taken her less than an hour to erase all evidence that they'd shared the same space.

Tyrone had to admit that his wife looked incredible. She'd brushed her hair off her face and it displayed her delicate features to their best advantage. She'd put on weight, it was obvious she'd spent time in the sun and her flawless face glowed with a mysterious inner light that could only come from within. Perhaps, he thought, she'd changed her mind about being a wife; perhaps she was willing to move back into his bed and act like a wife.

"Hey, baby," he drawled in a sensual baritone.

Bree's eyes narrowed. There was a time when just the sound of Tyrone's greeting sent shivers up and down her body, but no longer. All she felt was a deep-seated revulsion that caused a rush of bile to settle in the back of her throat.

"I'm not here to welcome you home."

Tyrone frowned as he shrugged out of his shirt, leaving it on the bench at the foot of the California-king bed. "Why, then, *are* you here?"

"I'm here to tell you that I'm filing for a divorce." Her pronouncement stopped all movement from him. "I also want to tell you that I'm pregnant. The baby will carry your name, and I'm not opposed to granting you liberal visitation."

An expression of hardness distorted her husband's beautiful masculine face. "Is it mine?"

Bree shot up from the chair. "You sonofabitch! Of course it's yours." She ran out of the bedroom.

"Don't leave, Breanna!" Tyrone shouted, taking off after her.

She'd made it to the staircase when Tyrone reached for her, and she threw off his arm. First she was standing, and then she found herself falling—headfirst down the stairs. "My baby, my baby," she screamed over and over. All she remembered before nothingness swallowed her whole was her husband leaning over her with an expression of fear—stark and wild in his eyes.

PART TWO

Love Found

chapter thirty-three

December 5—I arrived in Italy this morning.

Why I selected Rome as a temporary home is a question I've asked myself many times since I admitted to Ryder that I needed to live abroad for a while. Now that I'm here I know it's because of the Italian-language movies I watched day after day when I became a virtual recluse. I think of today as my day of personal emancipation. It is the first time I have written in my journal since I lost the baby. Even when I got the news that my divorce was finalized I couldn't bring myself to write about it.

I celebrated my twenty-fifth birthday a month ago today, and a week later came into my trust. After losing the baby and subsequently divorcing Tyrone I moved from my parents' house to live with Ryder.

Daddy dropped Tyrone from the label and the rumors as to why his role in the Will Smith movie was recast with another actor were fodder for the tabloids, entertainment television and weeklies. The paparazzi had a field day following him and Raina Hunter, who was photographed with a noticeable baby bump. Once our quickie divorce was finalized everyone thought Tyrone and Raina would marry, but when Raina revealed that Tyrone wasn't the father of her baby he dropped out of sight. There was talk that he'd moved back to Oakland to live with his mother.

I know I frightened my mother and father when I refused to eat or speak. Now I know what Mother went through when she was in the throes of her depression. However, what I refused to do was take an antidepressant. I preferred to dull the pain with the weed Sierra or Letisha would bring me—even if it was only temporary. When my father found out that I was smoking weed in his house he gave me an ultimatum—move out or go into rehab. I chose to move out. Ryder took me in and most times I was so high I didn't know what day it was. His relationship with Connor changed because his lover didn't want me living with them. This time it was Ryder's turn to choose and he chose me. Connor moved out and a week later hooked up with a female actress from one of his classes. They married two months later. So much for his being gay. I didn't want to tell my brother that the fake-ass was using him, but at least he found out before it was too late.

It was the best thing that could've happened to my brother, but seeing him so unhappy sobered me up enough to realize I wasn't the only Parker in pain. Ryder and I hung out together and I told him things I'd never told anyone—not even Mother. He did admit that he is ambivalent about his sexuality which led him to believe he is bisexual.

A year after Connor moved out Ryder began dating again. Lisa Bailey is a fourth-year medical student at Stanford University School of Medicine. Ryder said he was reluctant to become involved with a woman again after his relationship with Connor. He did tell me that being with Lisa offers him the peace that has always eluded him.

I'm living at the Internazionale Domus Relais Pierret

until I find a permanent apartment. The hotel is right on Piazza di Spagna, near the Spanish Steps. It occupies two floors of the seventeenth-century Pierret, considered an Italian "national monument." The rooms are large and some suites come with kitchenettes, but I decided to rent an apartment with a full kitchen.

Although I managed to sleep during the transatlantic flight, jet lag has hit me hard. I'm going to get something to eat, and then I'm going to sleep. When I wake I'll call Ryder to let him know that I arrived safely. I'll wait until the weekend to call Mother and Daddy.

As soon as I set up my laptop I plan to communicate via e-mail. Not only is it faster but also less expensive than using my cell phone. I find it ironic that I've put myself on a budget now that I'm solvent. When I was living at home it never mattered how much I spent because Daddy paid the bills. But living on my own reminds me of the time when I was a student in Paris. What's different is I'm no longer a student, but a grown woman in control of her destiny. I don't have to wait for a money transfer the first of each month, but I can't afford to engage in reckless spending. I'm paying a rate of three hundred U.S. dollars a day to live at the hotel, and it's a bargain. I don't have to clean, the furnishings are luxurious, the accessories are modern and the linens are of the finest quality. I'm planning to live here for a month, then go apartment-hunting. I have the name and numbers of several real estate agents who I hope will find something that will meet my needs. I want an apartment with lots of natural light so I can sketch for hours.

I chose an apartment with a kitchen in this hotel because I plan to prepare my own meals. Of course I'll eat out occasionally, but I think it's going to be fun cooking for myself. Purchasing cookware is a priority. Instead of going to a supermarket to shop for food I plan to take advantage of the open-air markets offering fresh fish and produce. This place also has a small balcony that looks out on the Spanish Steps. It's perfect place for sketching, eating and relaxing.

The steamer trunk with most of my clothes and sketch pads is scheduled to arrive at the end of next week. Until then, I'll use the spare time to tour the city, shop for food and relax!

Bree registered a buzzing sound, but it took a while before she realized it was the telephone. Reaching over she picked up the receiver, mumbling a sleepy greeting.

"*Ciao, bella.*"

She smiled as the vestiges of sleep vanished. "*Ciao,* Ryder."

"How was your flight?"

"It was very good. I slept until we crossed the international dateline. Once sunlight came through the shades I couldn't go back to sleep."

What Bree found so puzzling was that in the year and a half she'd lived with her brother she'd slept indiscriminately. It hadn't mattered whether it was two in the afternoon or two in the morning when she finally crawled into bed. It'd taken a single episode of substance abuse when she'd woke to find her heart beating so fast that she felt as if she were going into cardiac arrest to stop her from smoking marijuana. The initial impact of the drug after the first drag led her to believe it'd been laced with either crack or PCP. Once sober she realized Ryder was also hurting emotionally, but hadn't chosen drugs as a way of medicating his pain.

"How's Rome?"

"It's still magnificent—the little I've seen of it."

"Have you eaten?" Ryder asked.

Bree glanced over at the travel clock on the bedside table. It was nearly six; she'd been asleep for more than ten hours. "I will when I get up."

"How's the jet lag?"

Stretching, she smothered a yawn with her free hand. "Not bad now. I'm going to take it easy for a few days."

"Stay out of the clubs, Bree." Ryder teased.

She wrinkled her nose. "Very funny. If I wanted to party I could've stayed in L.A."

There was a noticeable pause before Ryder said, "Are you sure you want to live in Europe?"

Bree rolled her eyes upward although her brother couldn't see her. "I thought we talked about this, Ryder. I want to break into fashion, and that's not going to happen in the States. It's much too competitive. I plan to consolidate my sketches before I schedule appointments with some of the local designers."

"Isn't Milan the fashion capital of Italy?"

"It is, but that's why I'm going to concentrate on Rome."

"You're going to do all right, little sister."

Bree laughed softly. "You say that because you're biased, Ryder Parker."

"No shit, little sister."

"I'm going to say the same thing when you become a best-selling writer."

"Now who's biased, Bree?"

"It has nothing to do with you being my brother. I've read what you've written and you're very good, Ryder. I've always said that I want to write the story of my life, but I wouldn't know where to begin. Will you edit it if or when I decide to do it?"

"How much of your life do you want to tell?"

"All of it, Ryder."

"Have you thought of how a tell-all would affect Mother and Dad?"

"The book wouldn't be about them, but *me.*"

"I only asked because you can't tell your story without involving the family, Bree."

"As I said before, the book will be about me, not about Karma, Langston or Ryder Parker. No one will ever know that you and Connor were lovers."

"Have you forgotten I was the one who wanted to come out, not Connor?"

"I couldn't stand Connor." Bree wanted to say *hate,* but it was too strong a word.

"I know it sounds crazy, but I still think about Connor. Especially when I'm in bed with Lisa."

"Did you tell her about your relationship with Connor?"

"Yeah. I told her everything before our second date."

"I suppose she was cool with it since you're still together."

"She wasn't *that* cool until I was tested for HIV, not once but twice. When both tests came back negative she agreed to sleep with me and only with a condom. I realize this might too much information, but I always practiced safe sex with Connor."

Bree smiled. "Good. Now, when are you going to marry Lisa and make me an aunt?"

Ryder's laugh came through the earpiece. "I'll make you an aunt after Lisa graduates medical school."

"You've talked about marriage?"

"The *M*-word has come up a few times."

"Don't wait too long, Ryder."

"I won't."

"Give Lisa my love. I'm going to ring off now and see about getting something to eat."

"I want you to promise me you're going to eat at least two meals a day."

"I promise."

"Say it like you mean it, Breanna."

"I promise to eat at least two meals each day." She knew Ryder was concerned about her weight loss. She'd lost fifteen pounds, weight she could ill afford to lose. "You know how much I love pasta and bread, so it shouldn't take more than a month to regain the weight I lost. Now, please let me hang up so I can go and eat."

"Good bye, Bree."

"*Buono ciao,* Ryder."

Depressing a button, Bree terminated the call, swung her legs over the side of the bed and made her way to the bathroom. She would keep her promise to Ryder. She would eat.

chapter thirty-four

"Sta aspettando qualcuno, signorina?"

"No. I'm dining alone tonight," Bree replied in English. Whenever someone spoke to her in Italian she had to remind herself to reply in the same language. There was no doubt it would take her a few days before she began thinking in Italian.

She'd asked the hotel's concierge for the name of a restaurant within walking distance and he'd recommended a tiny restaurant that was literally off the beaten track. It was located in a narrow alley several blocks from the Spanish Steps. When she'd walked into the miniscule eating establishment with a seating capacity for no more twenty, Bree hadn't expected live music. Sitting in a corner of the dimly lit space was a man on a stool playing a muted trumpet. The tune was familiar and it took a while before she recognized The Eagles' classic hit "Desperado."

"Please, follow me," the waiter continued, speaking Italian.

She was shown to a table in a corner only a few feet from the horn player and given a menu. Another man appeared, setting a bottle of water and two goblets on the checkered red-and-white tablecloth.

"Gradirebbe vino, signorina?"

"No, grazie. Io appena voglio acqua."

The silver-haired man's eyebrows lifted a fraction. He hadn't expected the tall, thin woman with flawless dark skin who spoke English with a distinctive American inflection to speak fluent Italian. He gave her admiring sidelong glances as he opened the bottle of mineral water, filled one of the goblets and removed the other one.

"Mario will be your server tonight, *signorina,*" he said in heavily accented English.

"Grazie—"

"Enrico," he said proudly. "My name is Enrico Rotondo."

Bree gave him a warm smile. "Thank you, Enrico."

"Prego, signorina."

She took a sip of the cool sparkling water. Flickering candles on the tables and wall sconces provided just enough light for diners to discern the features of the person sitting across the table. Bree thought of it as rendezvous for lovers to drink and dine while enjoying the live music.

She directed her attention to the lone figure on the stool under a single spotlight, meeting his penetrating gaze. A shaft of light shimmered on his olive-brown lean face. She wasn't able to discern the texture of his hair concealed under a black felt hat with a short turned-up brim.

He nodded and she smiled in acknowledgment. They were dressed alike: black pullovers, slacks and boots. His short black leather jacket was slung over the back of his stool, while she had yet to relinquish hers. The forty-degree December night-time temperature in Italy's capital city was much lower than what she was used to in southern California.

The musical piece ended, and Bree, along with the other patrons applauded politely. The musician stood up, bowed and walked over to a nearby table and sat down as recorded music filled the restaurant. A softly played mandolin was the perfect complement for an atmosphere geared for intimate dining.

Bree pretended interest in the menu in front of her rather than stare at the tall man in black. Something about his coloring and features indicated he was mixed-race. His high cheekbones and slanting eyes made him look exotic. Leaning back in his chair, he rested an arm over the back of it and stretched out long legs. He signaled a passing waiter, beckoned him closer, whispering something in his ear. The waiter glanced over at her, nodding and smiling.

What now? she mused as the waiter approached her table. If the musician was looking to pick her up, then he was in for a very rude awakening. Tyrone Wyatt had turned her off on the opposite sex—forever. She was only twenty-five and had had two horrific romantic entanglements—one a married man and the other her husband, both of whom had gotten her pregnant.

Bree's impassive expression did not slip when the waiter stood over her. "*Signorina,* the gentleman would like to know if you'd be willing to share a table with him."

"Please tell the gentleman that the lady prefers dining alone tonight." A slight frown creased her forehead. Was she viewed as an anomaly because she'd chosen to eat alone? Women in the States did it all the time.

Bree flashed a saccharine smile when the musician doffed his hat and inclined his head in her direction. It was apparent he had taken her rejection well. She gave her order to her waiter then sat staring surreptitiously at her admirer through lowered lashes. When he'd raised his hat, she'd caught a glimpse of dark, close-cropped curly hair.

Boisterous male voices, shuffling feet and the scrape of chairs on the stone floor only feet from where Bree sat garnered her attention. Three young men wearing heavy ski sweaters and jeans crowded around a nearby table. The bistro tables seated two, so one of them took the empty chair from Bree's table and down sat heavily on it. Their flushed faces and slack mouths indicated they'd been drinking.

The man who'd taken the chair leered at Bree. "Do you

mind?" he asked as a silly grin pulled one side of his mouth downward. His accent screamed midwestern U.S.

"Not at all," she said, deadpan.

Inwardly she cringed. *Why do they have to be Americans?* she thought. She loved her country of birth, yet whenever she traveled abroad her fellow Americans, instead of blending in, stuck out like sore thumbs with their brash, and, at times, impolite behavior. She couldn't understand why, when traveling to a foreign country, they expected everyone to speak English, when they didn't attempt to speak the host country's language.

"Where are you from?" he asked, leaning in her direction, the stale odor of wine wafting into her nostrils.

"Come on over, baby. We got room for one more," another slurred, shifting his chair to create a space.

Instead of answering the obviously inebriated young men, Bree took a swallow of her water.

Reuben Douglas set down his wineglass and rose to his feet. He recognized the three young men as the same ones who'd come into the restaurant a week ago and had been unceremoniously shown the door when they'd had too much to drink and had begun annoying the other patrons. They'd complained loudly that the owner would hear from their lawyers, but the three-hundred-pound-plus chef wielding a cleaver convinced them leaving was preferable to losing a limb or digits.

Reuben's step was determined as he strode over to the table and rested his hands on the shoulders of two of the three. "Gentlemen, if you don't want to find yourselves in the alley missing a few of your teeth, I suggest you leave the lady alone."

Rheumy blue eyes focused on him. "What the fuck do—"

"Think hard and long about what you're about to say," Reuben said in a quiet voice. He gave each one a long, lingering stare. "Get something to eat, and then go back home and sleep it off before you wind up in jail for drunk and disorderly conduct. *Capisce quello che io sto dicendo, i miei amici.* You're six thousand miles from home, so your lawyers can't do shit for you, so don't start with that again." They nodded, then with downcast eyes pretended interest in the tablecloth. *"Buon appetito."*

Smiling, he straightened and winked at the object of the young men's attention. Returning to his table, he picked up his chair and sat down at the table of the pretty dark-skinned woman.

He extended his hand. "Reuben Douglas."

Bree stared at his hand, then reached out and took it. "Breanna Parker."

"You're American?"

"Yes. Thank you for taking care of those idiots."

Reuben missed the soft warmth of her hand when she withdrew hers. "It's the first time I've ever played rescuer and I must admit that it's something I could get used to."

Bree wondered if she gave off vibes that she needed rescuing, that she couldn't make it on her own unless she had a man. "I'm certain I would've been able to handle them, but again, I thank you."

Pushing back his chair, Reuben stood up. "If that's the case, then I'll go back to my table."

"*Buona sera,* Reuben."

The corners of his mouth lifted when he smiled. "*Buona sera,* Breanna."

He had one more week to fill in for the regular entertainer at his uncle's restaurant. The space for the restaurant was carved out of a section of wall wealthy Romans had erected centuries ago in what was one of the first gated communities. Reuben finished his glass of wine, then returned to the stool and picked up his father's trumpet, his gaze fixed on Breanna as she studied the menu on the table in front of her. There was something about her face that was vaguely familiar, and he searched his memory for where he'd seen or met her before.

Bree took another sip of her water as a rush of embarrassment heated her face. She'd thought the musician had asked her to share his table because he was coming on to her, being unaware of his attempt to shield her from the unwanted advances of men who viewed her as an easy pickup.

The waiter returned and she selected an appetizer of tuna in olive oil with small white beans and onion, and an entrée of broiled fish topped with garlic, parsley and bread crumbs with chopped tomato, caper and olive sauce. In lieu of pasta she'd chosen a chilled fresh fig for dessert.

After her meal, the waiter returned to ask, "Was everything good?"

Bree glanced up and smiled at her waiter. "It was delicious."

"You'll come back again?"

"Yes, I will come back again."

She took out enough euros to pay for the meal and a generous tip, then pulled out a few more euros, pushed back her chair and walked over to where Reuben played soulfully. Her gaze met his briefly as she placed the bills on the floor next to his stool.

"*Grazie.*" Bree felt a shiver of uneasiness when he glared at her. Turning on her heel, she walked out of the restaurant feeling the heat of his angry gaze on her back.

She lost track of time as she strolled some of the most elegant shopping streets in the world: Via Condotti, del Babuino and Sistina, stopping to peer into the windows of shops filled with creations from Bulgari, Prada, Versace and Gucci. She wasn't as interested in shopping as she was in what designers were offering for the upcoming fashion season. If someone were to ask her who her favorite designer was, her answer would be the late Christian Dior, whose designs she'd modeled on a Milan runway, then Oscar de la Renta, followed by Carolina Herrera. The clean lines and elegant simplicity of their designs were not only recognizable, but timeless.

The beauty of Rome wasn't only in its architecture, art, music, cuisine, wine or climate but also in its people. Their elegance, sophistication and impeccable sense of style never wavered, and she still marveled at the art of driving a Vespa in stiletto heels. When Ryder had asked her about Rome's appeal her response had been the sights, food, shops, hotels and nightlife—everything she needed to feed her creative appetite.

It was close to midnight when she returned to the hotel, her mind awash with ideas, and she didn't want to wait for the steamer trunk with her sketchpads to arrive. In addition to shopping for food she would also buy art supplies. She would become just another of the many artists and/or art students lining the streets or crowding squares and sketching portraits or ancient buildings.

chapter thirty-five

"Are you following me, *signorina?* I think they call it stalking in America."

Bree turned to find the musician from the restaurant where she'd eaten on her first night in Italy standing behind her. She almost didn't recognize him without his hat. She narrowed her eyes as she tried making out his accent. It wasn't Italian, but it also wasn't similar to any she'd heard in the States.

"I don't stalk men, Reuben." A slight smile softened his firm mouth, drawing her gaze to linger there. Seeing him up close in daylight verified that he was mixed race. His features were European, while his coloring and hair were African.

"They stalk you, Breanna."

"Are *you* stalking me?"

"How long have you been here?" he asked.

"I just walked in," Bree admitted.

She'd gotten up early to buy bread, cheese, fruit, herbs, vegetables and fresh fish from an outdoor market. It'd taken the better part of an hour to wash and put away her purchases. A call to the front desk had proven successful when she was given the name and address of an art-supply shop less than a quarter of a mile from the hotel. A shiver of excitement had raced up her spine as she walked in to see stacks of paper in various weights and colors, drafting tables, brushes, pencils, canvases and easels. It was as if she'd come home.

"Well, I have been here for twenty minutes, which means you are the stalker." Smiling, he revealed a set of perfect white teeth.

Reuben had thought he would never see Breanna again, believing she was a tourist. The glints of red highlights in her warm-brown shoulder-length hair matched the undertones in her flawless brown face. Her delicate face reminded him of the painted angels and sculptures from the Renaissance period, her nose and eyes in particular. She was taller and thinner than he'd originally thought. But, then, he'd only caught glimpses of her standing in the restaurant.

Bree's expression brightened when she realized Reuben was teasing her. *"Io pensai che Lei sia un musicista, non un attore comico."*

His smile vanished as if someone had suddenly turned out the light behind his eyes. "You speak Italian?" She nodded. "But, you're from the States."

"Yes, but I still speak Italian."

"Where did you learn the language?"

"At school. And you?"

"My mother taught me."

Bree stared at the tall, slender man dressed casually in a tan V-neck sweater, dark wide-wale chocolate-brown cords and matching hip-length suede jacket. "Your mother is Italian."

"Yes. My father was an American." Reaching into a pocket of his cords, Reuben took out a handful of euros and counted out several, handing them to Breanna. You gave me money. I don't play for money."

Although irked by his mocking manner, Bree did not show it. *"Mi perdonerà se io sono piuttosto ignorante della sua cultura?"*

Reuben stared at the American woman who'd introduced herself as Breanna Parker. "It's not about you being ignorant of the culture, it's the restaurant's policy."

She grimaced. "I'm sorry about that."

He dismissed her apology with a wave of his hand. "Are you an art student?"

"No. I came here for a pad and pencils."

Reuben moved closer to Breanna when two young women reached around him to examine boxes of charcoal and colored chalk. "What are you sketching?"

Bree studied the man who continued to intrigue her with each passing minute. So far he was asking the questions and she was supplying the answers. "I haven't decided." It was a half truth. When she had awoken that morning the notion of designing lingerie had come to mind. "Are you an artist?" she asked Reuben.

"I'm a fashion designer."

She took a quick breath of complete surprise. "Men's or women's?"

"Women's."

"Who do you work for?"

Reuben smiled again. "You ask a lot of questions, don't you?"

Bree was too excited to register his slight reprimand. She'd come to Europe to find herself and recapture her muse. Although not superstitious by nature, she believed walking into *il ristorante di luna blu* the night before and meeting Reuben Douglas again today in an art shop was predestined.

"I'd like you to take a look at my sketches," she said, her voice rising with excitement. Reuben was a professional and what she needed was feedback from someone in the business.

"How many sketches do you have?"

She smiled. "A lot."

"Where are they?"

"They're not here. Not yet," she added quickly.

He lifted his eyebrows. "Where are they?"

"They're in a trunk on the way from California."

Reuben found Breanna refreshing. He knew nothing about

her other than her name and that she was an American who spoke fluent Italian, yet he felt a vaguely sensuous connection that was almost palpable. But something stopped him—her age. She was young, and at thirty-nine he knew she was much too young for him. The only time he'd become involved with a woman ten years his junior it'd ended badly for both of them. Besides, he didn't know if the American woman was married or engaged. Just because she didn't wear a ring and had dined alone didn't mean she was not in a committed relationship.

"When do you expect your trunk to arrive?"

"It should be here at the end of the week."

Reaching into the breast pocket of his jacket, Reuben took out a small business card, handing it to her. "Call me when it arrives and we can set up a time to meet."

"Thank…" Bree's offer of gratitude died on her lips when she found herself staring at Reuben's back as he turned on his heel and walked out of the shop. Her gaze shifted to the card printed with his name and a handwritten telephone number. There was no e-mail, Web site or street address.

She wanted to believe that Reuben was still smarting because she'd given him money as if he were a homeless street entertainer. He probably thought of her as a pretentious American who viewed him as needy and inferior. He'd brushed aside her attempt to apologize for insulting him, and Bree knew she would probably make a few more social faux pas while living in Italy, but she was certain never to make the same mistake twice. She'd done that with her first lover and her ex-husband.

"Sta cercando qualche cosa?"

A salesclerk asking Bree if she needed help pulled her out of her reverie. Smiling at the petite woman with sparkling hazel eyes and dark curly hair, she shook her head. *"No, grazie.*" She'd come to purchase a pad and pencils, but what she hadn't expected was to run into the man who'd helped to diffuse what could've become an ugly confrontation between herself and fellow Americans.

Bree paid for her purchases and retraced her steps, stopping at a small sidewalk café to enjoy a midmorning snack of strong black coffee and biscotti. Her pulse had quickened with excitement when she opened the door to her apartment. Minutes later, she sat on the balcony, pad on her lap. Holding the pencil lightly, she drew a curving line. The seconds ticked off into minutes and the minutes in an hour and then into two.

The straight and curving lines became shapes, taking on a life of their own as she drew figures with fabrics that draped, flowed and swirled on the page. It was when she felt a slight stiffness in the back of her neck that Bree knew she had to stop.

The dizzying rush of creative energy had subsided, receding to her subconscious to wait for her call it up again.

chapter thirty-six

December 20—I've been in Italy two weeks and I still don't have my trunk. The Customs officer I spoke to promised it would be cleared tomorrow. I've already arranged for a messenger company to deliver it to the hotel. There's nothing of extreme value in the trunk except my sketches. The clothes and shoes can be replaced, but not my sketches. The few pieces of jewelry I decided to bring I'd stored in my carry-on.

I got my first e-mail from Mother yesterday. She always claimed to be electronically challenged, but after Ryder showed her how to go online she's like a kid in a candy shop—she can't get enough. Daddy said she's now an Internet junkie. I can't believe Mother actually wrote that she misses me, but when she mentioned coming to Rome for the Christmas holidays to be with me I called Daddy to talk her out of it. I left the States to put some space between myself and my mother and two weeks isn't enough time for me feel disconnected from my family or even remotely *homesick.*

Bree bit down on the cap of her pen as she reread what she'd written. She underlined the word *homesick* twice. She was an American, yet she didn't feel like one. How could she when she'd lived abroad for a total of seventeen of the twenty-five years of her life? She not only spoken Italian but now thought in the language.

> I thought of spending Christmas in Paris, but changed my mind, because I want to go to St. Peter's for Christmas mass.

Bree dialed the number on the small business card. Her trunk had finally arrived with her cherished sketches.

"*Ciao.*"

She hesitated when she heard the softly modulated baritone greeting. "*Ciao,* Reuben, this is Breanna Parker."

"You have your sketches?"

"Yes. The trunk was delivered a few hours ago."

"When would you like to meet?"

"It would have to be at your convenience."

There came a pause before Reuben said, "I'm free tonight."

"Perhaps we can meet over dinner."

"What if we look at the sketches first, then discuss them later over dinner?"

"Okay. Where do you want to meet?"

"I can come to your place."

Bree gave Reuben her address and then rang off, her heart pumping a runaway rhythm. It would be first time she would show her creations to another person, and the fear that what she'd drawn could be ripped off was never far from her mind. She wasn't certain why she was so paranoid about her work, but she had heard claims of designers passing someone else's work off as their own. Her wariness had led her to sign and date each design.

A uniformed police officer rerouted traffic away from the Spanish Steps and Reuben maneuvered his Vespa along a cobblestone street and parked it in an alley, pocketing the key. Barricades had blocked vehicular traffic to the streets leading to the Internazionale Domus Relais Perriet.

Breanna had chosen to live in Piazza di Spagna, in the center of Rome, which meant he had to walk six blocks instead of three to get to the hotel. He rechecked the slip of paper on which he'd written down her address before walking into the lobby and asking the clerk at the front desk to ring Breanna Parker. Minutes later he came face to face with the woman whose image had haunted him relentlessly until he'd uncovered where he'd seen her before.

Each time he saw her she looked different. Today she wore a white man-tailored shirt with a pair black of stretch slacks and ballet-type shoes. And with her hair pulled off her face with a black velvet headband she was the epitome of casual chic. If she'd cut it into a pixie style she could've easily passed for a young black Audrey Hepburn. Her body was willowy—model-thin—but with curves.

"Hello," he said, handing her a decorative bag. "I hope you like red wine."

Bree took the bottle, her smile mirroring her excitement that Reuben Douglas had followed through on his promise to look at her designs. "As a matter of fact, I do. Thank you. Please come in."

He walked into a living room with tall windows, colorful framed prints on the walls, gleaming parquet floors in a herringbone design, a fireplace, sofa, loveseat and a desk and chair. "I would've been here sooner, but some of the streets are blocked off."

Bree placed the bottle of wine on a table, then reached for Reuben's hand. His black attire made him appear taller, slimmer. "Come with me and I'll show you what's going on." She led him into the master bedroom with a marvelous view directly onto the Spanish Steps.

Reuben stood holding Bree's hand as he watched the preparations for a bridal-fashion shoot. His gaze shifted from the rail-thin models swathed in frothy white wedding gowns to the Piazza Trinità dei Monti.

"The view of the city from here is incredible."

Bree eased her hand from his, staring up at Reuben's distinctive profile. "Where do you live?" A shaft of light crossed his face and she realized that his eyes weren't as dark as she'd originally thought. They were more hazel than brown, with glints of gold and green. He'd cut his hair and the close-cropped raven strands lay against his scalp like the down of a bird's wing.

He smiled. "Not in Piazza di Spagna."

"I don't plan to live here after the new year."

"Are you going back to America?"

"No."

"Where are you going?"

"I'm not sure yet. I've contacted a local real estate agent to look for a flat close enough to the center of the city that I won't need a car."

Reuben smiled. He didn't know why, but he hadn't wanted Breanna to leave Italy. There was something about her he found intriguing *and* refreshing. He'd found her confident, not brash, and she projected a childlike exuberance when she'd talked about her designs.

"Don't tell me you're not used to our chaotic traffic," he teased.

Bree rolled her eyes upward. "I'm thoroughly *intimidated* by your chaotic traffic, whether driving or walking."

"If you plan to live here, then you should consider the Piazza della Repubblica. It is accessible to most of Rome's attractions and well-connected to public transportation. The neighborhood is lively during the day and quiet at night."

"Is that where you live?"

"No. I live in Trastevere."

Bree made a mental note to look up the areas on the Internet. She let out an audible breath. "I guess we should get started because you'll have a lot to look at."

She led Reuben to the balcony where she'd stacked her sketch books in chronological order, beginning with the oldest on top. She watched as he shrugged out of his jacket, hanging it over the back of the wrought-iron chair.

"I can make an antipasto if you'd like to eat something before we go."

"No, thank you."

"If that's the case, then I'll be inside." Bree didn't want to sit and watch his reaction to years of dreams she'd put on paper. She returned to the living room, sat on a chair with a footstool and reached for the novel on a nearby table. If she wasn't taking walking tours of the neighborhoods, sketching or cooking she rounded out her day reading. She'd packed classic novels that had been required for her English and literature courses. Rereading Steinbeck, Austen, Dickens, the Brontës and George Eliot afforded her a greater appreciation for the written word.

Reuben was anxious to see what Breanna had designed. He smiled when he saw that she'd signed and dated her sketches. Artists were certainly a strange breed, and he counted himself amongst them. Dusk had descended on the city, streetlights were coming on, a lantern affixed to a wall on the balcony illuminated the space when he finished. A rush of mixed emotions assailed him, but he knew he had to be open and honest with his assessment of designs that'd spanned years.

He found her in the living room, turning the pages of a thick novel. The light from a floor lamp next to the chair bathed her in a soft golden glow. "I'm finished."

Her head came up and she put the book on a side table. "That didn't take long."

"You have a lot of duplicates."

"I know. I'd stop and start several times because I wasn't certain what I wanted."

"We'll talk about it over dinner."

"Why do you sound so ominous?"

Reuben angled his head. He knew Breanna was apprehensive, because he'd gone through what she was now experiencing. He'd had teachers who had let him down tactfully when they told him that no one would ever wear his designs, and others who'd announced publicly that he would never make it as a clothes designer. Thanks to hard work, perseverance and an abundance of stubbornness he'd proven them wrong.

"All I'm going to say is that you didn't fail."

Clasping her hands together and closing her eyes, Bree whispered a silent prayer of gratitude. "Thank you."

"Don't thank me yet, Breanna. I still have to give you my critique."

"I'm always looking for corrective criticism."

Reuben wondered how she was going to react to his criticism. There was no doubt Breanna had her share of artistic talent, but it needed refinement, refinement he hoped he'd be able to give her.

"Are you ready to go?"

Bree held her arms out to her sides. "Should I change?"

"No. You're perfect."

She went to get a jacket, then closed and locked the windows. Reuben was waiting near the door when she gathered her keys and handbag. They took the lift to the street level, and when they emerged and walked out to the street, Reuben reached for her hand, holding it firmly as he led the way back to where he'd left his Vespa.

The shoot had ended, the police had removed the barricades, and lovers, backpackers and young Romans crowded the steps where models had posed and strutted earlier that day.

Reuben pointed to the fountain at the foot of the steps. "A couple of years ago a drunk vandalized one side of the fountain."

Bree leaned closer to capture some of his body's heat. Although nighttime temperatures were in the mid-forties, she felt chilled. "What happened to him?"

"All I'll say is that he's lucky the police got to him before the crowd did. However, artisans restored the fountain and you can't tell where it'd been damaged."

"Speaking of fountains, I haven't thrown a coin into the Fontana di Trevi."

Reuben placed his free hand over her fingers in the crook of his elbow. "Make certain you do it the proper way."

"How's that?"

"You have to hold the coin in your right hand, turn your back to the fountain, and toss the coin over your left shoulder."

"That's a lot."

"We Romans are very superstitious. According to the legend, the spirit of the fountain will see that one day you'll return to Rome."

"But, I've already returned without throwing a coin in the fountain."

Reuben slowed as they navigated around a group of tourists flipping through guide books and peering closely at maps. "This isn't your first trip to Italy?"

"No. I came here during school holidays the year I turned seventeen."

He steered her down a narrow street with tiny shops and restaurants tucked into buildings dating back to the Renaissance. "Did you go to school in the States?"

"No. It was in Switzerland."

Reuben gave her a sidelong glance. A light breeze lifted her hair, which brushed her cheeks. "Do you also speak French?"

"Yes."

"What about German?"

"My German is a little rusty. But I'm fluent in French, Spanish and Italian."

He stopped long enough to permit two fast-moving cars to pass, and then hurried her across the street. "How old are you, Breanna?"

"Twenty-five."

"You're twenty-five and you're living alone in a foreign country."

Bree heard the censure in his voice. "I've lived in foreign countries a lot longer than I've lived in the States. I was seven years old when I was sent to a Swiss boarding school. After graduating I spent five years in Paris—living on my own. I've been married, lost a baby, so I believe I'm qualified to live alone."

"I didn't mean to imply that you can't take of yourself."

"What exactly were you saying, Reuben?"

He lifted a shoulder. "I suppose my concern is that you're a single woman living here without male protection."

She smiled. "Does your concern have anything to do with those clowns coming on to me in the restaurant?"

"Yes."

"I'll be all right, Reuben." Breanna wanted to tell him that she never had a problem with men who weren't interested in her—just those who were. It was whenever she permitted herself to get involved with them that she was in for trouble. Unlike her mother, she'd always made poor choices when it came to men.

"Have you ever been on a Vespa?"

Bree stopped suddenly, causing Reuben to lose his balance before righting himself. "You came here on a scooter?"

"*Sì.* I promise to go slow."

She gave him a look that said communicated that she didn't believe him. No one in Italy drove slowly. Pedestrians daily played chicken with vehicular traffic just crossing the street.

"*Promesso,* Reuben?"

He chuckled softly. *"Sì, io prometto."*

chapter thirty-seven

Bree buried her face against the side of Reuben's neck as he zipped through the streets. The wind whipped her hair around her face, her teeth were clenched and her arms were wrapped tightly around his waist. She closed her eyes and prayed.

"Where are you taking me?" she asked when he came to a stop at a street light.

"To a restaurant in Trastevere."

The light changed, and Reuben took off again, Bree clinging to him as her heart beat a rapid tattoo against his back. The scent of his aftershave and the smell of leather wafted to her nose. "Why are we going to Trastevere when there are restaurants closer to my hotel?"

"This place has good food, good wine and has yet to be discovered by hordes of tourists."

"The food at the restaurant where I met you is very good."

"I know," he said over his shoulder, "but if we go there, then my uncle expects me to work, either waiting tables or filling in for the keyboard player."

"That was your uncle's place?"

"*Sì.* He and my mother are brother and sister."

"You're a fashion designer, part-time waiter *and* musician."

Reuben chuckled softly. "No. I'm a freelance artist and personal designer. I paint landscapes and reproductions for a shopkeeper with a lengthy client waiting list."

He felt Bree tighten her grip when he maneuvered around a corner at a forty-five-degree angle. Seconds later he sped across a bridge. "We're now crossing the Tiber River."

"Are we still in Rome?"

"Yes."

Bree drew in a deep breath when Reuben slowed as he entered the neighborhood across the river from Aventino. Straightening, she glanced around her. The buildings were carefully preserved, as if time had virtually stood still. Small streets were lined with restaurants and café bars spilling out onto the street.

"It's charming, Reuben."

He maneuvered into a narrow alley, coming to a complete stop. Reaching around, Reuben helped her off the scooter. "I like living here."

"Did you grow up here?"

"No. There was a time when Aventino was a little grimy because poorer workers and artisans settled here, but lately it has undergone a second renaissance as an artsy neighborhood with pretty lively night life."

"How old are these buildings?"

"They date from the Middle Ages to the Renaissance."

How different everything was from Los Angeles, Bree mused, with its glass-and-steel apartment and office buildings. She also noticed that here the streets were bustling with people heading toward the many restaurants and cafés. There were a number of couples bundled up against the cooler night-time temperatures sitting outside at tables drinking espresso.

"Would you prefer eating inside or outside?" Reuben asked as he reached for her hand and led her to a small café.

She shivered noticeably when the wind picked up. "Inside, please."

Reaching over her head with his free arm, Reuben pushed

open an ancient wooden door with leather hinges, the mouth-watering smell of grilling meat and fish greeting them. The restaurant, a former carriage house, was illuminated with candles and a roaring fire in a massive fireplace. It had become Reuben's favorite in all of Rome. Of course, he hadn't made that fact known to his uncle who probably would deny all familial ties while branding him traitor.

Angling his head closer to Bree, he said, "Follow closely behind me."

Bree glanced around the dimly lit space. "Did they pay the electrical bill?"

He smiled at her. "There's electricity, but the candles are for ambience."

She wanted to tell Reuben that Americans only dined in the dark with candles for illumination during blackouts. "Do they cook by candlelight?"

Reuben gave her a pointed look before he realized she probably couldn't see his face. He led her to a table not far from the fireplace, which was tall enough for a six-foot man to stand in it without bending.

He recognized one of the waiters as he came from the kitchen carrying a large bowl of pasta and another with a variety of grilled fish. "*Ciao,* Giuseppe."

"*Ciao,* Reuben. I'll be right with you," the waiter replied in rapid Italian.

Reuben pulled out a chair for Bree, then he removed his jacket, draping it over the back of the chair opposite her, then sat down. "Hungry?"

"I wasn't until I walked in. Something smells delicious."

She smiled across the table at her dining partner. The flames from the candle flattered the lean contours of his face. Bree knew nothing about Reuben Douglas other than his name and that he was an artist and designer who lived in Trastevere, yet she felt as if she'd known him for a long time. Earlier that afternoon she'd wondered whether he was married or engaged, but had dismissed the notion because their association would be one that was strictly business.

She'd kept her promise to Ryder to eat at least two meals each day. Instead of the customary continental breakfast of fruit, sweet breads and coffee or tea, she'd opted for granola cereal with fruit, toast and a cup of strong coffee. Her midday snack was gelato with thin anise-flavored wafers, or a frothy cappuccino with an oven-fresh *cornetto* or croissant. Dinner, when she decided not to cook for herself, usually was a small bowl of pasta with either chicken or fish with grilled vegetables. Bree knew she would've put on more weight if she hadn't walked so much. She walked everywhere, occasionally venturing eight to ten miles from the hotel. She'd return to her apartment exhausted, but pleased that she had explored another part of the city she hadn't seen before.

Menus appeared and Bree studied the handwritten selections. *"Cosa è coda alla vaccinara?"*

Reuben smiled at her. "Braised oxtail. It's delicious."

She narrowed her eyes. "Are you just saying that, or is it really good?"

His frown vanished. "Are you always this distrustful?"

"No."

She'd said no when she wanted to tell him yes. Her parents had told her that they loved her, yet had still sent her away. Her French lover had claimed to have loved her in order to get into her panties, yet he'd deceived her. Then, there was Tyrone Wyatt. He loved her enough to make her his wife, had raped her and lied about fooling around with Diamond and Raina Hunter. Even after their divorce a number of women had come forth to confess to sleeping with Tee Y while he was touring. Nothing had changed. The only person she still trusted was her brother.

"Then why don't you believe me?"

"I'll take your word for it and order it along with *aglio olio.*" Bree preferred garlic and oil on her pasta to other tomato-based sauces. "What are you ordering?"

Reuben glanced at the menu that hadn't changed in years. "*Cacio e pepe* pasta."

Her eyebrows lifted. He'd opted for a creamy and peppery pasta. "All you're having is pasta?"

"No. I'm going to have it with *guanciale.* That's pig's cheek. It's similar to bacon, but has a more delicate flavor."

"Does it taste like pancetta?"

"It's even better. I'll give you some so that you can judge for yourself."

A waiter came to take their orders, while another placed a small dish of antipasti and a basket with hot, freshly baked bread on the table, along with a bottle of red wine. Bree knew she had to eat sparingly or she'd never finish her entrée. The waiter uncorked the bottle of wine, filling two wineglasses with the dark-red liquid.

Reuben handed Bree a glass, then took the remaining one and extended it. "*Saluto.*"

She touched her glass to his. "*Saluto.*"

A slice of warm crusty bread along with marinated olives, artichokes and hearts of palm assuaged her preliminary hunger. She took a sip of the full-bodied wine, savoring the slightly dry flavor that lingered on her tongue.

Reuben ran a finger down the stem of his glass. "I suppose you want to know about your sketches?"

Bree stared at him with wide eyes. "Yes."

Lowering his gaze, he stared at the back of his hand. "You're quite talented, Breanna. But…"

"But what, Reuben? And, please call me Bree."

"Your designs need refinement. You need to take risks, because most are too simplistic. For example, you drew a basic sheath dress cut on a bias with a jeweled neckline. An inverted pleated bodice and a slightly flared hem would've made it more unique. And, depending on the fabric and accessories it could double for day or nighttime."

Bree listened intently over the most scrumptious dinner she'd had in Rome as Reuben offered constructive criticism of her designs. The candle had burned down to a nub before it was replaced with another pillar. What surprised her was that he'd been able to recall sketches of dresses, slacks, jackets, coats and skirts filling half a dozen pads.

Biting her lower lip, she glanced away. She'd secreted her designs, believing they were unique, but a thorough critique by a professional designer had shattered her dream to set up her own fashion-design house.

"Do you think I need more course work?"

Reaching across the table, Reuben placed his hand over hers. "No. You have the skill to be a dress designer. What you need is another set of eyes to fine-tune your work."

Bree felt the comforting warmth of the hand covering hers, stunned by the tenderness in his expression. "I can't ask you—"

"Then don't ask," he said, cutting her off. Attractive lines fanned out around his eyes when he smiled. "I've been where you are now. I came out of design school believing I was going to be the next Valentino, de la Renta, St. Laurent or Armani, but three years of rejections humbled me to the point I knew I had to ask for help. Meanwhile, I painted and sold portraits and landscapes to support myself in order not to become the stereotypical starving artist.

"Swallowing my pride, I contacted one of my instructors and told her of my dilemma. She put me through several exercises where I had to draw a simple jacket, shirt and blouse. The true test came when I had to convert those garments for day, business and evening wear with the accompanying accessories.

"Nothing was off-limits. I used epaulets, beading, rickrack and braiding. I also added peplums, velvet and fur trim, ribbons, silk and satin flowers and ruffles and hand-embroidered trim on the collar of one jacket."

Propping her elbow on the table, Bree rested her chin on the heel of her hand, her eyes shimmering with excitement. "How long did it take you to complete the assignment?"

"Four months. The results were phenomenal, her critique invaluable and it changed my life. I updated my portfolio, returned to Paris and contacted the people at the same fashion houses who'd told me that I'd never make it in the business."

"What happened?"

Reuben gave her a dazzling smile. "I got offers from three of seven."

"Who did you decide to go with?"

"A small couture house that eventually became a part of St. Michel."

Bree's eyebrows lifted. In the world of fashion, St. Michel was on a par with Chanel and Dior. "Why did you leave them?"

"I returned to Italy six years ago when my father was hospitalized with a rare form of cancer. He'd been a Vietnam Green Beret, and he believed his illness was a result of exposure to Agent Orange. He was in and out of the hospital for a year until he asked my mother to bring him home because he wanted to die in his own bed. This would've been a burden on my mother if she hadn't been a nurse. She fed him and gave him his medication, while I took care of his bathing and personal needs. He died quietly in his sleep, but that didn't make it any easier for my mother who'd lost her husband and her best friend."

"Are you an only child?"

Reuben released her hand. "Yes. My mother had two miscarriages before she had me. She's always referred to me as her *perlina di oro preziosa.*" I didn't mind being her precious gold bead, but she insisted calling me that in front of my friends. By the time I was a teenager my nickname was 'Il Dorato.'"

Bree closed her eyes. Reuben's mother had lost two children before bringing one to term, while she'd gotten pregnant twice and lost both her babies—one to adoption, the other when she'd fallen down a flight of stairs.

She opened her eyes, smiling. "The Golden One," she whispered. "I like that."

"It would be all right if I was an athlete, but it's a bit much for an artist."

"Claim it, Reuben, because apparently you're a successful artist."

"I don't mean to sound self-deprecating, but I prefer keeping, as they say, a low profile."

"But, I thought you wanted to be the next Dior or St. Laurent."

"I did when I was twenty-five. Now at thirty-nine all I want is to do is take care of my personal clients."

"How many clients do you have?"

Picking up his wineglass, Reuben drained it while staring at Bree over the rim. She was like a child, asking endless questions. And, she could've been his child. After all, he was fourteen years her senior.

"Two."

"Two?"

"Yes. Their husbands are in petrol."

Bree wondered whether they were the wives of Middle-Eastern sheiks who modeled their haute couture in private and when they ventured out hid it under flowing robes. "Are they Saudis?"

"No. They're Americans. I can't reveal their names except to say they consistently make the best-dressed lists."

Bree wrinkled her nose. "Good for you."

She continued to stare at the enigmatic man with eyes that changed color with his moods. Her gaze lowered to his sharp, aquiline nose and down to his firm mouth with a hint of sensuality in his fuller lower lip.

"What are you doing for Christmas?"

The question caught Bree off-guard and she sat forward on her chair. "I plan to go to St. Peter's for midnight mass."

"What are you doing after that?"

"I have to call the States and talk to my friends and family. Why?"

"I'd like you to celebrate the holiday with my family."

"I don't want to intrude—"

"How can it be an intrusion when I'm inviting you, Bree?"

"Reuben, I'm not good with strangers."

He smiled. "You've done all right with me. Christmas is a family holiday, and I know it's not going to be easy for you to be so far away from home and your family."

Bree wanted to remind Reuben that she'd spent more time away from her home and family than she had with them. "Thanks for the offer, but I'll pass this time."

"Do you have any plans for New Year's Eve?" She shook her head. "I'll take no for Christmas, but not New Year's. I'm meeting friends, and I'd like to take you as my guest. Please don't tell me that you have nothing to wear because I have the perfect dress for you."

Bree gave him a skeptical look. "You have the perfect dress when you don't even know what size I wear?"

Reuben studied her intently. "You're approximately five-nine, about a thirty-three in the chest, twenty-two or three in the waist and thirty-five in the hips."

"Smarty," she drawled. "What about shoe size?"

Leaning over, he peered at her shoes. "Thirty-seven and a half."

"Wrong." He thought she wore the U.S. equivalent of a seven. "I'm a thirty-eight."

"I was close."

"Yes, you were, but as they say in the States 'close, but no cigar.'"

Bree wanted to ask Reuben whether he'd invited her to celebrate the holiday with his friends and family because she was alone in a foreign country and he felt sorry for her, or because he was interested in her. She prayed it was the former. At this time in her life she needed a friend, not a lover or boyfriend.

"Okay, Reuben, I'll go out with you New Year's Eve. How much is the dress?"

"Nulla."

"Nothing?" she repeated. "No, Reuben I can't."

He leaned closer. "You can *and* you will. Think of it as a gift."

"A gift for what?"

"Christmas."

"I don't know you, and you certainly don't know me well enough to give me a gift."

"If you buy me one, then we'll be even."

Bree waved her hand. "You're incredible."

He winked at her. "Thank you."

"I don't mean *that* incredible." The waiter approached and placed the bill on the table. Reuben touched his napkin to his mouth before reaching for it. "Would you mind if I paid for dinner?" she asked him.

Glancing at the total, he reached into the pocket of his slacks and took out enough euros to cover the meal and gratuity. "Yes, I would."

Pushing back her chair, she stood up. "I'm going to the rest room."

Reuben stood up. "I'll meet you outside."

The rest room was so small that it could only accommodate one person at a time. She lingered long enough to pull a comb through her hair, apply a coat of lip gloss and wash her hands. Reuben was seated on his Vespa waiting for her when she left the restaurant. She swung her leg over the back of the scooter, angling for a comfortable position behind him.

"The next time I take you out I'll bring a helmet," Reuben said over his shoulder.

Bree didn't respond as she wrapped her arms around his waist and pressed her face to the back of his leather jacket. She couldn't say anything because she prayed she would make it make to her apartment without a mishap.

Her prayers were answered when Reuben maneuvered onto the sidewalk outside the entrance to the lift leading to her apartment. He rode with her, waiting until she opened the door.

Reuben held out his hand, smiling when Bree placed her hand in his. "I'll call you in after Christmas to arrange for a fitting."

Bree stared up at him. "Is it that important for me to wear one of your designs? Because I could always buy a dress."

He released her hand. "It's been a while since a woman under thirty has modeled one of my designs."

"How old are your clients?"

"They're in their fifties."

She knew arguing with Reuben would only serve to alienate him, and she needed him—needed him to help her perfect her designs so she could realize her dream. "Enjoy your Christmas."

"*Buon Natale,* Breanna."

Bree closed the door behind his departing figure, trying to make sense of her new and puzzling association with Reuben Douglas.

chapter thirty-eight

Reuben, holding a tureen of ravioli with truffle cream sauce above his head, pushed his way through the throng crowding his grandmother's dining room. There were more people in Carolina Rotondo's house this year than last, which meant her search to connect with as many of her relatives before she died was going well.

However, he suspected some of the named Rotondos weren't actually related to him but enterprising namesakes looking for a place to spending the holiday while eating and drinking to excess. Carolina usually hosted her Christmas dinner alfresco, but a steadily falling cold rain had forced the festivities indoors.

Silvana Rotondo-Douglas took the large bowl from him and managed to find a space on one of the two long tables against the wall. "Thank you."

Bending slightly, he pressed his mouth close to his mother's ear. "Who are all of these people?"

Silvana lifted her shoulders. "I can assure you that many of them aren't related to us."

Reuben smiled at Silvana, who'd recently celebrated her sixtieth birthday. Her short salt-and-pepper hair was stylishly cut to frame her round face and display her balanced features to their best advantage. The youngest girl in a family of two sons and two daughters, she'd always been referred to as *semplice* or "homely" when compared to her older, blond, blue-eyed sister, who was as waspish as she was beautiful. However, it was Silvana who'd caught the eye of an American army officer who'd spent his leave in Rome rather than return to the States following his second tour of duty in Vietnam.

Only fourteen at the time, Silvana didn't tell her parents that the correspondence she received from her American pen pal were actually letters from a man who was too old for her. It was another three years before Jesse returned to Italy with the intent of making Silvana his wife. By the time the Rotondos discovered that their youngest daughter, who had left home to attend nursing school, had married an *Americano* she was already pregnant. Silvana miscarried not once but twice before she finally gave her husband a son and her parents another grandchild.

Carolina reached up and rested a hand along her grandson's clean-shaven jaw. "Have you had anything to eat?"

Reaching for her wrist, he pulled her hand away, kissing the palm and then the snow-white hair pulled into a neat chignon. At eighty-two, Carolina, as the family's matriarch, had embarked on a campaign to see him married. She complained constantly that he was more American than Italian because at almost forty he should've settled down with a nice Italian girl a long time ago. She said only Americans waited until they're forty to become parents when they should've been grandparents.

"Yes. I had some *arrosto all acciughe e zucchini all menta.*" His grandmother had prepared her renowned roast veal in an anchovy sauce and fried zucchini with mint.

"Good boy," she crooned, smiling as a network of fine lines spread out around her blue eyes. Her smile faded quickly when she glanced around him. "Did you bring a girl with you?"

"No, Nonna."

Carolina squinted up at her grandson over her glasses. "Do you like girls, Reuben?"

Reuben stared, complete surprise freezing his features. "Of course I like girls, Nonna. Why would you ask me something like that?"

"I hear a lot of men who make fancy clothes prefer their own to a woman."

He couldn't believe his grandmother was asking him whether he was gay—not when she'd seen him with women he'd dated—to one of whom he'd proposed marriage. "I like women, Nonna. I like them a lot."

Carolina crossed her arms over her full bosom. "*Grazie a Dio.* Maria Corsi told me that she's looking to marry off her granddaughter—"

"*Abbastanza,* Nonna. Tell Mrs. Corsi that I can find my own woman." His voice though soft and quiet was pregnant with a warning that indicated the subject was closed. "I'm going outside to get some air."

"But it's raining, Rubino."

"I'll stand under the loggia," he said over his shoulder as he walked away.

Reuben ignored his uncle beckoning to him as he opened the front door and stood on the loggia staring out at the mist obscuring the view that never failed to inspire him. The farmhouse was erected on a rise that overlooked ten acres of olive trees and fields of sunflowers, staples that had provided a livelihood for Rotondos dating back to when the de Medici controlled Florence.

The structure reflected the colors and textures of the surrounding landscape, from the stone walls to the coppi roof tiles. Reuben remembered when his grandfather had replaced the now-worn window shutters with black shutters to complement the newly installed white windows.

He'd looked forward to going to the country in the summers to spend time with his grandparents and cousins. His days were filled with racing his cousins down the hill on their bikes, watching the workmen operating the olive press, gathering berries for Carolina's tarts and homemade gelato and lying on the grass while trying to identify the constellations in the summer night sky.

Leaning against a stone column, he recalled the first time he'd sketched a group of his grandfather's employees as they sat in the field under a tree eating lunch. It was the summer he'd turned six. Silvana was the first to recognize his artistic talent, and she convinced her husband to enroll him in art school.

Reuben turned around when he heard heavy footfalls behind him. His uncle had followed him. Enrico closed down his restaurant on Christmas, New Year's, Easter and in the month of August when most of Europe went on holiday.

Enrico Rotondo rested a large, gnarled hand on his nephew's shoulder. With the exception of coloring and hair texture, Reuben looked more like him than did his own sons. "It's getting a little crazy inside."

"It's madness. I can't understand your mother wanting to invite everyone in Italy named Rotondo."

Enrico reached into a pocket of his slacks and took out a pack of Turkish cigarettes. He put one in his mouth and lit it, drawing deeply on the strong, rich tobacco. His eyes narrowed as blue-gray smoke swirled around his face. "I had a long talk with Silvana, who believes Mama is reliving her past when she had to mother everyone, while I think she's becoming senile."

"She's not so senile that she's not trying to fix me up with Mrs. Corsi's granddaughter."

Enrico took another puff from his cigarette. "Mrs. Corsi is, as your father would've said, 'shit outta luck' trying to marry *her* off." He took another drag, then put the cigarette out in a nearby terracotta planter. "If I didn't have a woman for a year I still wouldn't want her."

"What does she look like?"

Running a hand through his silver hair, Enrico shook his head. "The only thing I'm going to say is that you wouldn't want to paint her. Speaking of painting—a customer offered to buy one of your still life paintings in the restaurant, and I told her that I had to speak to the artist."

Reuben met his uncle's eyes. "Sell it for whatever you want. After all, I gave it to you as a gift."

"What should I ask for it?"

"See what she offers you."

"I have no idea what it's worth."

"Take it to Constanza and have him appraise it."

"Is he the one who sells your paintings?"

"Yes."

"Can I trust him, Reuben?"

"Yes. But, Contanza may want to buy it from you, then have your customer come to him. This way you'll both make money."

Enrico frowned. "I thought you said I could trust him?"

"He's a businessman and you're a businessman. This time I'm going to take myself out of the equation because I'm not going to ask for a cut. Like I said, I gave you the painting as a gift."

"You don't need the money?"

Reuben swore softly under his breath. "This is why I don't do business with family, Enrico. I gave you the painting instead of selling it to you, because I don't like discussing money with my relatives."

Enrico held up a hand. "Okay."

He knew his family was curious as to how he earned a living, although he maintained a rather simple lifestyle. He rented the apartment in Trastevere, drove a Vespa instead of a car, dated women, but seldom introduced them to his family and traveled to the south of France for the month of August when the country went on holiday.

His private clients paid him very well for his work. An upcoming project included designing the wedding attire for one of his client's daughter's formal wedding. He'd electronically forwarded sketches of gowns for the bride, her attendants and mother of the bride.

Reuben thought about Bree, wondering if she'd followed through with her plan to hear the Pope offer Christmas mass at St. Peter's. She was six thousand miles from her home and family, while he was at his grandmother's house with close to sixty Rotondos who'd availed themselves of what appeared to be an inexhaustible supply of food and drink.

"Will you do me a favor and loan me your car for a few hours?" he asked Enrico. Silvana had picked him up in her car because she hadn't wanted him to ride the scooter in the rain.

"Sicuro," Enrico said, handing him the keys. "You don't have to bring it back tonight. I'll ask Silvana to take me home."

Reuben waited until he was seated in his uncle's Mini Cooper to take out his cell phone. Scrolling through the directory, he punched in Bree's number. *"Ciao, bella. Buon Natale."*

"Thank you. Merry Christmas to you, too."

"Did you get to see Papa?"

"Barely. I was so far—"

"Tell me about when I see you," he said, cutting her off. "I'm coming over."

That said, Reuben ended the call, not giving Bree the opportunity to tell him not to come. He had to see and talk to her again, not knowing what it was about the young woman who was strangely more European than American that had him thinking of her when he least expected to.

Bree opened the door when she heard the soft knocking. Reuben stood on the other side carrying a large bouquet of white roses with sprigs of pine. She had to admit to herself that he looked devastatingly handsome in a dark-blue suit, white shirt and blue-and-white-striped tie. Droplets of rain shimmered on his black hair like precious crystals.

He sniffed the air like a large cat. "Something smells good."

She smiled. "Come in. I just put a pork loin in the oven."

Reuben handed her the flowers before he took off his suit jacket and hung it on a wooden hook behind the door. "A little something to make your table pretty."

Bree brought the bouquet close to her nose, inhaling the sweet smell of roses mingling with the clean scent of pine. "They're beautiful."

"So are you."

The compliment was out before Reuben could censor himself. He'd found Breanna's scrubbed face mesmerizing. She'd pinned her hair up off her neck in a sensual disarray that called to mind photographs of a young, nubile Brigitte Bardot.

Bree stared at her sock-covered feet as a rush of heat stung her cheeks. Her gaze swung up and she caught Reuben staring at her as if she were a stranger. She wanted to be anywhere but where she was at the moment, and if she could have she would've fled to escape his disturbing presence.

"Thank you."

"Are you thanking me for the flowers or for the compliment?"

Her gaze swung back to him. Bree didn't want to admit how much his words buoyed her sagging spirits. She'd thought she would be able to deal with spending Christmas alone, but when she'd heard her brother's and parents' voices she couldn't stop the tears that flowed unchecked. Somehow she managed to complete her call without letting them know she was crying, then, she retreated to the bathroom where she washed her face and wiped away the evidence that reminded her that she wasn't as tough or as brave as she wanted others to perceive her to be.

Reuben had invited her to celebrate the holiday with his

family and she'd rejected his offer because she didn't want to feel like an interloper. Although she hadn't accompanied him, he'd come to her.

A sense of strength came to her when she realized she wasn't alone. A stranger, a man who'd offered to help her refine her designs, a man who'd invited her to bring in the new year with him and a man who'd voiced his concern because she was living in a foreign country without male protection had appointed himself her unofficial protector.

"I'm thanking you for both."

Taking a step, Reuben placed a hand on the nape of her neck, while his free hand went to her chin, gently lifting her head. Slowly, methodically, his head came down and he kissed her. Not the wet, fumbling kiss of a boy who didn't know how to angle his head so their noses wouldn't collide, but a kiss from a man who'd executed it countless times.

He smelled minty and male, his warm, moist breath seeping into her mouth when her lips parted. Bree wanted to get closer, but the flowers provided a barrier that kept them apart.

Reuben felt the flesh between his legs stir as if aroused from a deep sleep, and he knew he had to end the kiss before he embarrassed himself. He broke the kiss, though it was the last thing he'd wanted to do.

A smile tilted the corners of his mouth. "You can slap my face if you want to."

Bree bit down on her lower lip, tasting him again. "Now, why would I want to do that?"

"I kissed you without asking permission."

His explanation caught her off-guard. "Do you always ask women if you can kiss them first?"

"Yes."

"What if they say no?"

"Then, I don't kiss them."

"And, if they say yes?"

He lifted a shoulder. "Sometimes I kiss them, and sometimes I don't."

"If you don't intend to kiss them, then why do you ask, Reuben?"

"I ask to see if at a future time I'd want to kiss them. Not every woman I meet I want to kiss or sleep with. Many times all I want is their friendship."

She blinked once. "What about me? What is it you want from me?"

"I don't know. At least not yet. I do know that I enjoy being with you. At first I thought I'd be too old for you, but after spending time together I realize you're a lot more mature than most women your age. Perhaps it comes from living abroad, or maybe it is because you were married."

"Were you ever married?"

"No. But, I did come close at one time."

"What happened?"

"She decided she wanted to marry someone closer to her own age."

"How much older were you than she?"

"Ten years. I was thirty-two and she was only twenty-two."

"Twenty-two is young. I was twenty-three when I got married, and now that I look back I know I never should've married."

"You couldn't have been married very long if you're twenty-five."

"My marriage didn't survive my wedding night," she said softly as she turned and walked through the living room and into the kitchen, Reuben following. Songs she'd programmed into her iPod came through the wireless speakers from the dock resting on a shelf on the entertainment unit. She placed the flowers on the countertop before reaching into an overhead cabinet for a vase.

"What did he do to you?" Reuben watched as Bree filled the vase with water, her hands shaking as she attempted to arrange the flowers. He caught her upper arm, turning her around to face him. "What did he do?"

She blinked back tears. "He raped me, Reuben. My husband, who'd professed to love me, raped me not once but twice. He never touched me again, because I'd moved out of the bedroom."

"Had…had he done anything like that before?"

"No."

Bree told Reuben everything except the name of the man she'd married. A myriad of expressions crossed his face from horror to anger, then compassion when she told him of waking up in a hospital to be told that she'd lost her baby. She cried for the second time that day, this time in the warm, comforting embrace of a man who made her feel safe *and* protected.

He led her into the bathroom where he washed her face as if she were a child. Then he picked her up and carried her back to the living room where they huddled together on the sofa listening to music.

Bree stirred, loath to leave the warmth of the body pressed to hers. "I have to get up and check on the roast."

Reuben opened his eyes. "Don't move. I'll check on it."

Her eyebrows lifted. "You cook?"

"My uncle does own a restaurant."

"Can your uncle paint pretty pictures?"

"No."

"Just because your uncle owns a restaurant it doesn't mean you should know how to cook any more than he can paint or design clothes because his nephew does."

Lowering his gaze, Reuben stared at her mouth. "Has anyone ever told you that you have a wicked tongue?"

She laughed. "No. But I've been called impudent,

insolent and recalcitrant. But my mother's favorite word for me is naughty."

Reuben kissed the bridge of her nose. "I like naughty girls because they're always exciting."

"I don't think I'm that exciting."

He kissed her again. "Let me be the judge of whether you're exciting or not. After we eat your Christmas dinner I'm taking you home with me so you can try on your dress."

"I am not riding on a scooter in the rain, mister."

"We won't have to because I have a car today."

"Where did you get the car from?"

"I stole it," he said deadpan.

"No, you didn't."

"Yes, I did."

With wide eyes, Bree said, "Really?"

Reuben stared at her for a full minute before he broke down, laughing so hard his sides hurt. Bree pounced on him, landing soft punches to his upper arms until he caught her wrists, holding her captive.

"I'm sorry, *bella*."

"That wasn't nice," she admonished.

"Was I naughty?"

Bree stared down at the man staring up at her, unable to believe she felt so at ease with him and wondering if life would've been different if she'd met him before Tyrone or her French lover. She knew she couldn't dwell on her past or she would never move forward.

She gave Reuben a dazzling smile. "You were very, very naughty."

"Good." He reversed their positions, left the sofa and walked to the kitchen. She watched his tall, slender physique as he disappeared from her line of vision.

chapter thirty-nine

Reuben lived on the second floor of a row of buildings the color of salmon, the facades covered with tendrils of ivy that looked from a distance like spiderwebs. Rain beat a hypnotic tattoo on the curved terra-cotta roof, sliding off the baked-earth tiles in rivulets as he flicked on table and floor lamps in the apartment.

The space lacked walls, and the bricked room was separated into areas by the strategic placement of chairs and tables. A neatly made king-size bed occupied one corner, the kitchen, with a marble-topped table and antique leather chairs, another and a seating grouping that made up the living room. The remaining corner drew her curiosity as she walked over to a pair of massive armoires. The doors of one stood open to reveal bolts of fabric in various weights and shades, spools of thread and plastic containers with tubes of paint and brushes. Three dress forms stood side by side like sentinels not far from a drafting table and an easel. An industrial sewing machine sat under a trio of floor-to-ceiling windows in order to take advantage of the natural light. A table doubling as a desk held a laptop computer and printer.

Bree found herself drawn to a black silk organza sleeveless dress with a collar and hem of wispy black feathers. Reaching out, she touched the feathers that had been painstakingly sewn onto the garment. The design screamed simplicity *and* sophistication. Now she understood what Reuben was trying to tell her about her sketches. The dress was a simple sheath dress with a matching slip, but the fabric and the addition of the feathers made it unique.

"Is this the dress you want me to wear?"

Reuben came up behind her, resting his hands on her shoulders. "Yes. What do you think?"

"It's beautiful."

He pressed a kiss to the side of her neck. "Would you like to try it on?"

"Yes." Her heart fluttered wildly against her ribs.

Pointing to a door next to the kitchen, he said, "You can use the bathroom to change."

Bree waited until he took the dress off the form, then walked to the bathroom, closing the door behind her. She took off her boots, stripped off her jeans, sweater and bra. Clad only in a pair of black bikini panties, she stepped into the dress and pulled up the hidden zipper under her left arm. The mirror in the bathroom was over the vanity.

She opened the door and walked out, coming to a complete stop when she saw Reuben staring at her. The feathers ended six inches above her knees and if she were to wear stilettos then the dress would appear even shorter.

Crossing his arms over his chest, he decided that the dress looked as if it had been designed expressly for her body. Breanna Parker was thin, but not skinny. Her legs were long and shapely, her thighs slim and firm.

"Let me see you walk."

Resting her hands on her hips, Bree strutted across the room as if she were on a runway; she'd stepped back in time to when she was seventeen and had been given the opportunity to model the haute couture of Yves St. Laurent, whom she thought of as one of the fashion world's most celebrated designers.

Reuben closed his eyes for a second, unable to believe the sight of this woman wearing one of his dresses. "You are as beautiful now as you were the day I saw you in Paris modeling St. Laurent."

Bree stopped as if she'd been jabbed with a sharp object. "What the hell are you talking about?"

Lowering his arms, Reuben closed the distance between them. "When I first saw you at my uncle's restaurant I thought there was something that was familiar, but I couldn't place it. It was only when I saw you again in the art store that I remembered where and when. It was about eight years ago when attended a St. Laurent showing that I saw you. And I couldn't take my eyes off you. Each time you hit the runaway everyone around me gasped because you walked as if you owned that catwalk. You were truly fierce."

Bree felt her heart sink like a stone in her chest. "Is that why you wanted me to wear this dress? So you can get off on some resurrected fantasy?"

"Che è abbastanza!" he shouted, his eyes giving off sparks of green and gold.

"No, it's not enough! You used me, Reuben. All of my life men have used me for their own selfish needs, and I swore after I left Tyrone it would never happen again." She swiped at the angry tears pricking the backs of her eyelids.

"You're wrong, Breanna."

"No, I'm not!"

The fragile rein Reuben had on his temper snapped. "Get over yourself, Breanna. Don't forget you need me, because I *don't* need you for anything. And I mean *anything.* I could get any model to wear that dress, but I chose you."

She sobered quickly. "But why me?"

He lifted his shoulders. "I don't know."

Bree paced the floor, feeling the smooth wood under her

bare feet and the heat of Reuben's gaze on her. She knew he was right. He didn't need her, she needed him. Reuben hadn't asked anything for from her, except that she wear his dress.

Stopping, she turned and smiled at him. Why, she mused, did he look so devilishly handsome wearing only a shirt and slacks? He'd removed his tie and opened several buttons on his shirt to reveal his strong brown throat.

"I'm sorry, Reuben. I shouldn't have gone off on you like that."

He beckoned to her. "Please come here."

Bree walked over to him and closed her eyes. She didn't see him when he took off his shirt and draped it over her shoulders. He didn't drop his gaze when he unzipped the dress and slid it off her shoulders and down her waist and hips. Bending, he held each ankle as he helped her step out of the wispy garment, tossing it over the back of a chair.

"Open your eyes, Bree. I'm not the big bad wolf out to eat you. I'm sorry I barked at you." He didn't want to make the same mistake with Bree that he'd made with Lucia, who claimed he'd talked down to her as if she were a child and he her father.

Bree complied and wished she hadn't when she stared at his chest covered with a mat of crisp black hair. Reuben's clothes had concealed a lean, muscled body without a trace of excess fat.

"I accept your apology. Just make certain you don't bark at me again."

"What if I growl?"

"You're pushing it," she warned, buttoning the shirt in an attempt to cover her breasts. One minute she was standing and the next she found herself in Reuben's arms as he carried her over to the bed. "What are you doing?"

"We're going to take siesta together."

"It's after seven, and that's too late for siesta."

He placed her on the firm mattress, turned off all the lamps except the one on a table near the door, and then joined her on the bed. "Are you ever spontaneous? You're an artist. You're supposed to be a free spirit."

Turning on her side, Bree rested her leg over his. "You're wrong, Reuben. We're supposed to live in drafty attics, subsist on stale bread and moldy cheese as we ply our craft day in and day out and pray that we find someone to recognize our talent, or that we can catch the eye of a wealthy benefactor. But if that doesn't happen, then it is only after we die that the art world decides to acknowledge our genius."

Reuben rubbed her nose against his. "What do you want, Bree?"

"What do you mean?"

"What do you want for your future? Where do you want to live? Do you want to get married again? Do you want children?"

"I think it's a lot easier to answer your first question than the others. I want my own fashion house. I want it small, selective, so I don't have to compete with Donna Karan, Vera Wang or Monique Lhuillier. I'd prefer specialty boutiques to high-end department stores and select clients to mass production."

There came a beat. "I can help you realize your dream."

"How, Reuben?"

"I can help you with your designs, and provide the financial backing you'll need to get off the ground."

"Why me?"

He smiled. "I've been where you are now. I know what it is to want something so badly, but no one will give you that little break you need to prove yourself. The difference is that you've only shown *me* your work, so you haven't felt the bite of rejection after rejection. If I can help someone avoid what I went through, then I'll do it.

"We'll work together to refine your designs, then I'll make an appointment with my banker to transfer monies from my account to yours so you'll be able to secure a shop, hire workers and purchase equipment and supplies."

"How much interest are you going to charge me for the loan?"

"Nothing. I'm not a banker or loan officer. You repay me whatever it is I lend you."

"That's it?"

"Yes. That's it."

Bree looked at him as if he'd taken leave of his senses. "Do you know who I am?"

His eyebrows drew downward when he frowned. "What are you talking about?"

"Do you really know who Breanna Renee Parker is?"

"I only know what you've told me."

"You don't read American tabloids?"

"I don't read *Italian* tabloids, because I've never found a need to delve into someone else's salacious behavior."

Nervously, Bree moistened her lips, aware that what she was about to tell Reuben would either shatter or strengthen their fragile friendship. And she hoped it would the latter. "There was a time when I put the *S* in salacious."

She told Reuben everything. Why she'd been educated in Switzerland, her initial experimentation with drugs, the sex tape, drug overdose, up to and including her marriage to Tyrone Wyatt, going into seclusion and her decision to move to Italy to start over. What she didn't disclose were the circumstance leading to the child she'd given up for adoption.

"Now you know all about my sordid past." There was only the sound of his even breathing as he continued to look at her. "You can withdraw your offer to help and there'll be no hard feelings."

Cradling the back of her hand in his hand, Reuben leaned over and brushed a kiss over her parted lips. "Why do you think you're the only one with a checkered past? I've done things I'm not proud of, but at the time I believed it was okay. When I went to Paris it was the first time I'd been away from home and I played as hard as I worked. I got in with a fast crowd that drank, smoked and whored too much. We'd go to Amsterdam and get so high that we didn't know who or where we were."

"You were young and blowing off steam, Reuben," Bree argued softly. "At least no one filmed you having sex."

"Did you ever become a part of an orgy?"

"No!"

Reuben threw back his head and laughed at her shocked expression. "Well, I have. And, quite a few times. I've slept with women I should've never exchanged a word with, and I've gotten involved with others who made me question my sanity. We've all made mistakes, Bree."

"But, I made the same mistake with two different men."

"That's because you were young. We do a lot of crazy things when we're young because we believe we're invincible and immortal."

"Twenty-five isn't old, yet there are times when I feel old."

"You're not old, *bella.* You're young, beautiful and talented and when you launch your clothes line—"

"*If* I launch, Reuben."

"There will be no ifs. You are going to do it."

"Will you help me?"

Reuben pulled Bree closer. He knew what she was feeling, because there had been a time when he'd experienced what she was now going through. The fear of failure, the constant rejections had had him second-guessing himself so many times that he'd considered returning home to teach art. He'd wanted to quit, give up, but his former instructor wouldn't permit him to do that. She'd said that if he failed, then she'd also failed, because she hadn't given him what he needed to succeed.

"Yes, Bree, I will help you. I will help you because someone helped me. My mentor's mantra was: 'When you make it, reach back and help the next one.' You are *my* next one."

Bree lay in bed with a man—a stranger, who made her feel things she didn't want to feel. She knew she was attracted to Reuben Douglas because he was mature, erudite. But, there was more to the attraction. He was a man who took the time to listen to her, who attempted to understand her, and for that she would be eternally grateful.

But there was also something beyond the charisma and the compassion. He was confident, compelling and projected an energy that aroused feelings within her that had nothing to do with reason or common sense.

She knew she couldn't afford to get involved with Reuben, but that's what she wanted to do. For the first time in her life she wanted to have an affair with a man who met her on an equal footing. She was no longer a teenage girl who'd let an older man seduce her because he said all the things she'd wanted and needed to hear.

And, she wasn't the same needy party girl who, while under the influence, got caught up in the hype, believing that she and Tyrone Wyatt were Tinseltown's next A-list couple.

Reuben had appointed himself her protector. Three weeks ago she hadn't known Reuben Douglas existed, and in that time she'd changed—changed enough to know that she wanted the man holding her to his heart to become a part of her life *and* her future.

"Do you want something to eat or drink?"

Reuben's voice broke into her musings. She smiled. "No, thank you. But how can you mention food? Didn't we just eat?"

"I watched you eat."

"True. But I do remember you eating off my plate."

"I just wanted to sample what you'd made. Has anyone told you that you're quite the little chef?"

Her Christmas dinner of roast pork with fennel, couscous and grilled asparagus had exceeded her expectations. Reuben, who'd claimed to have eaten at his grandmother's, ate more than half of what she'd served herself.

"I shocked myself, because it's only the second time I've made couscous."

"Everything was delicious."

"Thank you."

Those were the last two words Bree remembered before she closed her eyes and fell asleep. This Christmas was one she would remember for a long time to come, because it would mark a turning point in her life. Reuben Douglas had become her friend and her confidant.

chapter forty

Bree pushed her feet into a pair of four-inch-high Christian Louboutin platform, black patent pumps. When she'd tried on the shoes with the distinctive red soles she'd immediately thought of Karma Parker, whose closet was lined with countless pairs of the sexy designs. It was New Year's Eve and she'd spent a week shopping and preparing to welcome in a new year with Reuben and his friends.

Reuben had altered her "gift" and she knew the dress would garner a lot of attention. When she told him that she had no intention of getting on the back of his scooter wearing haute couture he confessed to hiring a driver for the night.

Earlier that afternoon she'd visited a local salon to have her hair, nails and face done, and the results were startling, as evidenced by the number of stares and compliments thrown at her as she walked back to the hotel.

Reaching for an evening purse and a wool-lined silk shawl, she walked out of the bedroom to the living room where Reuben waited for her. Bree stopped short when she saw him staring at her sketches of lingerie.

"I'm not finished with those."

Reuben's head came up and he stared at Bree as if in a trance. Rising slowly, he closed the distance between them, his gaze taking in everything about her in a single sweeping glance. Her hair was parted in the middle and pulled back off her face in an elaborate twist behind her right ear. The stylist had pinned a jeweled hairpin with shimmering black feathers in the coil of reddish-brown hair.

He couldn't believe she could improve on perfection, but she had. Studying her critically with the eye of an artist, he silently admired the flawlessness of her complexion, the brilliance of her wide-set dark eyes and the lushness of that mouth he wanted to devour.

The last time he'd kissed Bree was Christmas, and it was something he wanted to do again, but he was reluctant to do so because he hadn't wanted to send the wrong signal. Yes, he wanted Bree, but he hadn't wanted to complicate their relationship. So far she hadn't given him any indication that she wanted more than a platonic friendship. Despite sharing a bed they still hadn't made love.

His grandmother had all but accused him of being gay because she hadn't seen him with a woman in a long time. He hadn't wanted to tell Carolina Rotondo that although he'd slept with women by mutual agreement they meant nothing to him. He needed them and they needed him for sexual release. However, it was the woman standing inches away wearing a dress that showed off her body to its best advantage that he wanted to sleep with. Her legs in the heels were magnificent. The diamond studs in her ears and the jeweled hairpin paled in comparison to the sensuality Breanna Parker radiated effortlessly.

"You look marvelous."

Bree heard the awe in her date's voice. "Thank you."

Reuben had come to her apartment dressed in a black suit with distinctive European tailoring not usually seen in the States. A stark white shirt and a silk tie in odd shades of silver and mauve, a matching pocket square and black leather slip-ons completed his sophisticated evening attire.

The stilettos put Bree at eyelevel with him. His gaze

lingered on her smoky-gray-and-muted-gold eyelids before slowly moving to her nose and coming to rest on the fullness of her mouth outlined in a red-orange lipstick.

"You know I want you."

Bree closed her eyes. "How?"

He leaned closer. "You know how, Bree, so let's not play childish games."

She opened her eyes to see lust in his eyes and on his face. "I know what you want, because I want the same."

Reuben pressed his mouth to her coiffed hair. "If I hadn't promised my friends I'd meet them tonight we would greet the new year with me inside you."

Bree felt her body warm with his erotic pronouncement. "You are going to have to use protection, because I can't deal with getting pregnant again."

"Mi permetta di preoccuparsi di quello, caro."

He didn't want her to worry, when that's what she had to do. If and/or when she got pregnant again she wanted it to be different. The next time she didn't want to have to be faced with the decision to give up her child or decide whether she wanted her baby's father in their lives.

If her marriage to Tyrone had worked out, then she would have been mother to a son or daughter and she never would have met Reuben. But fate had intervened and her life had turned another corner, bringing her back to Europe and to a man who, despite having an American father, was wholly European in bearing and deportment.

"It's not about you, Reuben. It's about me."

"Do you want a child?"

"I...I don't know."

Reuben saw distress mar her beautiful face, and decided to drop the subject. "Let's go because a driver is downstairs waiting for us."

They took the lift to the street level where a driver leaned against the bumper of a shiny black sedan. Straightening, he walked over and opened the rear door. Bree got in and moved over as Reuben slipped in beside her. A week of off-and-on rain had stopped, the skies had cleared and a warm breeze had raised daytime temperatures to an unseasonable seventy-five.

Bree stared out the window as the driver maneuvered slowly along the cobblestones streets to avoid the elegantly dressed pedestrians standing in crosswalks and crowding sidewalks and alleys.

Living in Italy made her even more conscious of style. It hadn't mattered whether it was cars, food or clothes—Italians were always elegant and sophisticated. Jeans, no matter how pricey, were relegated to students and tourists. The two dozen she'd shipped over from the States she'd only worn at home.

Reaching over, she laced her fingers through Reuben's. "Now, are you going to tell me where we're going?" Whenever she'd asked him where they were going for their year-end festivities, his response had been "wait and see."

He gave her fingers a gentle squeeze. "We're going to meet *our* friends at Etablì for an aperitivo. Then, we'll go to another place for dinner followed by live music at a nightclub. And, if we're still standing, then we'll hang out at Professionisti. It's an all-night café across the Tiber River that serves the most delicious pastries. The sun will probably be up by the time we make it back to my place."

Bree leaned closer, her shoulder touching his. "You should've told me we were having a sleepover."

"I wanted to surprise you," he whispered, chuckling softly. "While I was waiting for you I took a look at your lingerie sketches."

"What do you think?"

He smiled at her. "They're extraordinary. I believe you should switch your focus to designing lingerie. And, grouping the different garments into collections with monochromatic colors is ingenious. Victoria's Secret is going to have some serious competition if you decide to launch a sexy line of lingerie."

Bree stared at Reuben, complete shock freezing her features. She'd begun drawing bras, panties, bikinis, thongs, tank tops and pajama pants because she'd had recurring dreams about going into a boutique to buy undergarments.

"I drew them because I was mentally obsessing about underwear."

Reuben's thoughts were falling over themselves. "*Obsession* is a great name for lingerie."

"I don't think we can use Obsession. Calvin Klein would probably come after us for copyright infringement."

He smiled at Bree. "What about Naughty?"

"Naw-tee bras, naw-tee pan-tees and naw-tee thongs," she drawled in a British accent. "I love it, Reuben."

"You'll have to hire a British spokesperson if you want to go with that pronunciation."

"We'll need a logo."

"You'll also have to come up with a tagline."

Bree sobered. "Why do you keep saying 'you,' Reuben? I thought we were in this venture together."

"You don't need me to help you with Naughty."

"Not only do I need you, but I *want* you, Reuben. Weren't you the one who reminded me that I was a single woman in a foreign country and needed a man to protect her? You are that man, Reuben Douglas, and I'm not going to let you weasel out now."

"Are you calling me a weasel?"

"No," she laughed. "It's an expression that means you're trying to get out of, run from or circumvent your responsibilities."

Reuben winked at her. "Are you saying I'm responsible for you?" Bree nodded. "For how long?"

"For as long as you want, darling."

"I'm a very selfish man, so it just might turn into forever."

"Let's begin with ten years with an option for a ten-year renewal."

"It's either twenty years or no deal."

Bree closed her eyes, wondering if she could spend twenty years with a man who was certain to become her partner—in and out of bed. "Deal."

Shifting slightly until he was leaning over Bree, Reuben pressed his mouth along the column of her long scented neck. *"Grazie, il mio amore."*

"Prego, il mio caro."

Bree wavered in an attempt to understand the course her life had taken. She'd met Reuben her first night in Rome, he'd kissed her once, and she knew for certain that she was falling in love with the talented, compassionate artist.

Bree placed her hand on Reuben's outstretched palm as he assisted her from the car and escorted her into Etablì. She was impressed with the rustic bar in a seventeenth-century building with beamed ceilings, sitting areas and a fireplace. It was crowded with attractive young thirty-something Italians dressed to the nines.

Reuben wended his way through the crowd until he located his friends sitting together. The two men stood up at their approach, while their female counterparts exchanged glances before affecting practiced polite smiles. The men were medium height, dark and jaw-dropping handsome. Reuben released Bree's hand to rest his on the small of her back.

"Nicolas, Gianni, this is my very good friend Breanna Parker. Breanna, Nicolas and Gianni Cesàri. The two ladies with them are their wives Arielle and Chiara." He'd deliberately made the introductions in Italian.

Bree extended her hand to the bookend twin brothers and gave their wives a bright, friendly smile. The women were both blond with dark eyes and looked enough alike to be sisters. The two couples wore matching wedding bands. *"Il mio piacere."*

Gianni ignored her hand and kissed both her cheeks. "Your Italian is very good."

"I try," Bree said modestly.

Reuben waited until Bree was seated before dropping down beside her. He knew his friends were curious about his date because they'd expected him to bring a woman whom he'd been dating off and on for several years.

Arielle leaned forward. "Will it insult you, Breanna, if we speak Italian? My English is some time not so good," she asked in slightly accented English.

"Non si importa se Lei parla inglese o l'italiano. Io sono scorrevole nell'ambo," Bree rattled off in Italian. She'd just put them on notice that if they wanted to gossip about her in Italian, then don't.

Nicolas came to attention. "Where did you learn to speak Italian?"

Bree felt the intensity of the twins' dark-green eyes as they stared at her. "I picked it up in school."

"Where did you attend school?" Gianni asked.

"Switzerland."

"My sister and I went to school in Switzerland," Chiara said, speaking for the first time. "It is there where we studied English, French and German."

Bree gave the sisters a stunned look when Chiara mentioned the name of the exclusive boarding school; they'd attended the same school. "I went there, too."

Although Arielle and Chiara were older by eight years, the three had been taught by some of the same instructors. Reuben exchanged seats with Bree and the women launched into a discussion about some of the escapades they'd gotten into. The topic of conversation segued into fashion when Bree stood up to show off her dress and shoes.

Arielle lifted a leg to show off her black suede-and-satin Casadei ankle boots, while Chiara flashed a pair of Cesare Paciotti suede platform slingbacks. While chatting with the two women and nibbling on tiny appetizers of meat, fish and vegetables, Bree discovered the sisters were former flight attendants, while their husbands were partners in a family-run law firm.

Arielle, who'd just finished her second mojito, glared across the table at Reuben. "You must be very special to Reuben for him to design a dress expressly for you. I've lost count of the number of times I've asked him to make something for me, but his excuse is that he doesn't have the time. Please, Breanna, try and convince your boyfriend to think of something for me when Gianni and I celebrate our tenth wedding anniversary next summer."

Bree winked at Reuben. "I'll see what I can do." She'd eaten sparingly and hadn't ordered anything alcoholic because she wanted to save her appetite for dinner.

They remained at Etablì for two hours before Nicolas settled the bill and they walked out of the bar, climbing into separate cars to go to the next restaurant for dinner. Reuben had made the dinner reservations, and as soon as they arrived they were shown to a table.

This time Bree sat between Reuben and Nicolas, who kept her entertained with stories about some of their more eccentric, but extremely wealthy clients. The table conversation was lively, the food delicious and the wine excellent. It was close to eleven when Reuben paid the bill and they headed to a nightclub.

A DJ playing dance numbers alternating with recorded techno music reminded Bree of the times when she, Letisha and Sierra had hit the L.A. clubs weeded or coked to the gills and ready to throw down if someone stepped on their shoes.

But that was her past. She'd been clean for over a year and a half and the urge to abuse drugs was no longer there. Not only had she changed her behavior, she'd also changed her head.

She danced with Reuben, who was blessed with a natural rhythm that made him a standout on the dance floor. The music slowed, and she took turns dancing with Nicolas and Gianni, towering over them by at least three inches in her stilettos. As the clock inched closer to midnight the partygoers were given hats and noisemakers and champagne flowed from fountains like a waterfall. Five large televisions were turned on and everyone stopped to watch the clock count down an old year before welcoming in a new one.

Reuben wrapped both arms around Bree's waist, pulling her flush against his body. Everything about her seeped into him, making them one. He stared into her eyes, hoping to see what she was feeling at that moment, hoping and praying she would come to love him as much as he'd come to believe he loved her. He'd asked her to give him the next twenty years of her life when what he wanted was the rest of her life.

He'd thought his life complete, but Breanna Parker had proven him wrong. The women in his past paled in comparison to her once he realized the only fulfillment they'd brought him, by mutual agreement, was sexual gratification.

"Ten, nine, eight," he whispered against her lips.

"Four, three, two," Bree intoned, inhaling the scent of the champagne on his breath.

"One," they chorused.

"Anno Nuovo e felice!"

A shudder ripped through Bree as Reuben kissed her as if it was to be their last time together. Pressing closer, she wrapped her arms around his neck, returning the kiss. If she'd suspected she had fallen in love with him, now she knew she was.

"Let's get out of here," he whispered close to her ear.

"Where are we going?"

Easing back, he smiled. "Home."

chapter forty-one

Bree lay in Reuben's embrace as their driver steered the car toward Trastevere. "I have a gift for you," she said cryptically.

Reuben frowned. "For what?"

"You gave me this dress as a gift, so I decided to buy something for you."

"You didn't have to do that."

"I know I didn't, but I wanted to." Easing out of his loose embrace, she opened her beaded satin purse and took out a small tan felt sack.

Reuben recognized the logo immediately. He opened the bag to find a Louis Vuitton monogrammed canvas business-card holder. "You didn't have to—"

"Yes, I did," she interrupted. "When you gave me your business card it looked as if it'd been in a fight. If you're going to become a partner in a line of lingerie then your cards will have to be on point."

Palming the case, he angled his head and kissed her. "Thank you, baby."

"You're welcome, darling." Bree rested her head against the leather seat, smiling. It was the first time he'd referred to her in English as *baby,* and she liked it.

"Let us out here," Reuben ordered the driver. "We'll walk the rest of the way."

Pedestrians and vehicular traffic had clogged the narrow

streets, and it would probably be a quarter of an hour before the man would be able to maneuver anywhere close to his apartment building.

The driver slipped from behind the wheel to open the rear door. *"Io sono spiacente, Signore Douglas."*

"It's not your fault," Reuben said, smiling. He handed him a bill. "Happy New Year."

The driver bowed low. *"Grazie, signore."*

Reuben helped Bree out of the sedan. Bending slightly, he swept her into his arms. "I doubt whether you'll be able to walk one block on the cobblestones in those shoes."

"You can't carry me."

He winked at her. "You're not heavy."

"I will be by the time you carry me home."

Shifting her slight weight to a more comfortable position, Reuben began walking. "You have a choice, Breanna. Either I carry you, or you can take off your pretty shoes and walk in your stocking feet."

"Are you kidding? I'm not about to pick up bubonic plague. I'd rather take my chances in the heels."

"This is the twenty-first-century not the Middle Ages, and I'm not going to take care of you if you turn your ankle."

"I thought you promised to take care of me."

He walked in the direction of his building. "I promised to protect you, Breanna. And right now it means protecting you from yourself. I don't know how you were able to dance in those stilts."

"Practice, darling. When I used to come home on school holidays I used to sneak into my mother's closet and put on her shoes. By the time I was twelve I could rock in a pair of heels."

"It's a good thing you practiced, because you can rock a runway."

Bree tightened her hold on Reuben's neck. "That was my

first and only show. When my parents discovered I was modeling they had a fit. Mother thought I was going to give up school for modeling, and Daddy believed unscrupulous agents and bookers would take advantage of me."

"What did they do?"

"Daddy's lawyers threatened a lawsuit because the people who'd set up the show didn't get my parents' signatures. I was underage at the time, which meant the contract wasn't valid."

"That's too bad. You would've made an incredible model."

"Maybe yes, maybe no. If it'd worked out, then I never would've met you."

"Not true. We were destined to meet, *bella*."

Bree rested her head on Reuben's shoulder as he turned into an alley, skirting a couple locked in a passionate embrace and oblivious to everything going on around them.

It was a new year—a time for change and a time to discover and rediscover all that was lost. For Bree it was a time when she could actually formulate a plan and follow through. Following through didn't guarantee success, but she was certain to try.

It had taken twenty-five years for her to grow up, two and a half decades of looking for love in all the wrong places, and a quarter of a century to acknowledge that she had to take responsibility for her self-destructive behavior. Medicating herself with drugs had temporarily dulled her pain, yet when the numbing effects wore off the pain was still there, increasing in its intensity, triggering the vicious cycle of abuse all over again.

After she'd stopped smoking marijuana there were occasions when she believed that she, like Karma, was manic-depressive. Her mood swings had become more frequent and when she told Ryder he suggested she seek professional help. At first she'd balked but eventually she'd relented. The psychiatrist who evaluated her confirmed she was not a manic-depressive and refused to give her a prescription for an antidepressant. He'd concluded that her acting out was her way of getting attention—albeit negative attention.

She'd waited for her trust not to squander it away on top-of-the-line automobiles, jewelry, outrageously priced designer clothes or a house with more square feet than one person needed, but to control every phase of her business enterprise from marketing to design. In that way she was more like her parents than she was willing to admit. Langston Parker ran his recording company like a despot and Karma Parker had total control of everything and everyone within her household.

"I can walk from here," Bree said when she heard Reuben's breathing change. The street where he lived was at the top of an incline.

"It's not that far."

"Put me down, Reuben." His response was to tighten his grip under her knees.

Reuben felt his lungs laboring with the higher altitude and the additional weight. But if he'd taken on the role as Bree's protector, then he had to go all the way. He reached the top of the hill and walked down the cobblestones. The neighborhood with its narrow streets hadn't changed, except for the installation of electricity and indoor plumbing, in the houses, since it had sprung up during the thirteenth and fourteenth centuries.

He'd moved back into his mother's house when he'd returned to Italy from Paris, but a year after his father had passed away he decided it was time for him to live on his own again. Fortunately Silvana hadn't lapsed into the role of the grieving widow whose life had stopped when her husband's did. She continued to work at the hospital, volunteer at her local parish church and look in on her elderly mother several nights a week.

He'd spent weeks touring Rome before deciding that living

in Trastevere suited his temperament. It was located on the western bank of the Tiber River at the foot of the Gianicolo hill, and its quaintness appealed to his artistic nature. It was a popular site for photographers who wanted to capture images of an authentic Roman medieval neighborhood. When his Parisian friends came to visit him they were shocked when he revealed that they were still in Rome.

And, once he began a project, whether painting or sketching, he'd work around the clock, stopping only to eat and shower. He hadn't befriended anyone in his neighborhood, therefore he had no distractions. His neighbors recognized his face, the shopkeepers were familiar with his food orders and the proprietors of the local restaurants and cafés knew what dishes he preferred. Living in Trastevere was peaceful and relaxed.

He arrived at his apartment and gently set Bree on her feet. A private well, considered a luxury centuries ago stood by the front door, a picturesque memento of the past. "Can you make it up the staircase?"

Bree rolled her eyes at him and then pressed her back to his chest for support as she leaned over and took off her shoes. She winked at him. "I can make it now."

Reuben rested his hand over her hip, pulling her to his side. "Let's go."

She followed him up the stairs and into his apartment. Reuben had left a lamp on by the bed, and the shadows from the large, bulky furniture took on shapes that resembled the figures on the spires rising above Gothic-inspired churches.

He locked the door and tossed the keys into a clay pot filled with small, smooth, round white stones. He held Bree's steady gaze as she stood in the middle of the room, her shoes pressed to her chest.

"We don't have to do anything if you don't want to."

She gave him a weak smile. "Thank you for offering me a choice."

"I will always offer you a choice, Bree. It will never be all or nothing."

"I'm going to need something to sleep in and a cream or lotion, so I can clean the makeup off my face."

Reuben nodded. "I'll give you one of my shirts. The only cream I have is one I use when washing paint off my hands."

"I guess it'll have to do."

"I'm sorry I didn't ask you whether you wanted to spend the night with me. That way you could have brought what you need with you."

Bree wanted to go to Reuben, put her arms around his neck and kiss away the lines of concern creasing his forehead. "It's okay, darling. I'll be prepared for the next time. Do you mind if I use the bathroom first?"

"Of course not. Let me get the shirt and cream for you." Walking over to the armoires, he opened a lower drawer and took out a shirt wrapped in cellophane. Opening another drawer, he found the tube of cream, handing both to Bree.

She stared at the laundered shirt. "I thought you were going to give me a T-shirt."

"I don't wear T-shirts."

"But everyone wears T-shirts."

"I'm not everyone, Bree."

"Bene, mi scusi," she drawled.

"You are excused. You will find a towel and cloth in a basket under the sink."

"Do you have an extra toothbrush?"

"Look behind the mirror and you'll find some there."

"Grazie."

"Prego."

Bree put down her shoes and placed her purse on a table,

then walked in the direction of the bathroom, feeling the heat of Reuben's gaze following her retreat. He'd talked about being inside her and she wanted the same, and her concern was whether sleeping with him would change everything. Would he feel the need to control her? Would having a physical relationship jeopardize their business relationship? And, could she trust herself not to become emotionally dependent on him?

She forced herself to think of the new friends she'd made earlier that evening as she cleansed her face of makeup and brushed her teeth. At the last minute, she took the pins out of her hair before stepping into the miniscule shower stall, managing not to wet her hair as she directed the spray of lukewarm water from the handheld nozzle over her back and shoulders.

After drying her body, she slipped into the shirt and buttoned it; the hem ended at her knees. She emerged from the bathroom to find Reuben lying across the bed, clad only in a pair of boxers. The soft snores and the even rise and fall of his chest were a clear indication that he'd fallen asleep. Moving closer, she studied his face in repose. His classically handsome features were enhanced by the gold-brown skin pulled taut over the elegant ridge of his cheekbones. Her gaze moved down his hair-matted chest, and still lower to a flat, hard belly. Although slender, he must possess great strength to have carried her such a distance.

She turned away, afraid he would wake up and find her staring at him like a voyeur. Sitting down on the side of the enormous wrought-iron bed, she swung her legs over the mattress and lay beside him. Not bothering to turn off the table lamp, she slipped under the sheet and closed her eyes. This year had begun unlike any other she'd experienced. It would be the first one when she would go to sleep and wake up beside a man who had promised to protect her, a man she found herself inexorably in love with.

chapter forty-two

Bree woke to the smell of brewing coffee and the sound of Josh Groban's singing floating softly throughout the apartment. Rising on an elbow, she spied Reuben moving around the kitchen. He had on a pair of shorts, paint-spattered shirt and leather sandals.

"Buona mattina."

He turned, smiling at her. "Good morning."

"Anno Nuovo e felice."

"Happy New Year to you, too."

"What time is it?"

"Eleven-thirty."

Whipping back the sheet, she swung her legs over the side of the mattress. "Why on earth did you let me sleep so long?"

"Where are you going? Do you have a date?"

"No. I just don't want to sleep away the day." She hadn't wanted to slip back into the habit of sleeping for hours without regard to whether it was day or night.

Reuben came over, sat down and handed her mug of coffee. He ruffled her hair. "I didn't wake you up because you probably needed the sleep."

"It has been a while since I've gone clubbing."

"I should be the one apologizing for falling asleep on you last night."

Bree rested her head against his shoulder. "You probably were exhausted from carrying me."

Reuben grimaced. "It wasn't that. I had too much wine."

She took a sip of the strong, sweet coffee, then set the mug on the bedside table. "No harm done. That's why you hired a driver. Excuse me, but I have to use the bathroom."

He caught her arm as she stood up. "I went to your place to bring you something to wear when we go to see my mother later this afternoon."

"How did you get into my apartment?" She didn't think the hotel management would've let him in without her consent.

"I took your keys from your purse because I didn't think you'd want to wear a party dress and stilettos while riding on the back of a Vespa."

"You're right about that. What's happening at your mother's?"

"It's an Italian tradition that we eat seafood on New Year's."

Bree stared at the stubble on his face. "You want me to meet your mother?"

"Don't you think it's time I introduce my girlfriend to my family?"

"I'm your girlfriend?"

He ruffled her hair again. "Of course you are. Would you prefer I call you *la mia donna?*"

Bree wrinkled her nose. "I think *girlfriend* sounds better than my being your woman."

Reuben patted her behind. "Go to the bathroom, and then come back to bed where we'll have our morning coffee."

Bree completed her morning ablutions, smiling because Reuben had brought enough grooming supplies for her to leave half at his place. He was in bed, his back supported by a pile of pillows and his arms outstretched. She ran, jumped into his embrace and kissed him.

"Thank you for bringing my stuff."

Reuben tasted toothpaste and mouthwash on her breath

when his tongue slipped into her mouth. She went still before relaxing under his oral onslaught. "Can you forgive me for neglecting you last night?" he whispered hoarsely.

Breathing heavily, Bree closed her eyes. "There's nothing to forgive."

"Are you sure?"

"I'm very, very sure." Reuben combed his fingers through her hair, holding it off her face. He dipped his head and Bree felt his lips graze her cheek. They moved to her neck, then behind an ear. A shudder shook her. He'd discovered the most erogenous spot on her body.

"You don't know how hard it's been for me to sleep with you and not touch you," he whispered hoarsely.

Bree closed her eyes. She didn't want Reuben to talk; she wanted him to make love to her, needed him to help her forget every man who'd kissed and touched her. All those who'd lied, telling her what they thought she wanted to hear because they knew how needy she was for attention, how much she wanted to be loved.

"You can touch me now."

"Where?"

"Everywhere."

Reuben undid the buttons on her shirt, slipping it off her body; he became the sculptor, his hands and mouth mapping every dip and curve of her body. He needed to learn her body in order to bring her maximum pleasure. His mouth closed over her small, firm breasts, suckling and teasing them with his teeth until her nipples were erect. His hand slid up her thighs; he pressed his thumb against her clitoris and Bree gasped and arched off the bed.

He'd wanted to go slowly, but the dampness dotting his fingers, the rising scent of desire and the soft moans coming from Bree's throat caused the blood to rush so quickly to his penis that he suddenly felt lightheaded.

Reuben hadn't realized his hands were shaking until he attempted to divest himself of his clothes. In his frustration, he ripped his shirt buttons from their fastenings and pushed down his shorts and boxers in one sure motion.

Bree had asked him to protect her against an unplanned pregnancy and he'd promised her he would. Reaching for a condom, he slipped it on and returned his attention to Bree, who'd opened her eyes to watch him.

She smiled. "Thank you."

He knew she was thanking him for wearing the condom. When she'd told him that she'd lost a baby he wondered if she feared getting pregnant again. Whatever her reason, he would honor and respect her wish.

Lowering his body, he kissed her again, summoning a tenderness he hadn't known he had. Making love with Bree was different, because he wasn't the same man he'd been before meeting her.

It wasn't that he slept with women indiscriminately, but after listening to her talk about her childhood, her acting out as a young adult, he'd come to realize that Breanna Parker was a fragile soul, someone he had to treat as delicately as a newborn. He'd witnessed her spurts of temper, but instead of feeding into her anger he'd sought to defuse it. If she hadn't had such a volatile childhood he would've welcomed her fire. To him fire and passion in a woman were indivisible.

Bree clung to Reuben, his kisses warm and comforting. With each brush of his lips a delicious shudder rippled through her, bringing with it an increasing desire to surrender all of Breanna Renee Parker. In the past she'd offered up her body, but now she wanted to give Reuben whatever made her who she was.

"Love me. *Per favore mi ami,*" she pleaded in Italian.

"Open your legs for me, baby."

Bree complied, parting her knees as Reuben's engorged

penis pushed into her, gasping audibly at the slow, intense penetration that ignited a fire between her thighs that spread up and outward.

Reuben felt her heat, heard her moans, his groans matching and overlapping hers. In one quick motion, he reversed their positions, pushing into a sitting position, bringing Bree to straddle his thighs. Bracing his back against the pillows, he gripped her hips, bringing her down over his erection and watching her expression as she threw back her head and screamed his name. The hairs on the back of his neck stood up as he closed his eyes and surrendered to the release that stopped his heart and breath and numbed his brain.

Collapsing against Reuben's chest, Bree buried her face between his neck and shoulder and waited for her respiration to return to normal. He felt so good, his still-pulsing penis inside her. Her hips moved of their own volition as she rocked back and forth, her clitoris swelling with the friction. Her rocking intensified until the soft flutters grew stronger and stronger and she climaxed again. Tears streamed down her face and her lips quivered as she lay motionless, spent from a passion she'd never known. She issued a small cry of protest when Reuben withdrew from her and placed her on the damp sheet.

"Sleep, baby," he crooned softly, kissing her moist cheek.

He left her curled in a fetal position as he left the bed to discard the condom, still awed by the passion Bree had offered him. Making love with her was incredible, and he knew it would only get better.

He lingered in the bathroom long enough to wash away the semen. A wave of regret descended on him when he thought of the number of times he could've fathered a child, yet hadn't.

On April twenty-ninth he would turn forty, and he thought of his friends who were younger than him yet had married and started families. Whenever they asked when he was going to settle down, his response was he was having too much fun as a bachelor. It was only a half truth. He'd achieved success in his career, but his personal life was fractured. He dated and slept with women but hadn't committed to any of them. Most couldn't deal with his mercurial moods—the need to be alone when he sat down to fulfill the demands of his clients, the hours he spent over a drafting table sketching and erasing until some innate voice communicated he'd gotten it right.

Then there were the overseas telephone calls and drawings forwarded electronically for approval, followed by a finished garment shipped overnight to a professional dressmaker in the States for alterations, if necessary, and for a final fitting.

If he and Bree were to go into business together he knew she would understand his solitary existence only because she would undergo the same regime. A wry smile lifted the corners of his mouth. When he'd come to her rescue in his uncle's restaurant he hadn't known he was meeting his soul mate.

She'd told him that she was a trust-fund baby, but hadn't disclosed how much she was worth, and he hadn't asked because it was none of his business. He would help set up and launch Naughty, but would remain a behind-the-scenes partner. He hadn't had to share his success publicly with anyone, and he'd make certain Bree's experience would be the same.

And something in his gut told him that Naughty would become an international success. He still had enough connections in the fashion industry to make it possible. Bree's net worth would remain her secret, while his contacts would remain his.

chapter forty-three

Reuben cradled Bree's hand in his as he led her down the street leading to his mother's apartment in a section of Rome that was within walking distance of the Via Veneto. Flickers of apprehension swept over her when she realized she hadn't known Reuben a month and he planned to introduce her to his family.

She'd checked her hair and face so many times that Reuben had physically removed her from the bathroom so he could shave and shower. However, she did compliment him on selecting for her a pair of tailored charcoal-gray slacks, a white silk blouse with a tuck-pleated front, a black cashmere jacket and a pair of black leather wedge pumps for what he assured her was a casual gathering. Bree knew she could rely on him to select the perfect outfit for any occasion.

"Did you tell your mother you were bringing company?"

Reuben gave her fingers a gentle squeeze. "No."

"Why not, Reuben?"

He squeezed her hand again. "Don't panic, baby. I told her that I was bringing my very special girlfriend."

She gave him a sidelong glance. "Please define what you mean by *special girlfriend.*"

"My lover *and* that special woman that makes me a little bit crazy."

"All that, huh?"

"Yeah, all that."

Bree laughed. “Now you sound like an American.”

“Don’t forget I’m half-American. I grew up hearing English and Italian, but it was easier learning Italian than what I came to recognize as American English.”

“We Yanks do stray a bit from the king’s English.”

“That’s because you use a lot of slang.”

“I know. Every time I came home on holiday I discovered new words that hadn’t been in the lexicon. It took me a while to realize *phat* was spelled with a *ph* and not an *f*. There were times when I felt like an alien in my own country.”

“Living abroad will do that to you.”

“Did you feel the same when you lived in Paris?”

“No, because I’d hang out in Paris for a couple of months, then take the train back to Roma.”

“Have you ever been to the States?”

“No.”

“What about your American relatives?”

“I’ve never met them. My father didn’t talk much about his life in America. I think it had something to do with the war and the Civil Rights movement. I’d overheard him tell my mother that after the assassination of Dr. Martin Luther King, Jr., and the subsequent riots, he’d decided he was never going back.”

“But aren’t you curious about your father’s country of birth?”

“A little. Maybe one of these days I’ll go with you when you visit your family.”

“Where was your dad from?”

“I think he mentioned some city in Texas.”

“Texas is a very big state.”

“So are California and New York.”

Bree smiled when a man whispered something ribald to her as he passed. She’d become accustomed to the blatant stares and surreptitious remarks from Italian men of all ages that made her appreciate being female. Some had been bold enough to ask if she were a model and others if she were an actress. What surprised her was that they seemed genuinely disappointed when she said no. Their reaction to her was the same, and it didn't matter whether she alone or with Reuben.

"I'll take you to California and New York."

"My mother lives here," Reuben said as he guided her into a courtyard leading to a three-story building in a soft sand-beige color. "This was once the residence of a wealthy Roman businessman who'd opposed the Fascists, so in the end he lost his life *and* his property when the government confiscated it. Twenty years ago a private company purchased it, converting office space into apartments for professionals."

Bree tugged on his hand. "Wait, Reuben!"

He gave her the look that exasperated parents usually reserve for their children. "What now?"

"I need to stop and get something for your mother. I can't go to her house empty-handed."

"Stop worrying, Bree. I sent her a case of wine and flowers from us."

She exhaled an audible sigh. *"Grazie."*

"Prego."

Bree walked into the richly appointed lobby, taking note of the meticulously restored mosaics. The rich colors of the blue, green, red and yellow tiles formed images of wood nymphs and sprites frolicking in naked abandon. A few were copulating, much to the delight of others watching the lewd exhibition.

Reuben smiled when he saw Bree studying the wall. "These walls were once covered with large murals because the mayor felt naked images were a little too risqué in a building where governmental business was carried on." He pointed to a couple astride one another. "Isn't that what we did this morning?"

Bree was grateful for her darker coloring that concealed the flush stinging her cheeks when she recalled their sensual coupling. "Did you have to bring that up?"

Reuben punched the button for the lift. "Did I embarrass you?"

She averted her gaze. "You don't have to talk about it."

He caught her arm, turning her around to face him. "If it makes you comfortable, then I won't bring it up again."

Bree studied the features of the man with whom she had fallen love, hoping he couldn't read on her face what lay in her heart. "I'm not embarrassed, but what we have together is very new—at least too new for *me* to feel completely comfortable with you."

Reuben stared at her hair, secured in a chignon, a style much too mature for her face and age. Whenever the sunlight hit her hair it glowed richly, the color of red autumn leaves. He still hadn't figured out whether her hair color was natural or she employed the expert services of a colorist.

"How long do you think it'll be before you feel comfortable with me?"

"I don't know," she answered truthfully.

"Do I frighten you?"

Bree gave him a half smile. "Not as much as I frighten myself."

The lift door opened and they walked in. "What are you frightened of?"

Pressing her back to the wall, Bree closed her eyes for a second. "I'm afraid of letting go, of falling in love with you."

Taking a step, Reuben pulled her into the circle of his arms. "Do you really think I'd take advantage of your love, Breanna?"

"I don't know."

"The answer is no, baby. I've waited a long time for someone like you to come into my life, someone who understands my work, the highs and the lows of success and failure. And maybe I feel a connection with you because the blood of my father's ancestors that runs in my veins also run in yours.

I am Italian, but I am also African, and that is something Jesse Douglas never wanted me to forget. He might have criticized his country, but he always loved being African-American."

The lift door opened and Bree followed Reuben down a hallway, his words echoing in her head. She wondered if he'd ever been treated like a foreigner or an outsider in his own country because of his color. It wouldn't be unheard of, because it was still going on in the States with certain races and religions.

She all but forgot about race and politics when she walked into Silvana Douglas's apartment to find her waiting to meet the woman whom her son had referred to as his "very special girlfriend."

Silvana extended her hands to the tall, much too slender, young woman who apparently had enthralled her son. "Welcome, Breanna," she greeted in English. "It is Breanna?"

Bree took her hands, smiling at the petite woman with salt-and-pepper hair and soulful blue-green eyes. *"Sì. Grazie, Signora Douglas."*

Silvana's eyebrows lifted. "You speak Italian?"

"She speaks it as well I do," Reuben said in English.

"You should speak Italian, *nipote.* Are you not *un italiano?"* Carolina Rotonda mumbled loudly as she walked into the room, carrying a foil-covered dish from which wafted delicious smells.

Reuben went over to his grandmother, took the dish and kissed her cheek. "I wasn't talking about myself."

Carolina glared up at him. "Who were you talking about?"

"Breanna Parker."

The older woman turned and looked at Bree, her eyes sparkling like polished blue topaz. "You came with a girl," she crowed in delight.

Reuben winked at her. "A girl who understands and speaks fluent Italian."

Carolina approached Breanna. "So tall and so very pretty. She's so much prettier than that other girl who looked like a horse."

Enrico handed a large covered tray to his sister, while rolling his eyes at his mother. "Mama, come sit down and relax." He took her arm. "I will bring you a glass of wine."

"You know I do not drink wine until I eat," she said, shrugging off his arm. "Silvana, will you please fix me a plate?"

"What do you want, Mama?"

"Everything."

Silvana smiled at Reuben. "Please take your grandmother and Breanna into the dining room." She'd gotten up before dawn to prepare the seafood dishes ranging from calamari and *cozze* to *solgliola.* Her mother and brother had prepared the pasta dishes.

Bree found herself in an enormous room with twelve-foot ceilings and exquisite parquet floors. An antique table and chairs, with seating for sixteen, was set with china, sterling and crystal; a matching sideboard literally groaned with the many platters and chafing dishes.

Reuben seated his grandmother at the head of the table. Carolina patted the chair to her right. "Rubino, I want the girl to sit here with me."

"Her name is Breanna, Nonna."

"It's okay, darling," Bree said, sotto voce. Smiling, she sat beside the feisty older woman.

Carolina smiled sweetly at Bree. "You like my grandson?"

"Yes, I do. I like him very much."

She patted Bree's hand. "Good for you."

Bree angled her head closer to Carolina Rotondo, answering the older woman's questions as family members filed into the dining room, each stopping to greet Carolina, who held court like a reigning monarch. All gave Bree curious looks until Silvana told them she was Reuben's guest.

Reuben walked over to his grandmother. "Excuse me, Nonna, but I'd like to introduce Breanna to the family."

Carolina narrowed her eyes. "You bring her back. I'm not finished talking to her."

Bree mouthed the appropriate responses when she was introduced to Reuben's aunts, uncles and several cousins. He explained that not everyone had come because they were visiting with their in-laws.

Enrico, holding her hands in a firm grip, kissed her on both cheeks. "We meet again."

"I'm surprised you remember me." Bree gave the handsome restaurateur a warm smile.

"I remember all women who visit my restaurant. Especially the beautiful ones who dine alone."

Reuben patted his uncle's back. "I think you'd better stop before you get into trouble with your wife." Even after being married more than forty years, Enrico's wife was still insanely jealous of her husband.

Enrico looked around for his wife and saw thankfully that she was talking to his youngest sister. "The woman is just impossible."

"But you love it, uncle."

"*Sì, io faccio.* It is very good for an old man's ego."

Reuben shook his head at his uncle's antics. Putting an arm around Bree's waist, he led her over to the table with the food. "Let me fix you a plate before my grandmother talks your ear off," he said softly. "I know you like your pasta with garlic and oil, but what type of seafood would you like?"

"What do you have?"

"There's *aragosta* or Mediterranean lobster, *fritto misto,* which is deep-fried calamari and shrimp, *cozze* or mussels, *sogliola* or sole, *polpo,* which is octopus and *baccalà* or codfish stew."

She pointed to a platter of tiny fried fish. "What are those?"

"Fragaglie."

"I'd like to sample a little of each."

"Go sit and I'll bring you your plate."

Bree returned to where she'd sat beside Carolina, watching the interaction among the Rotondos. From listening to the animated conversations going on around her she knew they were a close-knit family. She thanked Reuben when he set a plate down on the table in front of her. Between bites of expertly prepared fish and sips of an excellent pale blush wine she felt herself relaxing enough not to feel like an outsider or interloper.

It was hours after Silvana had ushered everyone into the living room for dessert and after-dinner drinks that Bree found herself alone with Reuben's mother, while Reuben cleaned up the kitchen.

Silvana, who spoke English with only a trace of an accent, pointed to a photograph of herself holding an infant and her late husband. "We took this picture the day I came home from the hospital with Reuben." There was obvious pride in her voice.

Bree peered closely at the tall, slender black man wearing a double-breasted suit and hat, looking quite the dapper gentleman. There was something in the way he angled his head that reminded her of Reuben.

"This one was taken the day Reuben went to school for the first time."

"He looks adorable." Reuben was dressed in a white shirt, shoestring tie, short dark pants and knee socks. "Did he go to a parochial school?"

"Yes, but he hated it. Once he made his confirmation Jesse and I decided to enroll him in an academy for the arts. It was the best decision we ever made for our son. He excelled in all of his subjects. His art teacher said that his skills were exceptional for a boy his age. His ability to draw the human figure was uncanny. I must admit I was very embarrassed when he brought home his first sketch of a nude woman. He wanted to put it up in our home, but I wouldn't permit it. Jesse told me I was being silly, because there are nude statues all over Italy, and it wasn't pornography but art."

"Did you hang it?"

"No."

"Why not?"

"Reuben took it to an art dealer who paid him eight hundred lira, then sold it for three thousand to one of his customers. My son, at fifteen, had become a professional artist. He made enough money from his paintings to pay for his college tuition. The money Jesse earned giving private music lessons and what I had saved working as a nurse that we'd set aside for his college we gave to him as a gift when he graduated."

"Reuben is a very talented fashion designer," Bree said. She told Silvana about the dress she'd worn the night before.

Silvana stared at the young dark-skinned woman whose face reminded her of a doll's. "You must be very special to my son, if he gave you one of his designs."

A slight frown appeared between Bree's eyes. "Why would you say that?"

"He was very close to a model he met in Paris and she became his muse. He designed the most beautiful dresses for her, but after they broke up he stopped designing for young women. Now, he makes clothes for women my age."

It's been a while since a woman under thirty has modeled one of my designs. Now Bree knew what Reuben had meant when he'd said it was important that she wear the dress he'd made for her. And, she wondered about the woman from his past who'd left such an indelible impact on his career that he only wanted to sew for older women.

Did he see her as his new muse?

Would he, if she asked him, design another garment for her or was the feathered sheath dress something he'd done on impulse? She decided to wait before asking him to design another outfit befitting the launch of their line of sexy lingerie.

"Your English is excellent. Did you learn it from your husband?" Bree asked, smoothly changing the subject.

A flush darkened Silvana's face at the same time as her eyes turned a soft moss-green. "My husband taught me all the cuss words, because he said they were a universal language before he tutored me in English. Jesse studied music in college, but a few months after he graduated he was drafted and sent to Vietnam. He was wounded, but went back.

"I met him when I was fourteen and he had stopped in Italy on leave before returning to the States. He asked me for directions to get to the Fontana di Trevi and I told him that I would show him how to get there. I thought he looked so handsome in his uniform, and because he was an American I thought he knew all the movie stars. He laughed and said the only movie stars he ever saw were the ones who came to Vietnam to perform for the soldiers. I gave him my address and asked him to send me movie magazines."

"Did he?"

"Yes, he did. He sent me movie and fashion magazines. After a while I sent him pictures of myself with makeup or a new hairstyle I'd copied from a magazine. Jesse Reuben Douglas was twice my age, but I still fell in love with him. What I didn't know was that he wasn't the same man who wrote me such wonderful letters or encouraged me to stay in school to become the nurse I'd always wanted to be. It was only after I saw him again that I realized that not only did he look different, but inside he was very different. Your president had been assassinated and people were angry because of inequality and segregation."

"How had he changed?" Bree was so engrossed in the story that she found herself holding her breath.

"He had long hair that stood out all over his head and he wore a beard. I had left home to go to nursing school near Milan and when I met him at the train station I thought I'd fallen in love with Rasputin. He checked into a hostel a few kilometers from my school, but I told him I would not be seen in public with him unless he cut his hair and beard."

"Did he?"

"At first he refused, and then he did. I spent all of my free time with him and when he asked me to marry him I really thought he was crazy. It was when he admitted that he wouldn't sleep with me unless I married him that I gave in. We found a priest who agreed to marry us when I lied and told him that I was pregnant and didn't want to bring a bastard into the world. The lie came back to haunt me because I miscarried in my second month. I got pregnant right away and I managed to make it to three months before I started bleeding."

"Did your parents know you'd married?"

"No. I'd enrolled in an accelerated nursing-school program where I wouldn't take a break between semesters."

"Didn't they come up to visit you?"

Silvana smiled. "Yes, but they thought I was living in the nursing students' dorms. A lot of the girls were either secretly married or living with their boyfriends, so no one said anything. I didn't know how my family was going to react to my marrying an American, but I knew they would never reject their grandchild."

"I suppose it worked."

Her smile grew wider. "It did, but not before my father cursed my husband, using every conceivable dirty word in the Italian language. Jesse had taught me American curses and I'd taught him the Italian ones. His Italian still wasn't very good, but it was good enough to tell my father exactly what he thought of him. I thought Papa was going to have a stroke, but then he extended his hand to his new son-in-law and invited him to join him for a meal. Jesse and Papa became very close, and when my father died Jesse did not take it well. It was after that he told me that he didn't have much family back in Texas, and that my family had become his family.

"Although I miss my husband I'm left with wonderful memories and an incredible son. I still remember Jesse cooking what he said was a traditional Southern dinner with fried chicken, corn bread, sweet potatoes and macaroni with cheese. He tried to teach me to cook his food, but mine never came out like his. What I miss most is his Texas-style ribs. I can make Tuscan-style ribs, but they are not the same."

"I'll cook a Southern dinner you," Bree volunteered.

"You can make Texas ribs?"

"I can make something that's very close to it. My brother's girlfriend is from the South, and she taught me how to make Louisiana barbecue."

Silvana pressed her palms together. "Wonderful. I work part-time for a doctor which means I have a lot of extra time. Let me know when you want to come over and I will rearrange my schedule. You can invite Reuben if you want."

"Invite me where?" Reuben asked, walking into the living room.

Silvana stared at her son, recognizing the tenderness in his gaze when he looked at Bree. It was a look she recognized. He'd fallen in love with the delightful young woman.

"Breanna has promised to come and make Southern spareribs."

"Just let me know when, I'll be here." Reuben glanced at his watch. It was after ten. "If it's all right with you, Mama, we're going to leave now." Extending his hand, he pulled Silvana gently to her feet and kissed her cheek. "Thank you. Everything was delicious."

Rising on tiptoe, Silvana pressed a kiss to his chin. "Thank you for the wine, the flowers and Breanna," she added softly.

He kissed her again. "I'll call you in a few days."

Reuben waited for Bree to say her goodbyes, then escorted her down to the street where he'd parked the Vespa. It was the first day of the new year and if it was an indicator for the days to come, then he'd look forward to each sunrise.

chapter forty-four

Bree sat Indian-style on a chair, her journal in her lap, as she waited to use the sewing machine. The seeded-pearl bodice to a wedding gown was stretched over a dress form as Reuben pieced layers of satin and tulle together for the skirt. He'd worked practically nonstop to design gowns for the bride, three attendants and the mother of the bride for an early June wedding to be held on South Carolina's Isle of Palms.

It had taken him two weeks to sew on the tiny pearls in an intricate pattern—by hand. She'd offered to help him, but his glare spoke volumes. It was the first and last time she'd ever offer her assistance. She uncapped her pen and wrote down the date:

March 28—Reuben and I are living together.

I should correct that and write that I'm living with him. I'm still looking for an apartment. The ones I've been shown are either too small but are close to restaurants, cafés and shopping, or, if large enough, are too far from public transportation, and it is impossible to get to on foot.

When I mentioned my dilemma to Reuben, he suggested I move in with him to save money until I find what I want. At first I declined his offer, but I reconsidered when I calculated how much I was paying to live at the hotel. At three hundred a day, I would spend more than one hundred thousand a year—money that would be better spent purchasing a house.

I moved in with Reuben at the beginning of the month. He complained when I attempted to make the place look a little less like a bachelor pad by buying a new comforter for the bed, along with decorative pillows, sheets and towels, but after pouting for a day he admitted everything looked nice.

We make love—a lot. Reuben Douglas has become my drug of choice—one I never want to give up. I've finished my sketches for the lingerie. Thankfully, Reuben introduced me to a pattern-making software program that eliminated countless hours of configuring sizes. I've cut out different styles of panties, bras, cover-ups and lounging pants. All that remains is piecing them together.

Bree's head came up when the distinctive whirring of the machine stopped. Reuben sat with his back to her, staring out the window.

"Are you finished with the machine?" she asked.

"This is the third time you've asked in under an hour, and the answer is still the same. No, I am not finished."

Bree flinched at the tone of his voice. A year or even six months ago she would have come back at him with a barrage of expletives that would have stunned him into silence. But she'd changed and now weighed her words carefully before she spoke because once said they couldn't be retracted. She also held her tongue because she was in love with Reuben. Love had softened her and made her willing to compromise. It was no longer about Breanna—it was about Breanna and Reuben.

"We need another sewing machine."

Swiveling on his chair, Reuben stared at Bree as if she'd

taken leave of her senses. "Where would we put another sewing machine, Breanna?"

"Next to the one you have."

"No!"

She sat forward on the chair. "And why not, Reuben? I'll never finish my samples before the end of the summer."

"Then you don't finish. What's the rush? It's not imperative that you launch your line next spring."

"That's because it is *not* your line you're talking about."

"It has nothing to do whether it's mine or yours. I'm on deadline and you're not."

Bree's eyes narrowed as she stood up. "Thank you very much for reminding me that your work is more important than mine."

Pushing back his chair, Reuben stood up. "I didn't say that."

"You don't have to."

"Where are you going?" he asked when she reached for a sweater and her handbag.

"Out! That way I can't say something I know I'll regret later."

Staring numbly, Reuben watched as the woman he loved walked out the door.

He wanted to go after her, but he couldn't force his legs to move. Bree believed he thought more of his projects than hers, but she was mistaken. He'd worked around the clock to finish the wedding wardrobe weeks before his personal deadline so he could concentrate on helping her with her lingerie.

Bree projected that if she finished her samples by summer's end, then she would be ready to launch her line the following spring. If not, then it would be the following fall. What Reuben hadn't told her was that his Milan contact was willing to schedule a showing *this* fall if she completed everything before the end of spring. Reuben hadn't told her because he wanted it to be a surprise.

This was their first argument and it wouldn't be their last.

He decided to wait for Bree to calm down, and when she returned he would try and make it up to her.

Reuben sat in the dark, not attempting to turn on a lamp even though the sun had set hours before. He was waiting for Bree, who still hadn't returned. Even if he wanted to go look for her he didn't know where to begin. Before they'd begun living together he'd known he could reach her at her hotel.

He hadn't wanted to imagine something happening to her, yet there was always that possibility. She had the numbers to his cell phone, their apartment and his mother's. In an emergency she could always call Enrico at the restaurant.

The silence was shattered by two short rings of the phone, galvanizing Reuben. He came close to losing his balance as he dove for the receiver and snatched it up before it rang again.

"Ciao."

"*Ciao,* darling."

Frustration, fear and rage imploded when he heard Bree's voice. "Where the hell have you been?"

"I need you to meet me, Reuben."

He was too incensed to register her gentle tone. "Where the hell are you, Breanna!"

"If you stop yelling I'll tell you."

Reuben listened as she gave him an address. He repeated it aloud and said, "I'll be there as soon as I can."

Slamming the receiver on the cradle, he ended the call. It took a minute to slip into a pair of boots and grab his keys to the scooter. The address Bree had given him was near the Via Veneto. In fact, it was only a short distance from where his mother lived.

Bree and Silvana had established the habit of meeting every Sunday for dinner. They alternated cooking, and when he saw them together it was as if they'd known each other for years instead of only three months.

He knew Bree e-mailed her family in the States every week to reassure them she was enjoying life in Italy. He'd also noticed her writing in cloth-bound books, and when he asked her what she was writing her response was "my life story."

When he recalled his life at twenty-five he could truthfully admit that it was very uneventful. Even at thirty-nine it still wasn't spectacular enough for anyone to want to know the most intimate details. However, it was different with Bree. What she'd encountered in her young life others would probably not experience in the whole of theirs.

He hadn't wanted to believe that her mother had entertained thoughts of killing her daughter, but the alienation had been most profound. Even if Bree had been permitted to attend a boarding school in the States it would have offset some of her pain at feeling disconnected from her family and homeland.

What she did understand was that her negative behavior was a cry for help, a cry for attention and that in the end it was self-destructive. Reuben hadn't noticed any evidence that she was abusing drugs again. In fact, she rarely drank the wine which was customarily served at dinner.

The smell of the Tiber wafted in his nose as he crossed the river. Spring had come to Italy with daytime temperatures reaching the mid-sixties. He turned the throttle and the powerful four-stroke, four-valve Granturismo Vespa shot forward in a burst of speed as he maneuvered around a slower-moving sedan, the blue lights on the dashboard shimmering like waves of neon.

He made the trip in half the usual time, maneuvering onto the sidewalk in front of the address Bree had given him. He'd just cut the engine and parked the scooter against the side of the building when Bree and another woman approached.

Twin emotions of anger and relief swept over him when he realized she was all right. What he wanted to do was shake her until she lost her breath for making him worry about her.

Bree didn't see the scowl etched into her lover's face as she threw her arms around his neck and kissed him. "I have a surprise for you, darling."

He lifted his eyebrows. "And, I have one for you."

"Tell or show me later, Reuben," Bree said without taking a breath. "Signora Rispoli needs to get home, so we're going to be quick."

Reuben barely glanced at the dark-haired woman dressed in a business suit. "Be quick about what, Breanna?"

"I want you to see our new home."

His frown deepened. "What are you talking about?" Bree was talking in riddles, and he wondered if she *was* under the influence, because nothing she was saying made sense to him.

"I'm buying a house."

"Where?"

"Here." She pointed to the three-story palazzo. "We can use the first floor for our business, the second for entertaining and the top floor for our personal living quarters."

Taking her arm, he led far enough away so Signora Rispoli wouldn't overhear them. "Do you have any idea how much a building in this section of Rome will cost you?"

"Yes, and I managed to negotiate for a lower price if I forego a mortgage."

"How much lower?"

"I got her to take off three-fifty."

"Three hundred and fifty euros?"

"No, darling, three hundred and fifty thousand euros. It was going for two million, three hundred fifty, and once Signora Rispoli told the bank that I was willing to take the property without securing a mortgage, they agreed to drop the price."

"Where are you going to get two million euros?"

She smiled. "I'm going to call my father and have him

send a wire transfer. The funds should be in my account in a couple of days."

He stared at Bree as if she had a horn growing out the front of her head. "You have it like that?"

"I told you that I came into my trust. Have you heard of Sean "P. Diddy" Combs?" Reuben nodded. "Diddy is the biggest hip-hop impresario of the mid-nineties, and my father is the biggest R&B impresario of every decade since the 1970s. Yes, Reuben, you're looking at a troubled and misunderstood rich girl who has finally gotten her head *and* her shit together. I'm going to buy this building, and either you're going inside to look at it with me, or you can get back on your scooter and ride into the night."

Reuben tried processing what he was hearing. Bree had mentioned a trust fund, but he hadn't given a thought as to how much she was actually worth. He'd offered to underwrite the cost of her getting her company off the ground, and she had probably had a good laugh at his expense.

His hand slipped to her elbow. "Let's look at *your* palazzo so Signora Rispoli can get home to her family."

The three-story building, bank-owned palazzo, unoccupied for six months, was *magnifico*. The first floor boasted a two-story entryway with pale marble floors. Large rooms with high ceilings, floor-to-ceiling windows, a kitchen and two full bathrooms were ideal to set up the corporate offices for Naughty.

A curving staircase led to the second floor where there was a large ballroom, a kitchen and several dressing rooms with adjoining baths. The third floor contained a four-bedroom apartment with en suite baths, sitting rooms and a kitchen. A lift had been added to the property five years ago after the owner had been felled by a stroke and was unable to navigate the stairs. The previous owners had removed all of the furnishings before the bank foreclosed on the property, but had left chandeliers in the entryway, ballroom and the third-story living room.

Bree spun around on her toes in the living room. The herringbone parquet floors were covered with a layer of dust. "What do you think, Reuben?"

Crossing his arms over his chest, he angled his head. "I think you're crazy, Breanna Parker."

Bree saw a hint of a smile lift the corners of his mouth. "I think you like it."

"What's not to like, Bree? It's great place for a business."

"What about for a private residence?"

"That too," he said, deadpan.

"Then, you approve?"

"Yes, I approve."

She let out a small shriek, launching herself at his chest. He caught and lifted her off the floor. "I love you," she whispered, pressing small kisses to his face and mouth.

Reuben kissed her back. "I love you, too." He set her on her feet. "I'll call Nicolas and Gianni to have them execute a search on the property for liens and they'll also have an engineer check to see whether the electricity and plumbing are in working order. You don't want to spend your money for a white elephant, and then spend even more to make it habitable."

Bree kissed him again. "Thank you, darling."

Reuben smiled for the first time since getting her phone call. "Let me talk to your Signora Rispoli. I'm going to let her know that our lawyers will contact her to go over a few things before we conclude the sale."

"Should I have Daddy wire the money, or should I wait?"

"Wait until we get approval from the Cesàris' that everything checks out."

Bree wound her arm around Reuben's waist as they took the

staircase down to the first floor where the real estate agent sat on a stair waiting for them. Bree then stood off to the side while Reuben spoke to the agent, who nodded, and gave him her business card.

"I'm so glad your husband likes the property," she said when Bree joined her and Reuben. "So many times a wife will like something and the husband doesn't, and vice versa. I'm certain once you live here you'll really come to appreciate that you've made an excellent choice."

Bree waited until they were on the street to say, "I don't know why she assumed we were married, because I hadn't mentioned I had a husband."

Reuben lifted his shoulders. "Perhaps she just assumed we were married."

"Well, we're not."

"There's no need to get upset, Bree. It doesn't matter what others think. You know and I know that we're not married. Shouldn't that be enough?"

She gave him a long, penetrating stare, then said, "Yes, it is."

On the drive back to Trastevere, Bree thought about all that had occurred since she'd stormed out of Reuben's apartment. She'd been so incensed that she'd thought about moving out and checking back into the hotel, but she'd changed her mind during the taxi ride to Piazza di Spagna.

Sitting in the back seat of the taxi and staring out at the passing landscape, she saw what she couldn't from the back of Reuben's Vespa. She saw block after block of elegant palazzos along immaculate tree-lined streets. Reuben claimed there was no room in the apartment for another commercial-style sewing machine, but that wouldn't be the case in a palazzo.

She'd called Bernadette Rispoli, praying the woman was

available to show her several properties. The agent was gracious enough to cancel several appointments to meet with her. She'd shown her two residences—one occupied and the other vacant, and she'd decided on the latter.

As soon as she took possession of the palazzo, Bree planned to hire a cleaning company and painters to make the structure habitable. Hopefully, that all could be accomplished before the middle of April.

"Have you eaten dinner?" Reuben asked after they'd crossed the river.

"No."

"Would you like to stop and eat somewhere?"

She tightened her arms around his waist. "Yes, but I'd like to shower and change first. Can we go back to the restaurant you took me to the first time I came here with you?"

"You like candlelight dining?"

"Yes," she murmured against his back. She liked eating by candlelight, making love with Reuben and the love she felt for him defied description. He was gentle, compassionate, affectionate and supportive. Even when she'd accused him of thinking only of himself, she knew she'd lied. Everything Reuben did or said was predicated on her being in his life.

He'd suggested she live with him to save money, not to have a live-in maid or lover. He wouldn't permit her to clean or cook because the woman he paid to clean the apartment needed the money to supplement her disabled husband's limited income. They alternated eating at home and eating out, Reuben doing all of the cooking. It was only when she visited with Silvana that she was able to hone her cooking skills.

Bree slapped Reuben on his bottom when he emerged from the bathroom completely nude. "Very nice," she crooned. Opening a drawer in the armoire, she withdrew a pair of black bikini panties. In order to save time, she and Reuben had taken a shower together.

A loud gasp escaped her when his arm snaked around her waist, pulling her hips to his groin. "Yours is even nicer. I think you're putting on weight."

She smiled at him over her shoulder. "Baby's getting some booty."

Reuben kissed her under her ear. "Baby had booty, but it's filling out nicely."

Bree groaned when his teeth nipped the sensitive skin on her neck. "Don't do that, Reuben."

"Why not?"

"Because you're getting me excited."

Reaching around her, his hand went between her thighs. "I love getting you wet."

Her eyes closed with his erotic revelation at the same time as her knees buckled. She braced her arms against the shelves in the armoire to maintain her balance. "Oh!" The single word echoed in the apartment when she felt Reuben's erection searching for entrance between her legs.

Reuben parted her legs with one knee as he pushed his penis into Bree, gasping as her tight flesh closed around him. He loved taking her from behind because it permitted deeper penetration and increased the pleasure both for him and for her.

Tucking her body into the contours of his own, he thrust into her, pulling out a little more each time, only to thrust deeper and deeper, the rhythmic sound of flesh meeting flesh keeping time with their syncopated moans and groans.

Bree felt the flutters that quickly became contractions. They swelled until she felt as if she couldn't get enough air into her lungs. Then they came; the organisms kept coming, coming and coming until she lost count after three.

Gasping and crying at the same time, she slumped against

the massive piece of furniture as Reuben held her waist and drove his engorged penis into her over and over, while growling out his release against her ear. The pulsing continued until it ebbed completely.

Bree didn't remember Reuben picking her up and carrying her to the bed. She didn't remember when he reached over to turn off the bedside lamp, or when he pulled a sheet and lightweight blanket over their damp bodies.

What she did remember was them making love again as the sun rose to herald the start of a new day. Afterward, they lay together, smiling at each other, aware they'd made love not once, but twice without using protection.

Gathering her close, Reuben pressed Bree's face to his chest. "I love you so much," he said reverently.

Smiling, she kissed the crisp hair on his chest. "And I love you, too."

His fingers toyed with her mussed hair. "I let you run away from me yesterday because I knew you were upset."

"You let me?"

"Yes, because I could've stopped you if I'd wanted to, but I didn't. I don't want you to believe that I'm trying to control your life."

"I know you're not trying—"

"Please don't interrupt me," he warned softly. "If you decide you're going to run away again, then don't call me to come and get you. I stopped playing games a long time ago, and even when I did, I wasn't very good at it."

"I wasn't running away," Bree said in her defense. "When you said there wasn't enough room here for two machines I decided to remedy that."

"So, you just happened to go out and buy a palazzo."

Raising her head, she smiled up at him. "Call it an impulse purchase."

"A two-million-euro impulse buy?"

"I'll probably never spend that much again for a single item. Besides, it's going to be our home and place of business. Can't you be happy for us?"

"I'm very happy for us. But, there's something I need to tell you. Don't look so frightened," he said, when her expression stilled and grew serious.

Reuben told Bree about the arrangement he'd made with a friend in Milan who hosted two showings each year where he permitted a new designer to showcase his or her talent at the beginning of each show.

"As soon as I finish with my wedding project I'm going to help you finish your samples for his fall lineup."

A piercing scream rent the air as Bree hugged Reuben so tightly around the neck that he reached up to extricate himself from her arms. "Thank you, thank you," she cried over and over, while raining kisses over every inch of his face. "Why didn't you tell me?"

He gave her a dazzling smile. "What? And ruin the surprise?"

"Not telling me has put a two-million-dollar dent in my bank account," she countered.

Reuben ran his forefinger down the length of her nose. "Remember, it's going to be our home and the corporate office for Naughty lingerie. And once your designs take off you'll realize your initial investment within the first two years."

She lifted her eyebrows. "You think so?"

"I know so. After the line takes off we'll have to come up with a signature fragrance. We can call it Naughty Girl."

A smile trembled over Bree's lips as she stared at the man who'd become her partner in the truest sense of the word—in and out of bed. It was the first time he'd said *we* and not *you.*

"We're going to make an awesome team, Reuben."

He cradled her face between his hands. "We're not going to, *bella,* because we're already an awesome team."

chapter forty-five

October 18—It seems as if I've been waiting years for this day, and now that I'm in Milano I'm frightened—even more frightened than when at sixteen, I had to endure eighteen hours of labor to give birth to a baby girl, only to have her taken from me without having a chance to see what she looked like.

Although I find myself pregnant for the third time in ten years this pregnancy is different from the other two. This time I'm completely and irrevocably in love with my baby's father, my ob-gyn has reassured me that I should deliver a normal, healthy child and sonogram pictures indicate that I'm carrying a boy.

I know what kind of father Reuben's going to be—overprotective—because I can't grunt or groan without him asking me *what's wrong.* The only thing that's wrong is that I'm scared out of my mind about showcasing my line of lingerie later tonight. I never would've gotten to this phase in my professional career if not for Reuben Douglas. He is the one who has helped me complete the sample pieces for a showing with the renowned Milan-based fashion promoter-cum-designer Aurelio Taurino. Reuben and I had dinner with Aurelio last night and he reassured us the models he'd contracted to wear the Naughty lingerie are some of the most professional in the business.

He's signed on ten of the top models from the States, Russia, the Caribbean, France and several African countries.

Mother called me before we left Rome two days ago, but that doesn't mean she called me every day. I probably shouldn't have given her the name of my hotel in Milano, but then she still would my cell. I know Mother is concerned about the baby, but each time I come back from the doctor I give her an update. She has taken to the notion of becoming an *abuela* like a duck to water.

Reuben and I plan to visit the States next week, where we'll marry and I will live until giving birth. I'll use the time to wait for a response from the fashion industry about the success or failure of a line of lingerie certain to become Victoria's Secret's direct competition.

I hear Reuben opening the door. He's returned, I hope with my peach gelato. Even before my pregnancy was confirmed I craved peach gelato. The doctor said I could have it as long as I don't have more than two ounces a day. I've gained a total of twelve pounds, and would've probably gained a lot more if I didn't work out on the treadmill. Reuben set up an in-home gym in a back room on the first floor.

Decorating the palazzo is still a work in progress, because we've focused much of our time and energy into getting ready for the show and setting up the first-floor office and the nursery. We've ordered furniture for the two guest bedrooms, but it isn't expected to arrive until after the first of the year. Silvana has promised to babysit whenever Reuben or I have to travel or want a few hours to ourselves. I told her I can't think that far in advance, because all I want is to make it through the next three months to bring this baby home when I leave the hospital.

Bree stood backstage with long-legged, scantily-clad models wearing Naughty lingerie. Aurelio, also known to his friends as Auggie, had decided on a Venetian Carnivale theme. All the models' eyes were outlined in black kohl that made them appear ghoulish behind the decorative masks with colorful ribbons and feathers that, along with stiletto heels, added even more height to their statuesque figures.

Auggie explained that the Goth look was a dramatic complement to the scraps of silk and satin in sensual shades ranging from jonquil to amethyst and magenta. Murals depicting images of Venice's watery canals, alleys and footbridges were barely visible through the swirling gray mist coming from a fog machine. The models were lining up as the sound of Enigma's new-world, old-world culture Gregorian chanting set the tone for the shadowy fabricated world of medieval Venice.

Bree sat on a stool in a corner, because she didn't trust her legs to support her quaking body. She didn't know whether it was the driving baseline beats coming through the powerful sound system or an attack of nerves, but the baby was kicking vigorously. Placing a hand over the black silk smock top she'd paired with a matching knee-length skirt in a stretch fabric, she rubbed her swollen belly. Just for tonight she'd slipped on a pair of stilettos for when she joined the models on stage at the conclusion of the show. She'd practically pleaded with Reuben to join her backstage, but he'd refused and insisted on sitting in the audience because he didn't want to intrude on her special night.

She tried concentrating on the music, but the sound of Auggie shouting to the models added to her increasing anxiety. The man was a creative genius because the models were magnificent-looking in the garish eye makeup and decorative masks.

Bree hadn't realized it was over until Auggie eased her off the stool to take the stage with the models. "It was *stupefacente!*"

She pushed back the drape and stepped onto the catwalk,

smiling and applauding the young women who'd lined up to applaud her. The lights were turned up and she spied Reuben on his feet with the others clapping and whistling loudly.

Bree met his gaze, blowing him a kiss as flashbulbs distorted her vision. On cue, the models strutted back behind the drapery, with Bree following. Auggie met her and returned her to the catwalk as the applause escalated. She didn't have to wait to read the trades the next day. Judging from the audience's reaction the launch of Naughty was a rousing success.

Reuben waited for Bree to join him, shielding her body from the crush of photographers and reporters who wanted to capture her image up close and/or interview her. Her fingernails dug into the back of his hand as she moved closer.

"Please get me out of here," she pleaded softly.

He forced a smile. "Ladies, gentlemen, please give me your business cards and Signorina Parker will contact you at a future date," he lied smoothly. Bree had been explicit when she'd stated that under no condition would she grant an interview until she was assured her line would achieve a measure of success.

A noted fashion columnist tapped Reuben's arm to get his attention. "Signore Douglas, what is your contribution to the creation of Naughty?"

Reuben knew the journalist wanted information about Naughty, and she would pump everyone mercilessly to give her editor something to print for the weekly. "I offered moral support."

"I've heard rumors that Signorina Parker is with child. Will you confirm this?"

"Again, you'll have to ask her that when she contacts you for an interview."

He wasn't going to publicly admit or deny that Bree was

carrying his child. They'd agreed to have a civil ceremony in the States, and to repeat their vows in a nuptial mass after the birth of their son. They would've married sooner, but preparing for the showing and settling into the palazzo had taken precedence.

When Bree had informed him that she was pregnant he'd wanted to marry right away, but she wanted to wait. He hadn't pressured her, only because she hadn't said no. One morning she woke to tell him that she would marry him in a place called Las Vegas, Nevada, in a small ceremony with her parents, her brother and his girlfriend in attendance. And if he wanted an Italian wedding, then she was amenable to repeating her vows at a church for his friends and relatives.

Now, looping an arm around her shoulders, he pushed his way through the crowd. Auggie had invited them to attend a reception following the showing, but he planned to take Bree back to their hotel room. He would call his friend in a few days and send him a gift for his generosity for allowing Bree to showcase her line of lingerie.

Reuben flagged down a taxi, giving the driver the name of their hotel. Bree had pulled her legs up under her body and rested her hand on his chest within minutes of climbing into the rear of the cab with him. She was sound asleep when the driver maneuvered up to the front of the modern hotel. Reuben paid the fare, then lifted Bree from the taxi and carried her into the lobby, remembering another time he'd carried her.

Some things had changed, while others had remained the same; certainly she'd put on weight—she was pregnant with their child. When he'd broken the news to his mother she'd smiled, saying that Jesse Douglas had looked forward to becoming a grandfather. It was Bree who'd suggested naming their child Jesse if a boy and Jessica if a girl.

Reuben managed to unlock the door to the hotel room

without waking Bree. She stirred when he undressed her and covered her with a sheet, first pressing a light kiss to the rounded belly.

On a Friday evening, at a wedding chapel in the Nevada desert, Breanna Parker became Breanna Douglas. She wore a champagne-colored coat dress that artfully disguised her baby bump. Reuben wore a tailored dark-gray suit with a lighter gray tie. Ryder had stood in as his best man and Lisa was Bree's attendant. Langston and Karma were on hand to witness their daughter marrying a man as different from Tyrone Wyatt as night is from day.

Reuben was older, worldly, and, above all, patient with Breanna. Karma had watched the interaction between her daughter and Reuben, resentful that he'd gotten Bree to turn her life around when all of her warnings had fallen on deaf ears. His quiet composure had a sobering effect on Breanna that made her more of a stranger than she'd been when she'd returned from Europe two years before.

She'd come to Vegas to see her daughter married, not because she approved of what she declared to be "tacky nuptials," but because she didn't want to have a bastard grandchild. Her father hadn't married her mother and she didn't want the same for her daughter.

As much as she tried, she wanted to be happy for Breanna, yet something wouldn't permit her to feel the joy that radiated in Bree's eyes as she exchanged vows with her Italian husband.

Karma had managed to concoct a plausible story for the women in her circle about her daughter's short-lived marriage to an R&B singing sensation, but how was she going to explain that her daughter had married again—this time at a wedding chapel in Vegas no less. She could count herself blessed that Bree hadn't requested an Elvis impersonator be in attendance.

She was an expert when it came to faking it, but what Karma couldn't fake was her excitement at wanting to see her grandchild. Once she'd come to the conclusion that she wasn't too young to be a grandmother, she looked forward to spoiling her grandson. She'd wanted a granddaughter to take shopping and to do all the things she hadn't had the opportunity to do with Breanna, but a grandson would still do nicely, because she would make certain that he would make the best-dressed baby list along with Suri Cruise—the daughter of Tom Cruise and Katie Holmes.

Touching a tissue to the corners of her eyes, Karma smiled up at her husband. "It was beautiful, darling," she crooned facetiously. "Let's hope she can stay married this time."

Langston glared at his wife. "Can't you be happy for her?" he whispered harshly.

"I'm trying, Lang."

"Don't try. Just do it."

Karma swallowed the acerbic words poised on the tip of her tongue. She didn't want to argue with Langston—at least not today, because she'd end up on the losing end. Her purpose in life was keeping her husband happy, which in turn made her happy.

"I'm sorry, darling." There was enough contrition in her voice to make her sound believable.

Langston reached for his wife's hand, bringing it to his lips. "It's okay."

He turned his attention back to his daughter as she slipped a gold band on the finger of her husband. They exchanged a chaste kiss and it was over. His baby girl was now a married woman.

Grinning broadly, he extended his hand to his new son-in-law, pumping it vigorously. "Congratulations."

"Thank you, Langston."

Reaching for Bree, Langston cradled her gently against his

body, ever mindful of her condition. It appeared this time he and Karma *would* become grandparents, and he looked forward to bouncing his grandson on his knee. He didn't know what Bree and Reuben planned for their son, but if the boy inherited a love for music, then he could prepare him eventually to take control of LP Records.

"Congratulations, baby girl," he crooned, kissing her cheek.

Bree smiled. "Thank you, Daddy, for everything." Langston had arranged for them to fly from L.A. to Vegas in his private jet, and he'd also reserved luxury suites for everyone at the Bellagio.

"You know I'd do anything for my favorite girl." And he had to admit that his daughter looked beautiful. She'd pinned up her shoulder-length hair in a fancy twist and her lightly made-up face radiated excellent health. He stared at the circle of diamonds in an eternity band on her delicate finger, hoping this marriage would last longer than her first. But there was something about Reuben Douglas that said he was in it for the duration.

"There are limos waiting to take us back to the hotel," Langston announced, ushering everyone outside the chapel where a number of couples waited their turn to become husband and wife.

Bree stood at the window, staring at the landscape beyond the glittering lights of the Vegas strip. The sun had disappeared behind the mountains, turning the desert into shades and colors that defied description.

She smiled when she felt the heat of her husband's body as he came up behind her. "How are you, Mr. Douglas?"

Reuben dipped his head and pressed a kiss to the side of her neck. "I'm good, Mrs. Douglas." He kissed her again. "You don't know how long I've wanted to call you that."

"How long has that been?"

"December fifth will be a year."

Turning around, Bree stared numbly at Reuben. "That's the day I arrived in Rome."

He smiled. "I knew there was something very special about you the moment you walked into my uncle's restaurant. I didn't know how special until we ran into each other at the art-supply shop."

Smiling, Bree patted her belly under a floor-length white satin nightgown. "Look what being special got us."

Resting his hand over hers, Reuben felt the slight movement under their fingers. "I think he's going to be a football player. As soon as he's walking I'll get him a soccer ball."

"Don't you want him to paint beautiful pictures?"

"I want him to be whatever it is he wants to be."

"You're right." She and Ryder had disappointed their father when they refused to become involved with his recording company.

"Are you ready to go to bed?"

"Yes." And she was. They'd come back to the hotel where Langston had arranged for the chef to prepare a wedding banquet that included everything from appetizers to a carving station. Ryder had accused him of overdoing it, but Langston gave him a baleful look that prompted Ryder to keep his comments to himself.

Bree had eaten too much and had to waddle back to their suite where she lay on a recliner until the food settled enough for her get up and change out of her wedding attire. How different her wedding to Reuben was from the spectacle Karma had staged for her and Tyrone Wyatt. The millions spent then on flowers, food, champagne and security could have been donated to charity, because her marriage was over almost before it began.

Reuben, wearing a pair of pajamas pants, picked her up and carried her to the bed. He now affected a mustache and goatee, and the facial hair enhanced rather than detracted from his overall good looks.

Bree knew this wedding night would be nothing like her prior one as she extended her arms to her husband. He came into her embrace, supporting his weight on his arms to avoid putting weight on her belly.

She smiled. "In another month I doubted whether we're going to be able to make love because my belly will be in the way."

"We'll just use another position. You can always lie on your side."

"I still prefer doggy-style."

Reuben laughed softly. "I think that's how I got you pregnant. Up against the armoire doggy-style"

"It was incredible."

"That's because you're incredible."

"When are you going to stop talking and make love to your wife, Reuben Douglas?"

Needing no further prompting, he undid the many covered buttons on the front of her gown, exposing her full breasts. Bree's body was voluptous, lush, and as she bloomed with the ripeness of impending motherhood his desire for her increased exponentially with her expanding waistline. He woke up with an erection and whenever he caught a glimpse of her naked body he was helpless to control the rush of blood to his penis. Breanna Douglas was sexy in and out of bed—with or without clothes.

He was fully aroused by the time he relieved her of the satin garment. Stripping off his pajamas he lowered himself over her body as she opened her legs. There would be no foreplay because Bree had become very demanding, declaring she didn't have to be warmed up because she was always hot and ready.

Reuben pushed his erection into her moist body, sighing as he felt her pulsing flesh pull him in and hold him fast before releasing his rigid flesh to begin the exercise again. He feared moving because it would be over too quickly. But, move he did, setting a rhythm that short-circuited their senses as they climaxed simultaneously.

He withdrew from his wife and lay beside her, awed by the passion and love she evoked just by their occupying the same space as him. What he didn't want to think of was that he would be leaving her. He was to remain in the States for another week, then he had to return to Italy on business. In return for Aurelio Taurino showcasing Naughty, he'd promised the man he would design a collection of evening wear for the following year's fall show. He would draw the sketches, meet with Auggie, then return to Los Angeles to await the birth of his son.

chapter forty-six

Bree slipped out bed in an attempt not to wake Reuben. The pains in her lower back had intensified. They weren't that sharp, yet they were enough to make her aware that they weren't Braxton-Hicks contractions. The pains seemed to come and go as she showered and brushed her teeth.

"Are you all right?"

Her head came up and she stared at Reuben, who'd come into the bathroom without making a sound. "I'm good."

He glared at her. "If you're good, then why are you gritting your teeth?"

"I have a few pains in my back."

"That means you're not good," he countered. "Please go back to bed and stay there. After I shower I'm going to call your doctor."

Holding the small of her back with two hands, she duck-walked out of the bathroom. "I'm not due for another week."

"We'll let your doctor determine that, Breanna," he said to her back.

Bree lay in bed, eyes closed; she was trying to remember what she'd felt before the onset of labor ten years before. She failed. The only thing she remembered was screaming and screaming, which had resulted in her not being able to speak above a whisper. It had taken a week before she'd regained full use of her voice.

Another pain hit her—this one in her lower abdomen, and she bit down hard on her lip to keep from crying out. She waited, counting off the minutes before another pain seized her, this one stronger and longer than the one before.

When Reuben returned she knew her baby was ready to be born. "I think I'm in labor."

"Breanna Parker-Douglas, 26, gave birth to a seven-pound-two-ounce baby boy on December sixteenth at a private L.A. hospital. Breanna and her Italian fashion designer husband named their son Jesse Langston Douglas in honor of his grandfathers."

Karma closed the magazine, smiling. "At least they got the facts right." Her daughter, after three attempts, finally had a child she could claim as her own.

"Reuben said he got an e-mail from a magazine asking if we would give them an exclusive on baby pictures."

"What did he say?"

Bree glanced over at her son, asleep in a bassinette beside her club chair. He looked exactly his father. The exception was his hair; it was more red than brown. "He wants to wait to see what some of the others are offering before he commits. Whatever we get we plan to donate to charity."

"That's nice." Karma couldn't pull her gaze away from the tiny baby, because her first grandchild—a girl—had also had red hair. Colin Ryder had certainly passed along his gene for red hair to his grand- and great-grandchildren.

"Reuben told me that you're going back to Italy the first week in January."

"Yes. Daddy offered the jet because I wouldn't fly on a commercial carrier with the baby until he gets his first set of immunizations."

"Why don't you wait until you get your six-week checkup?"

"I've already set up an appointment to see my ob-gyn in Rome for the checkup." Bree gave her mother a pointed look. "You know you can always come to Italy and stay as long as you'd like. We have plenty of room, and we live within walking distance of the most delicious shops in the world."

"The next time Lang gets on my nerves I'm going to take you up on your offer."

Bree rolled her eyes. "Daddy doesn't bother anyone—especially you, Mother, so stop the drama."

"He's getting old and cranky."

"We're all getting old and cranky, Mother. Jesse's a week old and he's already cranky."

Karma's eyes misted. "He's beautiful."

"You say that because you're his grandmother."

"Reuben's mother is his grandmother. I'm going to be *abuela*."

Bree smiled. Karma came to visit her every morning after she'd fed and bathed the baby. Reuben usually went for a jog, leaving her and Karma time to bond with each other and the baby.

"I'm glad you're here, because there's something I need to tell you."

"You're getting a divorce."

"That's not funny, Mother."

"Well, I never know what to expect with you."

There came a beat. "I know. That's why I want to tell you something before you hear it from someone else. I'm writing a tell-all book. No—I'm actually not writing it."

Karma sat up straighter. "What are you saying?"

Bree told her mother about her journals and how she felt it was time for her tell the world how she had dealt with issues that included abandonment, substance abuse, her adolescent affair and her short-lived marriage to Tyrone Wyatt. "I've given Ryder my journals, and he's going to write the book."

"How can you…how can you expose your family—"

"The book isn't going to be about you, Mother. It's about me. If I can help and inspire other young girls to turn away from drugs and alcohol, then I'm willing to sacrifice the Parker name to do so."

"How can you say that, you selfish little bitch!"

Bree stood up. "Perhaps it would be better if we didn't wait until the new year to leave."

"Go!" Karma screamed. "And don't bother to come back. You're no longer welcome in my home."

Bree walked out of the sitting room and into the walk-in closet to retrieve several pieces of luggage. Nothing had changed. She and her mother couldn't get along and probably never would get along. When Reuben returned from jogging she planned to tell him that she was ready to return to Italy as soon as she made arrangements for a private airline to take them to Rome.

chapter forty-seven

"Maybe Karma was overacting," Reuben said when Bree told him she and the baby were going back to Italy.

"Karma is being Karma, Reuben."

Reuben exhaled an audible sigh. "Jesse's too young to travel. And you still haven't healed."

"I'll arrange for a private jet to fly us directly to Rome. I'll even pay extra for us, other than the crew, to be the only passengers to lessen the risk of Jesse being exposed to airborne microorganisms."

Reaching out, Reuben held his wife's shoulders in a firm grip. "Why don't you call Ryder and ask if we can stay with him until Jesse gets his shots?"

"No. I'm not going to impose on Ryder again, and not with an infant. He can't write to noise, and it's the same with Lisa when she's studying. This is her last year in med school and she has to pass her exams if she hopes to graduate."

"Maybe you should try and make peace with your mother."

"All of my life I've tried making peace with my mother, but nothing I do is good enough for her. She's still pissed because we had a Vegas wedding. How on earth can she tell her phony-ass friends that her daughter went to Vegas to get married? Next they'll ask for a souvenir wedding photo replete with an Elvis impersonator. Right now, I'm done. Karma wants me to leave and Karma always gets what she wants."

"Why don't you ask your father to fly us over?"

"I don't want my father to have to choose between his daughter and his wife, because I'm certain he'd choose his wife over me."

"This sounds like a *telenovela*."

"That's because it is, Reuben. And, what makes it so sad is that we believe we're normal."

Reuben knew no amount of arguing would get Bree to change her mind. Besides, the doctor had cautioned him about the ravages of postpartum depression. So far, Bree hadn't exhibited the signs that she might be depressed and that's how he wanted it to stay.

"Okay, baby. We'll go back whenever you want."

Bree took a step and wound her arms around her husband's waist. "*Grazie,* my love."

He smiled. "*Prego, il mio amore.*"

Bree celebrated the new year at home with her husband, son and mother-in-law. The day marked a milestone: it had been a year to the day that she'd first slept with the man who was destined to become her husband and the father of her child.

Jesse was gaining weight, she was losing her pregnancy weight and orders for Naughty were beginning to trickle in. Reuben had found vacant space where they would set up a factory for production of the mostly handmade items. Only the seams were machine-sewn. He'd also assumed the responsibility of interviewing experienced seamstresses, offering them competitive salaries when he evaluated their handiwork. Several women who'd learned the art of lacework from their mothers and grandmothers became immediate hires.

She and Reuben decided to sell the baby pictures to a British tabloid, who'd outbid *People* magazine. The contact sheet showed frames of them at home with photos of the three of them,

Reuben and Jesse together, she and Jesse and one of Jesse smiling while asleep. The photographer had captured the essence of the love she felt for her husband and son in every frame.

Bree discovered running a household while caring for a baby wasn't as easy as it had been before she'd had Jesse. She'd given up sketching, reading and exercising on the treadmill. When her doctor gave her approval to resume sexual relations with Reuben she was usually sleeping soundly before he came to bed. Early-morning lovemaking was no longer an option because she had to get up and breast-feed Jesse.

Karma had extended an olive branch by e-mailing her an apology. Bree replied to the e-mail, updating her mother about everything. She found it easier to communicate with Karma long distance than in person.

Bree had just put Jesse down for a nap before joining Reuben to go over sketches for a collection of loungewear for their Naughty label when their housekeeper knocked lightly on the door of their sewing room.

"There's a man at the door asking for Signorina Parker."

Bree exchanged a look with Reuben. Most people knew her as Douglas, not Parker. "Did he give you his name or a business card, Rosa?" she asked.

"No, *signora.*"

"Do you want me to see what he wants?" Reuben asked.

"No. I'll take care of it."

Bree walked down a wide hallway and into the living room. A tall, slender man with jet-black hair and equally intense dark eyes watched her approach. It was hard to pinpoint his age, but she put him somewhere between forty and fifty.

"I'm Breanna Parker-Douglas. How may I help you?"

The man handed her a business card. "My name is Philip Cook, and I represent Mr. and Mrs. Gilbert Keane."

The address on the card indicated the man standing in her living room was an American from the Bay Area. "I'm sorry, but I don't know anyone named Keane."

"The Keanes are the couple who adopted the daughter you gave up ten years ago."

Bree froze, unable to believe what she was hearing. "What are you talking about?"

"Ms. Parker, you signed over—or should I say your parents relinquished—your parental rights to your baby to the Keanes, who were unable to have children of their own. Unfortunately, their daughter has a rare blood type and needs a kidney. What I need is your permission to be tested as a potential match and donor. I'm aware that you now have a son, but I appeal to you as the child's mother to agree to be tested."

Bree knew she couldn't lie and say she hadn't had a child, because why else would the man come to her if he hadn't had proof? The secret that Langston and Karma Parker believed to have been buried had resurfaced. Ten years ago she'd been faced with the dilemma of giving up her child for adoption, and now that child needed her. If she didn't agree to the test, then she'd never know if she could have saved a life, but if she did and proved to be a match …

"Where would I go to be tested?"

Philip Cook murmured a silent prayer. "We can have a local doctor do the test."

"And, if I prove to be a match?"

"Then, we'd ask you to come to the States. Jessica—they named her Jessica—is too weak to travel."

How ironic, Bree thought. What were the odds of her biological son and daughter sharing the same name? She closed her eyes for several seconds. "Please sit down, Mr. Cook. I have to talk to my husband."

Bree returned to the sewing room and stared at Reuben's broad shoulders as he sat at the drafting table. "Reuben?" He swiveled on the stool to look at her. "I have something to tell you."

Rising slowly to his feet he closed the distance between them. "What's the matter?"

"Sit down, Reuben. I have something to tell you."

She told him everything from her affair with her ski instructor to going into seclusion in at a convent in Brussels and giving up her parental rights to an infant daughter. "My daughter needs a kidney transplant and her parents want to know if I'm willing to be tested for a possible donor match."

Reuben's open hand came down hard on the table, scattering pencils and gum erasers. "Dammit, Breanna, when were you going to tell me you had another child? Did you think I wouldn't have fallen in love with you and married you? What the hell else are you hiding from me?"

Bree felt like crying, but she refused to let him see her cry. "Nothing."

"Are you sure?"

"Yes, Reuben, I'm sure. And, I never hid it from—"

"Don't!" He held up a hand. "Just don't say it. Go and do what you have to do to clear your conscience."

"This is not about my conscience, Reuben."

"If not, then what is it about?"

"It's about righting a wrong. I never wanted to give up my baby, but I wasn't strong enough to stand up to my parents. Don't you think it hasn't haunted me all these years? Never to hear my baby cry or touch her? Not to know what she looked like? To have passed her on the street perhaps, and not know who she is? It's not about out of sight out of mind, because she's never been that far from my mind." She couldn't stop the tears welling up in her eyes. "They named her Jessica. If our son would've been a girl we would have named her Jessica. How crazy would that have been to have had two daughters with the same name?"

Reuben felt his heart turn over when he saw the tears trickle down his wife's face. Taking four steps, he pulled her against his chest. "It's okay, baby. If you're the one who can save her life, then you have to get tested. I'll go with you."

Tilting her chin, Bree brushed her mouth over his. "No, darling. I need to do this on my own."

"Remember, I'm here if you need me."

She kissed him again. "I know. Come with me when I tell Mr. Cook that I'll take his test."

Naughty Girl's Secret Love Child

The headlines blared from tabloids from Europe and across the Atlantic to the States. Bree's housekeeper had repeated what she'd heard to her boyfriend who had leaked the news to the media. Reporters and photographers had taken up positions outside the palazzo, hoping to catch a glimpse of Bree, making her a prisoner in her own home until Reuben hired a private security firm to keep them at a distance.

Bree was confirmed as a donor match and she made arrangements to fly to San Francisco for the procedure. Again she took advantage of the media's greed for gossip and sold her story and gave the money to her daughter's adoptive parents to defray the exorbitant medical costs of the organ transplant.

Bree stood at the gate where her father's jet sat fueled and ready for takeoff, holding her son to her heart. He was five months old, sitting up and babbling constantly. His curly hair had darkened slightly, but in the sunlight glints of red were still visible. She kissed his cheek, leaving a smudge of lipstick on his mocha-colored skin.

"Now it's your turn to give Mama a kiss." Jesse leaned forward and pressed his open mouth to her nose. "Mama loves you so much."

Reuben took the child from her. "Go. Now."

She kissed Reuben, then turned and walked through the door and down the stairs to the tarmac where the sleek jet awaited her. She was going back home to save the life a child she'd never met.

Her heart felt like a lump in her chest when she sat down and buckled her seatbelt. She waited until they were airborne and the seatbelt light went off before she reclined her seat and went to sleep.

The media was waiting when Bree arrived at the hospital, but she was able to avoid them by slipping in through the Emergency Room entrance. She'd signed the documents giving the surgeons permission to remove her right kidney. What she hadn't agreed to was meeting Jessica Keane. She hadn't wanted a face to haunt her if the transplant proved unsuccessful. The child wasn't her daughter, she'd relinquished the right to call her that ten years ago. Jessica belonged to the Keanes, and if in the future she wanted to meet her birth mother, then Bree would meet her.

She was prepped for surgery and, as they wheeled her into the operating room, her last thoughts before she went under were of her husband and her son.

chapter forty-eight

"Hey, kid."

Bree opened her eyes when she heard the familiar voice. "Hey," she said, smiling at Ryder. "How long have I been asleep?"

"Hours. Do you feel like getting out of bed?"

"Yeah. I need to use the bathroom."

"Wait here until I get Lisa to help you."

Bree closed her eyes again. The doctors had said the transplant had gone well, and now they were waiting to see whether Jessica's body accepted her new kidney. Bree had spent three days in the hospital before she was discharged. Instead of going to Bel Air she had asked Ryder to take her home with him.

It had been two weeks since the surgery and her recuperation was going slowly. Waves of fatigue swept over her when she least expected. A few times she'd nearly fallen because she'd made the mistake of closing her eyes and fallen asleep while standing.

Internet blogs were humming with the news that she'd abandoned her husband and son in Italy and that Reuben Douglas was taking legal steps to declare her an unfit mother and was seeking sole custody of their young son. The gossip elicited disturbing dreams that had her waking up in a cold sweat.

Lisa Bailey stuck her head in the doorway. The future Dr. Bailey was tall and full-figured with waist-length dreaded hair, which she promised to cut when she graduated from medical school. "How's my patient today?"

"I'm ready to go home."

"I don't think so, Mrs. Douglas. You still have a low-grade fever."

Bree swung her legs over the side of the bed. "It comes and goes."

"That's what disturbs me, Bree."

"I'll be all right." Her temperature had been normal when she'd been discharged, so she didn't know why it was fluctuating between 98.6° and 101°.

She was determined to go home because she missed her son. Lisa helped her to the bathroom, and when she returned to the bedroom she picked up the phone and placed an international call to Italy.

"Ciao."

She smiled when hearing Reuben's soft greeting. "*Ciao,* yourself. I'm calling to let you know that I'm coming home."

There came a pause. "Do you feel well enough to come home?"

"Yes, I feel well enough to come home. What's up, Reuben?"

"What do you mean?"

"Are the rumors just rumors, or should I believe them?"

"I don't know what you're talking about."

"It's in all the tabloids and all over the Internet."

"I told you I don't read those things."

"Are you trying to take Jesse from me?"

"Breanna, you're delirious."

"I'm not delirious, Reuben. I miss you. I miss my baby."

"And we miss you, too. Just get well so you can come home."

"I'll talk to you tomorrow." She ended the call, then dialed information. When she ended this call she knew she'd made the right decision. She *was* going home.

Bree was packed and ready when the taxi maneuvered into the driveway to Ryder Parker's Hollywood Hills home. She'd chartered a private jet to take her to Rome. Despite feeling as if she was going to fall over at any moment, she knew she had to make the attempt.

Once aboard the aircraft, she asked the attendant for a cup of water so she could take a couple of aspirins. Half an hour later, the chills subsided and she felt well enough to eat all of her dinner.

They'd crossed the international dateline when she bolted from her seat to make it to the bathroom in time to purge her stomach. Bree stayed in the bathroom so long that the attendant tapped on the door to ask if she was all right.

"No, I'm not," she groaned. "I'm sick."

"Please unlock the door, Mrs. Douglas."

Reaching over, she slid back the lock and collapsed. The last thing she remembered was someone shouting something about radioing ahead to have medical assistance waiting when they touched down.

Ryder forcibly pulled his mother off the chair where she'd maintained a vigil at Breanna's bedside for the past week. "Mother, you have to get some sleep."

Karma waved a hand. "I'll sleep when my daughter opens her eyes."

Ryder turned to look at his father, who'd kept his own vigil in a corner of the sunny room in a Rome hospital. "Dad, please say something to your wife."

"Leave her alone, Ryder."

"You both look like shit! When Bree wakes up she doesn't want to see her parents looking as if they're ready to go to their graves. The doctors are giving her the best care she can get."

Karma dabbed her eyes with a crumpled tissue. "God is punishing me. He's punishing me for being a bad mother."

"Stop it, Mother!"

"Don't you dare tell me what to do!"

"Is there something I can do to help?" A young priest stood in the doorway.

Karma jumped. "Yes, Father. Can you please pray for my daughter?"

The priest walked in and stood next to the bed. "Of course." Reaching into his jacket pocket, he took out a small book, opened it and crossed himself. He prayed, his voice soft and soothing, saying that not all illness ends in death.

Karma buried her face in the pillow under her daughter's head, sobbing, while Langston buried his face in his hands and cried. The last time he'd cried was when he buried his mother. He got up and walked out to grieve in private.

His daughter's bedside had become a media circus, with reporters, photographers and the curious gathering outside the hospital for news of the Naughty girl. Everyone had a different story as to why she'd been hospitalized: she'd attempted suicide, she'd undergone a botched abortion, overdosed on drugs. The media tapped their cell phones, calling in stories that a priest had visited Breanna Douglas to administer the last rites.

Bree heard voices, familiar voices—male and female, but they sounded so far away. And why, she thought, did she feel so thirsty? She tried opening her eyes, but her lids felt weighted.

"Water. Can I please have some water?" The scent of a familiar perfume swept over her. "Mother?"

"Yes, yes, yes. It's me, baby. Open your eyes, Breanna."

She struggled to open her eyes and finally succeeded. "Mother."

Karma pressed kisses all over her face. "It's me, baby."

Bree frowned. "What happened to you? Your hair is a mess."

Laughing and crying at the same time, Karma combed her fingers through her mussed curls. "How about that? It's been more than thirty years since anyone has seen Karma Parker with a ratty do."

"You look good. Natural."

"Thank you, baby."

Bree stared at the clear liquid dripping into her veins. "How long have I been here?"

"Eight days. The doctors believe you picked up a staph infection when you underwent surgery. That's the reason for your fever."

"I want to go home."

"You are home, Breanna. You're in Rome."

"Where's Reuben?"

"He's on his way. He can't bring the baby to the hospital, so he's been spending his time between here and Silvana's."

Bree touched her hair. It was moist and plastered to her scalp. "Help me, Mother. I can't look like this when he sees me."

"Trust me, he's seen you look worse."

"Mother!"

Karma smiled. "I wouldn't worry too much about your husband. He'd love you even if you were bald and toothless."

"Did he say that?"

"Yes, he did."

"Damn! Well, since I still have my hair and teeth, please help me get presentable."

Karma helped her daughter take a sponge bath, brush her teeth, comb her hair and change out of the hospital gown and into one with the Naughty label. "Now, all you need is a little lip color and you're ready for your sexy husband."

* * *

Reuben walked into the hospital room to find his wife sitting up with her back supported by a pile of pillows. A slow smile became a full grin when she winked at him. *"Ciao, bella."*

"*Ciao,* darling."

He approached the bed, leaned over and kissed her, his mouth caressing hers. "Thank you for not leaving me."

Bree understood he wasn't talking about her walking away from him, but of her dying. "I will never leave you."

Karma stood up, patting her son-in-law's shoulder. "I'll see you later."

Reuben kissed her cheek. "Thank you for being here."

"You may come to regret those words. I love what little I've seen of Rome. Perhaps I'll stay here a little longer to see some of the city, bond with my grandson and get to know my daughter better." Karma smiled at Breanna. "I'll see you later, darling."

Bree waited for her mother to leave, then patted the side of the bed. "Get in, darling."

"I don't know, baby. You're looking kind of sexy in that nightgown. And based on your present condition I don't think you—"

"Get into bed, Reuben."

"Yes, ma'am."

Reuben got into bed with his wife, holding her to his heart. There were so many things he wanted to say, but they could wait, wait until he brought her home. But right now all he could think of was how much he loved her and how close he'd come to losing her.

He dropped a kiss on her hair. "I love you."

Bree emitted a soft sigh. "I love you, too."

'I'm going to check with the doctor to see when I can take you home."

Bree smiled. "I'm already home. You're my home, Reuben Douglas."